Swimming with the Fishes

Swimming with the Fishes

An Ozarks Lake Mystery (#2)

Marc Jedel

BGM Press
San Jose

Published in the United States by BGM Press.

ISBN 978-1-7327164-5-2 (Paperback edition)

Cover designed by Molly at CozyCoverDesigns.com

Other Books by Marc Jedel

OZARKS LAKE MYSTERY SERIES

Book 1. Fish Out of Water

SILICON VALLEY MYSTERY SERIES

Book 1. Uncle and Ants
Book 2. Chutes and Ladder
Book 3. Serf and Turf
Book 4. Hit and Mist

Sign up for Marc's mailing list to receive free content, learn of new releases, and receive special offers:

http://www.marcjedel.com

1

Wednesday Dawn

Jonas

"Wait. Did you just drop that in the water?" demanded Dale Cooper.

"Yeah," I admitted sheepishly, surprised he could tell what I was doing in the predawn light.

"Why in tarnation are you wasting perfectly good lures?" He stopped reeling in his line, and now I could make out his expression, a combination of annoyance and confusion that twisted his brows so tightly I doubted he could see much of anything. "Have you been doing that since we got out here? Is that why you haven't caught any fish?"

"I said I'd pay for all my supplies."

"It's the principle of it." Dale, a hearty outdoorsman in his early fifties with graying hair, seemed flabbergasted as he realized I had deliberately thrown away some of his fancy new fishing bait regardless of the money.

"Mr. Mayor, I do believe I'm the only principal out on the lake this morning," said Lester Stapleton, the principal of Jenkins High School, where I now taught biology. He chuckled at his own pun. "If Jonas doesn't want to catch any fish, that's his right."

I was nodding thanks for his support, but stopped as Lester continued, "He's a fool, but he can be a fool if he wishes."

I defended myself. "I told you I'd go out on the lake with you, not that I would try to catch any fish."

"Why on earth not?" Dale shook his head, utterly confused. "Don't tell me you don't eat fish either? I know vegetarians don't eat meat, but fish ain't meat."

Realizing this wasn't the best time to educate them on the difference between vegans like myself and vegetarians who also didn't eat fish, I simply said, "I enjoyed coming out on the lake with you."

"Dang early to go out on the lake if you're not gonna fish," grumbled the mayor.

I glanced around the still-dark lake, barely making out the wisps of fog that were drifting across the quiet scene thanks to the temperature inversion near the water. It was still too early in the day for turtles to be out sunning themselves, but I could hear some baby ducks nearby splashing in the water as they learned to swim. The air smelled clean, with a distinct overlay of pine mixed with the late spring flowers blooming along the nearby hills. "I like when it's quiet," I said softly.

"Quiet, ha!" Dale pointed to the southern sky with a disgusted wave of his arm.

I looked where he was indicating. "Is that . . ." I peered into the distance, trying to make out the dark shape moving against clouds still almost as dark with the sun just peeping over the horizon. "Is that a helicopter?"

"Yeah. Some moron's been flying one around for a few days, disturbing everyone's mornings," complained Dale.

"There it is," said Lester, an overweight but cheerful man about Dale's age. He started to stand in excitement, then must have remembered he was still on the boat because he plopped back down heavily into his seat. "Looks to be flying way over by Stillwater Cove now."

"Pretty early in the morning to be flying around," I said. The distant blades made a soft whooshing noise only detectable because the rest of the town was still asleep.

"Disturbing all the fish," complained Dale as he reeled in another empty line. He needed to blame something besides his fancy lures.

"What're they doing, you reckon?" asked Lester.

"I dunno. Maybe it's them Fish & Wildlife guys. Or maybe State Roads & Highways people surveying the land. There's been talk about extending that old county road forever." Dale shrugged.

"Well, at least we had some quality fishing time before that fish-disturbing helicopter ruined everything." Lester gestured at his nice haul of fish, chuckling at his old friend's expense.

"Would have been even earlier if your silly dog hadn't put up such a fuss when we was leaving." Dale directed this complaint at me, but the growling and muttering sounds he made as he shifted the lonely, melting ice cubes around in his empty fishing cooler suggested the real cause of his frustration.

Reminded of my normally sweet dog, I looked to shore to check if Daisy was still lying on the dock. She'd been waiting by the front door this morning when I crept down the hallway, trying not to wake Elizabeth and her mother. Although I knew Daisy didn't like the open water, she had jumped onto Dale's motorboat without much hesitation. He had a nice boat with four cushioned seats, space on the floor where I could spread a towel, and a back bench—plenty of good options where Daisy could have comfortably slept while we were on the water. But as soon as Dale started the engine, she had jumped up onto a seat, leapt onto the back bench, and then propelled herself onto the dock.

I had climbed more slowly out of the boat before picking her up and carrying her back onboard. Petting her to calm her while I sat with her on the boat, we had just pulled away from the dock when Daisy jerked away, raced along the boat's deck, and hurdled herself gracefully back onto the dock. She proceeded to lie down on an old towel left on the dock. She obviously heard us calling her because she cocked her ears in our direction, but she kept her head down on her paws and refused to come back to the boat.

She had done well by herself after we'd motored off, except for a brief stint of barking about thirty minutes after we left the dock. The light breeze must have caused a boat to clunk against another and startled her. The sun hadn't brightened the sky enough to make her out against the shore, but I'd called her name across the water and told her to calm down, which seemed to do the trick.

"Why don't we head back? You're getting grumpy from not catching anything," Lester said to Dale. "Besides, Jonas and I have school to get to." Lester reeled in his line and carefully removed the fancy lure, replacing it in his tackle box.

Going fishing before work was a new experience for me. Elizabeth and I had moved here to the Ozarks from the West Coast to help her mother recover from an attack and to rebuild a house on the land that used to belong to her grandparents. Ever since arriving, I'd been enjoying the new aspects of living out here—well, most of them. I still missed great coffee and a wider array of vegan restaurants. But this morning's sunrise on the lake had been special. Sure, I'd be a bit tired today, but I only had to proctor the kids' finals, not do any actual teaching.

Dale closed his cooler and stowed his gear as he made ready to head back. "Ah, what a way to start the day." He grinned despite his lackluster results. Making certain to catch my eye, he said, "Next time, don't waste my special lures. Just say so if you only want to sit there and shoot the breeze with us."

"Hard to get in much talking when you're in one of your story-telling moods," Lester teased his longtime friend.

"Well, I ain't nothing compared to ole CB. You ever go fishing with him, I recommend you bring some earplugs." Dale laughed. Although knowing Colton Buck, a local old-timer who liked to narrate the world as it evolved around him and couldn't pass up a good fried chicken lunch, earplugs weren't such a bad idea.

Dale pointed at the sky. "Red skies at dawn, all cares be gone."

Lester scoffed. "Your mama teach you that silliness?"

"Don't be making fun of my mama now, ya hear?"

"It's 'sailor take warning,'" I told Dale.

"What sailor?" Waving off my attempt to explain, he started up the engine. "This here is a motorboat." Then he steered us back to shore. "We should take you catfish noodling when the season starts." He smirked at me. "You ever noodled?"

I hesitated, cautious about his expression and wondering if he was pulling my leg. It wouldn't have been the first time someone here in Jenkins had tried to play this big-city boy for a fool. I figured Lester's head shake from behind Dale was a warning to me.

"You're making that up," I accused Dale, then put on my teacher's voice. "You know, it's not very nice to take advantage of a newcomer like that. What if tourists find out the mayor isn't very hospitable."

"No, no." He laughed. "It's totally legit. There's even an official catfish noodling season in Arkansas. Starts next week, on June first. You can look it up." Grinning like the cat who ate the canary, he said, "You thought I was pulling your leg, didn't you? Now you've got to come with me. In fact"—he drew himself upright in the driver's seat—"as the mayor of Jenkins, I hereby declare it a mandatory part of your cultural acclimatization."

I shrugged, pretty sure he was overstepping his statutory authority but impressed with his ability to throw out the mumbo-jumbo at this early hour. "Well, okay, I guess I'm game to trying out something new."

"Well, you can count me out, Dale. I told you after you dragged me out there last time that I'm never doing it again." Lester shook his big body as if to ward off a bad memory.

"Um," I said, starting to reconsider.

Dale interrupted me. "Nope, no take-backs. You've got to try noodling once if you're going to truly experience living in Arkansas. No backing out." He cut the engine down to idle as we slowed in the approach to our docking berth. The birds calling to each other signified that day was officially breaking.

Motion on one of the boats moored on the other wing of the dock caught my eye. I could make out a dim figure moving around on the boat, but even though we were getting close, things were still too shadowy to see clearly.

"Who's that?" I pointed at the person, who straightened momentarily as they exited the boat before crouching on the dock by the driver's seat of the next boat.

"I don't see anyone," said Lester, straining his older eyes to see into the shadows.

I could now see Daisy standing near where Dale's boat would dock and growling.

"Next time, you should leave her at home," remarked Dale. "Or teach her to swim. What dog doesn't like to play in the water?"

I partially stood, kneeling on a seat to get a little higher in an attempt to make out what was going on as we coasted into the dock.

No one seemed too close to Daisy, and it wasn't like her to growl or bark at other people, especially when I was nearby.

"Sounds like she's got her hackles up about something," said Lester. "Maybe she doesn't like fish either. A vegetarian dog, now that's funny." He chuckled to himself.

Then everything seemed to happen at once.

Daisy barked loudly. Twice.

Then, gathering herself, she leapt off the dock into the lake.

"Daisy!" I yelled as I jumped up onto my seat, putting one foot on the gunwale.

I balanced there precariously for a second, scanning the water for Daisy, while our boat drifted in to the dock. Before the other men could react to my standing on the seat, I spotted Daisy struggling in the water.

"There she is," I yelled.

I dove in after her, my head going under briefly but the rest of me belly-flopping into the water as the life jacket prevented me from going completely beneath the surface.

Suddenly, a fiery blast surprised me with a burst of blinding light, noise, and heat right as my head resurfaced.

2

Wednesday Very Early

Jonas

I spun in the water toward the explosion but couldn't identify the source.

Hearing Daisy flailing in the water shifted my focus back to her. "I've got you, girl," I called as I swam to her side and hugged her to me. Luckily, she calmed in my arms. It would have been quite tough to manage a thirty-five-pound dog thrashing around and fighting me in the water. "Smart dog," I told her as I rolled onto my back and looked up, breathing hard.

Debris rained down. Fortunately, none of it, especially the flaming parts, fell near me. My ears were ringing, but I rotated in the water, holding Daisy tight while searching for Dale and Lester.

There!

Dale must have looped one of the boat's ropes around a dock stanchion and killed his motor. He was bending over inside the boat, but Lester was not in sight.

"Dale," I called as I scissor-kicked toward him. My shoes and jeans felt like lead weights but the life jacket did its job, keeping Daisy and me afloat as I made my way to the boat. Despite my exertions, the chill from the water started to make its presence known. I had dressed for a predawn fishing trip in May. A swim hadn't been part of my planning process.

"Jonas!" He looked up, eyes wide with alarm. "Oh, thank goodness you're okay. Lester got hit by something."

I shivered, but not because of the cold water. "Is he okay?" Lester wasn't in the best of shape. I doubted he exercised regularly, unless walking up and down the hallways of his high school and yelling at misbehaving students counted.

Dale turned away from me and looked down into his boat. "Something knocked him out. There's blood, but he's breathing." He sounded distracted and worried.

I reached the boat. "Could you give me a hand here?"

Dale's head swiveled from Lester to us and back before he decided it was okay to leave his friend for a moment. He carefully shifted away from Lester's side of the boat, then leaned over the edge and grabbed Daisy. She didn't resist, but as soon as her paws gained purchase, she pushed off the edge of the boat to get out of the water faster. Her momentum caused Dale to flop backwards onto his back, landing on the boat's deck. Then he gasped as Daisy's full weight landed on his stomach before she leapt off onto a seat.

Dale had just sat up when Daisy decided to shake herself, spraying water everywhere. Then, deciding she'd had entirely enough of this water business, she darted up the middle of Dale's boat, knocking over a tackle box before jumping out onto the dock. She stayed near us, not venturing toward the smoke still rising in the air on the other end of the large dock.

I worked to pull myself onto the boat while Dale wiped the water off his face and shook his head at the disarray she had left behind. He reached to help me out right as I kicked the water hard to propel myself up. I knocked him over backwards again, landing on top of him before rolling off.

He lay on the bottom of the boat once more, coughing and catching his breath a bit longer this time.

"Sorry about that," I said, and helped him back to his pilot's chair as I stole a look over my shoulder at Lester. I was very pleased to see his chest and stomach rising and falling—the bulk making it more obvious from a few steps away. Relieved that he was still alive, and now feeling thoroughly cold, I asked, "Do you have another towel?"

He pointed. "Under that seat cushion."

I tossed one to him, and he used it to wipe his face again. Then he groaned slightly as he stood and moved slowly to Lester's side, dabbing at some blood on Lester's temple before wrapping the towel around him to keep him warm.

Sirens wailed in the distance. Our near-miss experience had not gone unnoticed.

Suddenly remembering that shadowy figure I had seen on the other boat before the explosion, I whipped around to look down the spur of the dock where the other boat had been berthed.

A smoldering wreck greeted me. Little of the boat's back remained above the water line. The rest had chunks blown off or shattered, with light wisps of smoke curling up from hot spots.

I stood up to see better. A rope from the front of the boat was somehow still attached to the dock, but the boat didn't look like it would remain floating for too much longer.

Lying on the dock a few feet from what remained of the captain's seat was a body.

I turned away, not wanting to see any more details. "There was . . ." I swallowed and continued softly, "Someone was by that boat."

"What?" Dale exclaimed much louder. He straightened up and twisted to look at the destroyed boat. Then, glancing down at his friend, he said, "Here, hold this. There's still some blood oozing so maybe we should apply pressure until the ambulance gets here."

I took over Dale's spot while he scrambled out of the boat.

Lester's glasses were missing and he had some cuts and black smudges on his head. Most concerning was the slowly growing red stain on the side of his shirt. The blood wasn't gushing out, but any blood was more than I wanted to see.

"She's dead." Dale's voice was quiet as he spoke to me from the dock.

I focused on keeping pressure on Lester's side, hoping that was the right thing to do. "Are you certain? Maybe you could apply some pressure on any bleeding too," I said.

"Nah. There's no head," he answered in a matter-of-fact tone.

I felt slightly nauseated. Dissecting animals in my biology class hardly served as preparation for encountering an actual dead human body, especially one without a head. There was a reason I didn't go to medical school. I kept my gaze focused firmly on Lester and tried to avoid thinking about how the body had lost its head.

The arrival of a sheriff's car drew my attention back to shore. Deputy Trent Walker emerged and ran up the dock. "Y'all all right? What happened?" he shouted as he approached.

"That boat exploded and killed somebody," explained Dale, pointing to the charred remains. "Lester got hurt. Are the paramedics . . . Oh . . ."

Answering his unfinished question, the ambulance raced up and parked alongside the deputy's squad car.

"Over here," I shouted as they hurried up the dock. The lead paramedic paused, glancing at the destroyed boat and then the deputy. At his gesture, they approached Dale's boat first.

I backed away as they took over, wiping my bloodied hands on the towel around my shoulders. Climbing out of the boat, I looked for Daisy. She'd be cold and scared as a result of her unwanted swim in the lake, the explosion, and then all these sirens and flashing lights.

She slunk over from a hiding place near the next boat, her tail between her legs. I wrapped her in a clean towel and stood, lifting her soggy bulk. I looked around, trying to figure out how to get out of the way and put her down somewhere safe.

"Let's get y'all off the dock so the paramedics can help Mr. Stapleton and the firefighters can do their thing," said the deputy as he started to guide us back to land. Partway back to shore, the deputy paused and pulled a rope across the dock, looping it around a pole on the other side and setting a chair in the middle of the dock as a barrier. It wouldn't stop someone from getting past, but it served as a good enough warning for now.

Dale said, "What about my boat? I could help with—"

Deputy Walker put his hand on Dale's back and pushed. "Mr. Stapleton's in good hands. Your boat will be safe. Come on, let's go talk out of the way. The firefighters are on their way too."

Before reaching the end of the dock, Dale stopped at his Bait, Boat, and Float shop and used the keypad to unlock the back door. "Do y'all want to warm up inside here?" he asked as he flipped on the lights and headed toward the back.

"No, thank you," answered the deputy. "I've got to keep an eye out here to stop any looky-loos from interfering."

"Be right back. I'll turn on the heat and put some coffee on." Dale ducked inside his store. He liked to talk big about new schemes to make money or drive more visitors to Jenkins—and in his mind, the two typically went hand in hand. I had yet to see evidence of action from all his dreaming. Whenever I encountered him, either outside Harps Grocery Store yakking away with CB or here in his own store, he always seemed to be in the midst of elaborating on a variety of grand ideas for expanding his shop's offerings in time for the summer travel rush. But in the two months that I'd known him, nothing had actually happened. For all that, I liked Dale. He was an outgoing, friendly man who seemed to genuinely care about the town and its residents.

"I'll be right back too," said the deputy. He left me at the shop while he checked with the paramedics and then got some police tape from his cruiser. He quickly attached it to a few light poles near the parking lot, moving alertly, his eyes swiveling from side to side. He was acting more nervous than I'd ever seen him, but that was understandable since he needed to manage an unexpected crisis. Of course, I didn't know him well as he tended to keep his distance from Elizabeth and me ever since he'd arrested her for murder when we first got to town.

Dale returned from his back room holding some thick wool blankets. I took one gratefully and Dale wrapped another around himself, then I set Daisy down and unwrapped the towel around her. She darted inside the store, but I let her go. She wouldn't get into trouble inside, and I knew I'd find her curled up on the ground in the sunny spot near the heating vent.

Dale and I stood there in silence, warming ourselves for a minute. I knew both of us were worried about Lester. As we watched people gather in the parking lot, I was about to ask him if he wanted to go with Lester in the ambulance when he spoke. "Guess I better go turn on the bigger coffee maker and call Hanson to come in early. Lots of people gonna be wanting some coffee and I want to go to the hospital to make sure they treat Lester right." He headed back into his store.

In both his store owner and mayoral personas, Dale enjoyed playing host. His bait shop was a frequent gathering place for men in the community. Serving as mayor of the small town of Jenkins certainly didn't require Dale's full-time attention. I'd observed that the role seemed more ceremonial than anything. It scratched Dale's itch for attention and his sense of self-importance.

Dale soon returned outside, and when the deputy beckoned us, we joined him behind the blocking chair on the dock where it split into different forks.

Glancing between the paramedics and the onlookers in the parking lot, Deputy Walker took a breath, apparently comfortable that things were under control for the moment. He gestured out to the water. "So tell me what happened."

Between the two of us, Dale and I told him what we'd seen. The deputy frowned when he heard about Daisy's barking when we were out on the water but didn't interrupt.

After we finished, he asked, "Now you said she"—he pointed toward the store where Daisy was likely asleep—"jumped into the water right before the explosion? Was it like she knew something was about to happen?"

I nodded. "Yeah. Pretty crazy. She hates getting in the water. Something must have spooked her into jumping off the dock. Maybe she smelled something." I paused, taking time to think. "Daisy has had certain quirks ever since I got her. I've always thought something must have happened to her before she was taken in by the dog rescue group."

Shaking my head at my dumb comment, I pressed my lips together. Of course something had happened to her. Dogs—even sweet dogs like her—didn't wind up at rescue adoption agencies unless something bad had happened to them.

I was glad I had adopted Daisy, although it had been an uncharacteristically impulsive move on my part. Not my typical style, but the bold move seemed necessary in order to impress the woman I had just met at my running club. Normally I was slow and cautious in my decisions, but I had really liked Elizabeth and worried I'd been too cautious to catch her eye. She had seemed as smitten with Daisy as I was when we met her at the adoption booth after Elizabeth's run in the park was cut short. The gesture had worked. Elizabeth and I were now happily married. Still newlyweds even. And as a bonus, Daisy had proven to be the better running partner.

"It's a dang shame," said Dale. "But boats do explode sometimes. There was one that exploded maybe five years ago." He turned to the side, apparently looking for confirmation from his buddy, but grimaced. "Forgot Lester wasn't here. He'd know for sure." He shifted his weight, anxious to check on his friend. "We done here?"

"Just a few more questions," answered the deputy. "Was the victim on the boat when it exploded?"

"Uh, I must not have been looking in that direction. I didn't see anyone," replied Dale.

"No, the dock," I answered more confidently. My eyes were younger than his. The person had been on the dock before the explosion. I was sure of it.

"Interesting." The deputy scratched his cheek. "Was the other boat's motor running?"

Dale jumped in again. "It, uh . . ." Then his face scrunched up. "I guess I'm not sure about that either. I didn't hear another motor, but . . ." His voice trailed off as he turned to me for confirmation.

I closed my eyes, remembering. "No. When Dale cut the motor to idle and we were drifting in, the lake was quiet."

"Yeah, that helicopter had flown away by then." Dale shook his head, then scoffed, "Tourists!"

I turned to him, raising my eyebrows. I'd never heard Dale complain about having tourists in the area. Rather, he typically complained there weren't enough of them.

"The birds." Dale snapped his fingers as he stared out at the lake. "I remember hearing birds calling overheard." His eyes widened as he whipped his head around to stare at the deputy. "Do you think they were trying to warn us?" His voice rose in excitement.

Deputy Walker snorted. "No, Dale. I think the birds were just being birds."

"But what about the dog? You wanted to know if she knew something before the explosion. Why not the birds?" sputtered Dale.

The deputy smiled, trying to hold back a laugh. "Well, if you'd like, I could add something to your statement for the official police record about how the birds were talking to you. What exactly were they saying to you again?" He cocked his head, pen in his hand, and looked hopeful that Dale would say yes.

As the siren from a fire truck approached, Dale returned to his senses and waved him off. "No, no. Don't be rude. I was just thinking out loud." He took a deep breath and glanced out toward his boat where the paramedics were still working. "Mind if I go see if he's doing okay?"

At the deputy's nod, Dale thanked him and turned to go. As he walked off, he mumbled under his breath, "The birds were definitely making noise."

"Hey! Stay off the dock, please," the deputy called to one of the more aggressive bystanders. I didn't know the folks who had gathered but recognized a few as locals.

He turned back to me, his demeanor serious. "Could you stick around a little longer for just a few more questions after I get the firefighters sorted?"

"Sure." I checked the clock hung on the side of Dale's store so boat renters would know when their time was up. I didn't have much to spare. The fire truck had taken a long while to get here. It was a good thing that the destroyed boat didn't appear to be on fire.

I moved to the side while he went to greet the fire truck and point them in the right direction. He waved the onlookers back a few steps and then returned to me.

"Thanks," he said. "So, about that earlier time when y'all were out on the water and Daisy started barking, are you sure you didn't see anything?"

"No. It was right around dawn and the hills are to the east of here." I pointed in the direction of the low mountains that rose outside of town. The land that Elizabeth had inherited from her grandparents was up on one of the nearby ridges, about fifteen minutes from downtown Jenkins.

"Come again?" He looked puzzled.

I shook my head. I'd forgotten again that not everyone had a scientific mindset. "The docks were dark. They were still in shadow from the mountains to the east even though it was lighter out on the water."

"Hmm," was his response. He took a step to the side, looking out and around the parking lot, not just where the onlookers were gathering. Then, he rotated as he studied the side of Dale's store with professional attention and then along the dock back to the burned-out boat.

"What? Do you see something?" I asked, curious despite my time crunch.

"Unfortunately nothing," he answered cryptically.

"What were you hoping to see?"

"Wondering if anyone had put up a security camera closer than the bank down the street, but I don't see any. I'll have to do a more careful survey." He put his hand to his forehead to block the sun.

Surprised by his implication, I asked, "You think it wasn't an accident?"

Still staring up the street, Deputy Walker murmured, "I think it was murder."

"What?" I stood there in shock. "How do you know that?"

The deputy winced and then shook himself as he realized I had heard him. "I shouldn't speculate."

I pressed him. "But why? Why do you think it's murder already?" I was curious now. What clue had he discerned that I had missed?

Turning to give me his full attention, he said, "Timing's certainly suspicious."

"Timing? What? Because it's morning?"

Deputy Walker looked down at the ground and shifted from one foot to the other. "Well, uh, we have some information, and, uh . . ." His voice trailed off.

Puzzled by his unhelpful answer, I asked, "Couldn't it have been an accidental gas explosion?"

This he answered more confidently. "Hard to get an accidental gas explosion if you haven't started the engine or done something really dumb like smoke while you're fueling your boat."

"I didn't see any sparks," I agreed.

The deputy jotted this down in his notebook too. Then he looked at the destroyed boat again. "I'm pretty sure that was where the *Full Throttle* docked." His body stiffened when he noticed me staring at him. "Please don't spread any of this around."

"Of course," I said.

"Thanks for your cooperation. We don't want word to get out before we can notify the woman's next of kin. And, of course, the Arkansas Boating Commission will send someone out to investigate. And then there's the . . ." He stopped speaking and sighed. "It'll get complicated. It's a boating incident on a state lake that borders a national forest with the boat still attached to Jenkins land. I better go make some calls."

I latched onto something he had said. "How do you know it was a woman?"

He smiled grimly, regaining his earlier confidence. "I'm pretty sure it's Courtney Stanton. I recognized her car in the parking lot when I pulled up. She lives next door to me so I know her car well. Hers was the only other car here besides yours, the mayor's, and Principal Stapleton's. She owns the *Full Throttle*."

"What did you mean about the suspicious timing?" I asked.

Deputy Walker paused and then cleared his throat. "I'm sorry, but I can't discuss ongoing investigations."

"But we've been talking this whole time," I objected.

"I think we're finished here. I appreciate your discretion in not sharing anything we've discussed." He placed his sheriff's hat back on his head and walked off. After only a few steps, he paused and turned back. "Thanks again for your assistance, Mr. Trout."

Hurrying in the opposite direction to my car, I wondered if the deputy was right. I had been right there and didn't realize there was anything suspicious. Why had he been so confident this was a murder?

Somehow the intellectual exercise of thinking about a possible murder helped me compartmentalize this morning's tragedy and push the queasy feeling in my stomach aside. As Daisy and I wound our way through the onlookers, I mindlessly repeated, "Good morning," and "Excuse me," without responding to their questions.

After all, I couldn't hope to address the most important question of all—why would someone want to kill Courtney Stanton? Indeed, any value I could contribute in this matter was at its end. I didn't even know who Courtney Stanton was.

3

Wednesday Breakfast

Elizabeth

"Ella Mae! It's so good to see you." Vanessa Martini stood from her table in the cafe to hug me. "Thanks ever so much for meeting me earlier than we'd planned for breakfast."

"Of course, sis. I was already up," I lied with a smile as I stifled a yawn. She wasn't actually my sister, but as my after-school buddy from third through eighth grade, I considered her the big sister I never had. We hung out together nearly every weekday while I soaked up as much of the wisdom and life experience that came from her being five years older.

Then we both turned our heads as a siren echoed around the restaurant from a few streets over. I frowned. The harsh sound broke the town's early morning serenity. It was way too early for someone to have gotten into such a bad fix. At least beyond what a good cup of coffee could resolve.

Vanessa had called me at my mother's house a few days ago. We had arranged to meet at nine-thirty, a perfectly reasonable time for breakfast. Meeting instead at seven-thirty was a new experience for me. I couldn't remember when I'd last been up and out of the house by this point. One of the perks of working for myself was that, under normal conditions, I only saw seven-thirty once a day.

I wouldn't have been here now if I hadn't missed Jonas's warmth in bed this morning. When I rolled over to check the time, I noticed someone had texted me. But it wasn't Jonas sending me pre-dawn texts. He knew better.

"What were you doing up so early?" I asked Vanessa.

"I couldn't sleep. I went out for a walk while it was still dark and then wondered if you might be available early—Oh!" She stepped back and ran an affectionate hand over the head of a young girl who was squeezing past us to the table. "Let me introduce you two. Olivia, this is my friend Ella—no, she prefers to be called Elizabeth." She looked at me. "Right?"

I nodded and then paused, unsure what to do. Finally I decided to treat Olivia like anyone else I might meet, only shorter. So I bent down, looking into her bright blue eyes, and shook her hand. "Nice to meet you, Olivia."

Olivia beamed and gave me an exaggerated handshake in return. That may not have been how other adults typically greeted her, but it seemed to do the trick. "I'm going back to my old first grade class this morning," she announced, sounding fully awake despite the hour.

"Well, good for you. That will be fun." I smiled at her as I sat down with them.

"Did you wash your hands?" asked Vanessa.

Olivia nodded, and I watched my friend interact with her daughter while I pretended to study the menu. In a town as small as Jenkins, I'd already eaten in every place multiple times so the menus held no mysteries.

Vanessa seemed so motherly, even though she was in her mid-thirties and not old like my own mother. She looked cute, with her hair worn long and tied in a loose ponytail. She was dressed in actual work clothes, unlike me. I was lucky if I remembered to throw on a nice blouse over pajamas for video calls with clients.

Vanessa and I had been as close as sisters until she graduated from high school and went off to the Marines. After she got out, she went to college, and then got married and gave birth to Olivia in the same month she graduated.

Turning to Vanessa, I asked, "Why did you decide to bring Olivia back right at the end of the school year?"

"With everything just finalized with you-know-who . . ." She paused to check that I understood her reference to her ex-husband, Adam.

I nodded and she continued, "Olivia and I moved to my mother's place near Little Rock when everything kind of fell apart. It was fine to handle my clients remotely for a while, and it allowed me to avoid . . . him."

I nodded again. It made sense she'd want to avoid her husband during a painful divorce.

"But now, the judge decided I get to keep our accounting office here in Jenkins and he has to go out on his own." Vanessa's smile flashed positively predatory for a moment. "So now it's time to get on with my life. Besides, it will be good for Olivia to have these last ten days of school to reconnect with the other kids in her class. That way it will be easier for her to go to playdates with them during the summer."

I smiled but didn't respond because I had no idea whether it was a good thing for Olivia. It sounded logical, but since when did children obey logic? I certainly hadn't, as my mother would readily attest to. At first glance, Olivia seemed fine. Her parents' divorce and having to spend most of the year in a different school didn't appear to have turned her into a juvenile delinquent or cause hopeless depression. At least not visibly. But she was seven, so who knew? And who knew whether it was best to have her change schools again? More importantly, how had Vanessa figured all of this out?

I laughed quietly to myself while Vanessa and Olivia ordered. After all the crazy things she'd taught me when I was young, this would be relatively tame. Heck, simply remembering to pick up her daughter after a party or showing up to the science fair would make Vanessa a mother-of-the-year candidate compared to my mother. Dr. Mary Banks always prioritized her patients' needs over mine. Maybe kids weren't so tricky. Just look at me; I turned out fine. Mostly. I mean, we got my murder charge thrown out a few months ago. So all was well.

After I ordered, Vanessa and I started catching up on the last ten years while Olivia doodled on the paper placemat with some crayons. I'd only had a chance to meet her for a brief lunch halfway between here and Little Rock since I'd returned to Jenkins. Now that she was moving back, it was time for a more complete story.

Vanessa chewed her lip. "Are you going to the reunion stuff this weekend?"

"Yeah." I gave a half-hearted shrug. "Not really sure how much I'm looking forward to it, though. Everyone judging each other and pretending they're happy to see people they didn't even like back in high school." I sighed. "But it's kind of hard to avoid attending when I'm living here again."

Vanessa shook her finger at me. "You should go. I didn't make mine and now I regret it."

I rallied some enthusiasm. "Yeah, I suppose it will be fun." Then I had an idea and brightened. "Do you want to come to lunch on Friday with me, Kelsey, and the 'ABC' gang?" I was referring to my old friends, Angela, Brooke, and Carlita, who hung out with me and Kelsey during high school.

Vanessa nodded eagerly. "Sure. I remember a few of them and it will be fun to meet some new people here."

"Sure!" I said, excited to act as a guide to Vanessa for once. "Oh, and Crystal, she just had a baby. You gotta go visit her."

Vanessa broke into a grin. "Crystal, huh? I remember her as a tiny little thing. Her baby must be teensy-weensy. And what about your husband? I want to meet him. Is he going to all your reunion stuff?"

"Yes, Jonas is weird," I said, and then, noticing her look of surprise, I hurried to explain. "He actually *wants* to go to my reunion. We're even going to tomorrow's go-kart mixer thingy. Who thought up that ridiculous combination?"

She laughed. "It does sound kinda fun, in a funky sort of way. *He*—" she emphasized with a hidden finger pointed at her daughter, "won't be back from Vegas until Friday afternoon so I won't even have to worry about running into him around here."

I pounced on the idea of having another friend to hang out with. "Oh yes, please come. You can come over to my mother's house first and meet Jonas. He said he wants to meet the people behind my stories."

Vanessa raised an eyebrow. "Which stories have you told him?"

"Not all of them." I winked. "He's not ready to swim in the deep waters of my history."

She snorted. "Is anyone?"

"He'll be fine with them. He doesn't get too worked up about stuff." I paused to smile. "But I do think there is only so much *me* that I can inflict on someone all at once. We just got married, you know. I'm letting my more notorious episodes trickle out slowly." I shook my head, a mischievous grin spreading on my face as I remembered a few particularly infamous incidents that were aided by Vanessa. It was a wonder I graduated.

"Well, if you don't hurry, the good people of Jenkins won't be shy about volunteering their more embarrassing Ella Mae stories. You don't want a tidal wave to swamp that poor man."

"Yes, I've noticed the gossip mill here has remained in prime form," I said dryly. "Well, whatever." Jonas knew I was more free-wheeling than him before he married me. That's what we artsy types were famous for.

Across the cafe, a hubbub arose from a table where three women were eating breakfast. The women, who looked to be in their forties, got all excited by something the man standing near them must have said. The man had his back to us but his presence was quite notable. He wore tight, dark slacks and a colorful silk shirt with swirls of blue and brown on a white base. Neither dress slacks nor expensive, fashionable men's dress shirts were common sights here in Jenkins.

Not as bright but just as notable was a much larger man standing behind the first, watching the room with his well-developed arms crossed in front of him. He wore a lightweight, black, form-fitting turtleneck shirt that emphasized his chest. His hair was trimmed very short on the sides and was only a bit longer on top. He had that vaguely Eastern European look and gave off more intimidating vibes than our local country bumpkins.

"Who are they?" Vanessa asked, her voice rising in surprise.

I kept my focus on the unusual sight. "Don't know. Never seen them before."

She laughed. "Well, you'd have remembered if you'd seen two guys who look like that around here. It's like Schitt's Creek came to Jenkins with a Secret Service detail."

I looked again. The man with the fancy shirt and slacks did sort of resemble someone off the set of a TV show.

When Mr. Fancy Shirt straightened, he turned to the next table and I saw his hair was dark and curly, meticulously groomed in a modern style. He looked to be in his mid to late forties but still in good shape despite his age. No dad bod to interfere with the cut of his expensive clothes. Although he wasn't classically handsome, the women continued staring at him even as he moved to speak with the couple sitting at the next table.

An air of restrained aggression enveloped his companion, or bodyguard, warning people of danger. In contrast to the local tough guys who needed large quantities of alcohol to work up their belligerence, this guy seemed to generate his "stay away" aura naturally. Our locals were mostly softies, living off their old high school football or wrestling reputations. They liked to sound tough once in a while and make much ado about meaningless exploits. On Saturday nights—or Fridays during football season—they drank too much and got rowdy as they staggered along the street at closing time.

"Tourists, I suppose," I commented.

"Man blouse," snickered Vanessa.

We both chuckled at her comment, then ignored the other side of the cafe while we returned to eating and chatting. A few minutes later, we looked up in surprise when a shadow fell across our table.

"Good morning, ladies." Mr. Fancy Shirt now stood next to us. "My name is Giuseppe Lucchesi." His accent sounded vaguely Italian, although I was certainly no expert. "I am in town scouting for movie locations. It is my great honor to introduce myself to all the beautiful women in town." He smiled and bobbed his head briefly in greeting before turning to Olivia. "And who might you be, young lady?"

"I'm Olivia and this is my mom Vanessa and her friend Elizabeth," said Olivia.

"Olivia!" Vanessa admonished her daughter. "Do you remember what we've discussed about telling strangers your name?"

Abashed, Olivia looked down to the table. "Not to tell them my name," she mumbled.

"That's right." She glared at her daughter for another moment before turning back to Giuseppe. "Sorry about that, but she needs to learn."

"Oh no, it is entirely my fault. I did not mean to get young Olivia in trouble. If she is to be punished, please allow me to take the blow for her." Turning to Vanessa, Giuseppe spread his hands wide and offered his chest for a sword strike.

Olivia looked up with wide eyes as if to check the surroundings for previously undetected swordsmen.

His over-the-top gesture completed, Giuseppe returned his attention to Olivia. "Well, Ms. Olivia, now that you know my name, we are no longer strangers. All is good, yes?" He bowed again and straightened, smiling broadly at Olivia, who by then was returning his smile unabashedly.

Vanessa's continued glare at Giuseppe made it clear that she planned to have another conversation with her daughter soon about not falling for smooth-talking, strange men, regardless of how well they were dressed. Indeed, maybe my mother should have had the same talk with me before I left for college.

While this was going through my head, Giuseppe turned his attention to me. He clasped his hands together in front of his mouth, touching his fingers to his lips before taking in a deep breath. "Ah, Liza." He uttered the name on his exhale, as if the name itself were a sigh. He paused, admiring me.

"It's Elizabeth," I corrected. His glibness wasn't going to take me in, although I did attempt to respond with at least a bit of Southern hospitality rather than telling him to get lost. Since returning to Jenkins two months ago, I'd been trying not to act so "big-city."

"Yes, yes." He waved a hand dismissively. "But I shall call you Liza. In honor of my mother."

"Was her name Liza?" asked Vanessa, far more politely than how I almost responded.

The man looked puzzled. "No. She was Maria, may God rest her soul." He crossed himself. "But Liza Minelli—you have heard of that great Italian beauty, have you not?"

"She's American. Her mother was Judy Garland," I said, frowning at his mistake. If someone was going to talk about an actress, they should know what they were talking about.

"But Italian-American," he said with an emphatic flourish. "And she is from New Jersey. Just like me."

"Um . . . she was born in Los Angeles," I said. My grandmother, Mimi, had loved Liza Minelli too. Growing up, I had seen many of her old movies and shows on television at Mimi's house.

His hand erased the air again, as if to wipe away anything that contradicted his own ideas. "Ah, Liza—my mother's favorite. She was exquisite. God bless her memory."

I was starting to get annoyed. "Liza Minelli's still alive."

He placed a hand to his heart. "Alas, my mother has passed." He paused and sighed deeply. "You are very beautiful, just like her."

I gave up. I wasn't sure if he was comparing me to his mother or Liza Minelli and I didn't care. Everyone in the cafe was staring at us, and I had no intention of speaking to this fool again anyway.

"Beautiful women, please forgive my interruption of your meal. Liza and Virginia, it was so very good to meet you both."

"Vanessa," she interjected.

"Yes, yes, of course." He waved off the distraction before leaning down toward my hand.

I snatched it away before he could do something gross. Calling us by the wrong names was one thing, but a stranger kissing my hand was definitely off-limits.

My move didn't seem to faze him as he turned his attempt into an elaborate bow, sweeping one arm across his body. He rose, winked at me, and then flicked a hand in the direction of the hulking, silent man who stood behind him. "Drosnic, let us be off. It's time for our meeting."

At the door, he paused, swiveled to survey the room, and announced, "And a lovely day to all of you." Then he pushed open the door and was gone.

When I turned back, Vanessa's mouth was still open.

"He was funny, Mommy," said Olivia.

Her words snapped Vanessa out of it. "Yes, he sure was, honey. Wipe your face. We've got to get you to school." She opened her purse to pull out some money. "With the napkin," she added without even looking up as Olivia stopped her arm just before her sweater touched her face.

How did Vanessa know? She was only five years older than me and yet she had skills I couldn't match. Skills I didn't even know existed.

"Drosnic? Giuseppe? Man blouses. Are we really still in Jenkins?" Vanessa chuckled. "What do you think that was all about?"

At my shrug, she continued, "Do you mind coming with me to drop Olivia off at school? It'll take a jiffy and then we can catch up more while I settle back into my office after all these months."

"Sure. Sounds fun." It was just after eight and my first client call wasn't until eleven. I smiled despite the early hour. I loved the freedom that came from working as an independent graphic designer. Being my own boss meant working from anywhere and pretty much whenever I wanted. I'd only lasted a few years working in a marketing communications agency before striking out on my own. If I never attended another early morning staff meeting, that would be soon enough.

As we walked to her car, an ambulance drove up the street from the direction of the lake, heading to the state highway. Frowning, I turned to watch it zoom out of sight. Since we didn't have any ambulances stationed in downtown Jenkins, this meant someone was on their way to the hospital.

For some reason, I thought of Jonas, out there on the lake in the dark this morning. I shivered despite the warmth. I'm sure he was fine. Otherwise, I'd have heard from Dale—and even Stapleton would have managed to figure out how to reach me. Pulling my windbreaker closed, I pursed my lips. What was the ambulance doing here? What could have happened?

*****

"Can't you just let her walk from here?" I asked Vanessa. We were only a few blocks from the elementary school. Cars were backed up and edging forward at a snail's pace.

"That's just not done," she said.

"But we can see the school from here. What's the problem?"

"I'd never hear the end of it from the other first-grade mothers," said Vanessa as she darted through the intersection as the light turned red.

"Who cares what other moms might think? What would happen—the cool moms wouldn't talk to you?" Seeing her expression, I added, "They're grownups now, for Pete's sake."

"Oh honey, you have no idea of the school mom politics," said Vanessa.

I gulped. I'd hoped that cliques were a thing of my past.

"Who's Pete?" asked Olivia from the back.

"When I was growing up, I walked all the way here and home by myself," I muttered. Then, realizing who I sounded like, I added, "In the snow, uphill, both ways," and snorted. Pawpaw used to call me soft if I complained about the cold or rain. My grandfather would have fainted if he saw this line of cars taking kids a few blocks to school. Well, not fainted, but he certainly would have expressed his opinion with some choice words.

"It's just a saying, sweetie, that people might say when they're frustrated," Vanessa answered Olivia.

I glanced back at Olivia to see her face twist in concentration as she filed this new tidbit away. My eyes widened as I took in her reaction. I had ignored what sounded like a rhetorical question to me. How did you learn how to talk to kids?

All of a sudden, we heard a loud thump right by my window, nearly making me jump out of my skin. Two hands wearing skater's gloves with long red fingernails sticking out of the open finger holes gripped the door by my open window. "Why good morning to you, Vanessa dearie," said the woman whose face was still out of my view.

She continued, "I see you must have been in such a state this morning that you didn't have time to put yourself together before rushing out to school."

I watched Vanessa check herself reflexively in her rearview mirror with a perplexed look. I didn't see anything wrong, either, but Vanessa reached for her lipstick before stopping herself.

"Well, I'm sure you've heard the news already about Courtney Stanton's death," the woman said.

"What?!" Vanessa's mouth dropped open as she stared up at the woman at an angle through the front windshield.

The name didn't ring a bell for me, but it took a toll on Vanessa. She sat there in shocked silence.

"Yes. What a terrible tragedy, just terrible. There was an explosion down at the lake this morning," said the woman, although her scornful tone belied her words.

I inhaled sharply. At the lake. I suddenly became concerned about whether something had happened to Jonas or his friends. I pulled out my cellphone, but before I could call him, the woman bent over to look inside the car at me. As she did, I could see enough to make out the pretty brunette woman who was connected to the hands gripping my door frame. And to remember her.

It was Sarah Hill. She had been between Vanessa and me in school. She was still a few years older than me now, although evidently her interest in rollerblading hadn't changed, because she was using the toe stop on one of her bright pink in-line skates to keep herself from sliding away. Her skintight, hot pink camo yoga pants and fluorescent orange sports bra appeared optimized to attract as much attention as possible.

"Why, Ella Mae, it's you. I could hardly recognize you. You look so different, after all this time," said Sarah.

Still stunned by her news, I made just a few incoherent sounds. Sarah didn't wait for me to recover as she returned her attention to Vanessa. "I imagine you must be relieved to hear the news," she said as her face twisted into a sneer.

"What? Why would I be happy to hear someone's dead?" asked Vanessa.

Sarah smirked. "You know . . ." She paused as she took in Olivia sitting in the back seat staring at her, then rolled her eyes. "Less competition. Fewer bookkeepers around to share your spreadsheets with."

Vanessa stared mutely at her.

"If you know what I mean," jeered Sarah as if anyone could miss her innuendo.

Recovering, Vanessa snarled, "Just as rude as ever. Go away, Sarah."

As Sarah pushed off, Vanessa shouted, "And I'm an accountant."

Sarah rotated in the narrow space between the car and sidewalk, showing off her skating skills, and threw us a huge, fake smile. "Oh bless your heart, I didn't mean nothing by it. I'm just teasin'. Y'all have a great day now, ya hear." She blew us a kiss, stepped onto the sidewalk, bent over as if pretending to stumble, and then did another rotation to show off her assets for the man who was admiring her in the car behind us.

In the sudden silence, Olivia spoke up from the back seat. "Who was that, Mommy?"

"She's a witch on wheels," answered Vanessa, and then muttered, "Or something like that," under her breath.

No one spoke for the next minute until we reached the designated drop-off spot. "Okay, off you go, honey. Give me a kiss and take your backpack," instructed Vanessa. She forced a smile, but it was tight and her voice was still tense. Olivia obviously could tell something was wrong, quietly following her mother's instructions and scrambling out of the car.

Operation Drop-Off completed successfully, we pulled away from the curb when the traffic monitor whistled and gestured for us to move along. It was as smooth an effort as any air traffic controller might manage.

Sensing the steam still coming out of Vanessa's ears, I waited to speak again while I tried Jonas on my cellphone.

No answer. I tried not to panic as it was school time and he was probably busy getting started with his class. I tried to convince myself there was nothing to worry about. I left a message for him to call me back as soon as he could.

As we pulled up at the small office building that contained the city office, I finally made a comment. "I see Sarah hasn't changed a bit. As pretty as she is, she never stopped being ugly."

Vanessa nodded grimly, and I added, "Guess some things don't change. In fact, I think the last time I saw her, she was also on skates, delivering burgers at the Sonic Drive-In."

Vanessa forced a small grin at my attempt to lighten the mood. As she led me to the building, I said, "Oh, I didn't realize you worked here."

"Well, I've been working remotely from my mother's place over yonder." She gestured generically out of town. "Come in for a minute," she added in a quiet voice. "I've got to pick up some stuff from the office before Adam gets back."

"Sounds devious." I winked but then noticed Vanessa had turned pale. Maybe this actually was something she didn't want her ex-husband to know about.

We hurried inside the building's front door and up the stairs, not stopping to say hi to Ethel in the town office. I only hoped the chatty town clerk, and would-be winner of any gossip competition, didn't see me in the lobby. I'd never hear the end of it if she knew I'd been in her building without stopping in for a quick chat to say my howdies, but my client call did start in a few hours, after all.

The building's second floor contained a larger realtor's office in addition to Vanessa and Adam's small accounting office. Not far from her office door, Vanessa paused by a large pot with a fake tree. She bent over and dug around the wood chips.

At the same moment she grabbed some jingling keys, the realtor's door swung open and Giuseppe stepped through with one hand already raised as if to greet his admirers outside. His sharp eyes latched onto Vanessa's hand, where keys dangled as she straightened up from the planter, but then a wide smile spread across his face. "Liza and Victoria!"

"Vanessa!" we both said in unison.

4

Wednesday Morning

Jonas

The warning bell sounded as I rushed into the school. Normally, I arrived at school with ample time to greet colleagues, politely turn down the school secretary's daily, solicitous offer of the foul coffee that Lester liked as I checked my mailbox in the main office, and address any student concerns in my classroom before class started. I'd never cut it this close before.

Deputy Walker had been thorough in his questioning, taking a long time with me. Afterwards, I raced home to shower and change. I couldn't show up for finals looking like I'd taken a dunk in the lake. Washing away the memory of witnessing someone die was harder to manage.

Had Deputy Walker's suspicion been right? Who would murder that woman and why?

Although still shaken by the explosion and death, at the moment I was more focused on Lester's condition. Realizing that probably no one had notified the school, I poked my head into the school's main office. "Mrs. Crosby, Principal Stapleton was hurt in an accident this morning and is in the hospital. I'm sure he won't be in today."

Her eyes grew wide. "Goodness' sakes alive. What happened?"

"I can come explain later, but I don't think his situation is too serious. I better run. I have to give a final right now."

Mrs. Crosby stared at me, her body still as she processed my update. Then, she nodded firmly. "We will somehow have to stumble our way through an entire day without Mr. Stapleton's wisdom and leadership." She said this without any expression, her eyes never leaving mine.

She stepped away from her post at the counter and turned toward Stapleton's closed office door. As she moved, her posture straightened, her shoulders drawing back and her chin lifting. Pausing halfway, she looked back at me. In a clear, commanding voice, she said, "Well, go on then, get to class, young man." She whisked me on my way like I was one of the wayward students. "Don't you worry. I'll call the hospital to check on Mr. Stapleton shortly. You tend to your own responsibilities."

I hurried off, wondering whether I had just witnessed a successful coup. Other than our daily coffee rejection ritual, I hadn't talked much with Mrs. Crosby over the few months that I'd been a substitute teacher at the high school. If Elizabeth had made that same comment about Lester's wisdom and leadership, I'd have known her words were facetious. My wife had a long-standing dislike for Lester ever since her days as a high school student. Considering Mrs. Crosby's rapid adjustment, I wondered if I should warn Lester to be careful not to drink anything she handed him in the future.

The final bell rang before I made it into my classroom. As I opened the door, a voice called out, "Aren't finals cancelled if the teacher is late?"

Amidst a burst of laughter, I responded, "Sit down, Tristan. Finals are still happening." The class clown, he preferred to hog the spotlight than study. He was smart enough but didn't put forth the same effort in his studies that he did on his football game.

I continued, "Sorry I'm late, but let's get started." Hanging my jacket carefully on the hanger behind the door, I added, "Please clear your desks except for your pencil and cheat sheet." Moving to my desk, I rummaged through my bag for the tests and then turned back to the class.

"Sydney, what are you doing?" I walked toward a girl who had pulled an empty chair close to her desk and was propping a large foam-core poster board on it. The poster board was filled with writing and paper charts.

"Why, Mr. Trout, I'm just setting up my cheat sheet where I can see it," Sydney answered with what had to be her best attempt at an angelic smile.

"But, uh, you can't—"

"You told us we could have a three-by-five cheat sheet," she insisted, her eyes now flashing with determination.

"Yes, but that's not what I—"

She interrupted again. "You didn't say three inches by five inches, just 'a three-by-five cheat sheet.'"

I paused, noticing the rest of the class staring, their index cards sitting on their desks.

Sydney added, "This follows your rules—it's three-by-five. Just feet instead of inches." She crossed her arms. "You're always telling us that units matter. You deduct points from our homework if we forget the units or get them wrong. Seems like the rules should apply to everyone—even teachers," she finished in a burst, and stared defiantly at me.

I covered my mouth with a hand to keep from laughing out loud. 'Hoist by my own petard,' as the Shakespeare saying went. Well, it seemed like poetic justice indeed. At least it meant that some of my lessons had taken hold.

Deciding to reward her cleverness—not to mention the huge studying effort it must have taken to fill the entire poster board with her tiny writing—I nodded. "Okay, you're right. It's clear you've learned that lesson. Just move your chair over there so no one can read your cheat sheet." As the rest of the class groaned and grumbled, I spoke over them. "I've told you for the last few months that units matter in science. Make sure you don't forget to include units as you work on the final." I cut off further debate by handing out their finals.

The room grew quiet and I settled at my desk, reading a book while keeping half an eye out for cheating.

Perhaps twenty minutes passed before loud noises from the hallway startled all of us. The whole class looked up, glancing between the door and me. After another outburst from the hallway, I stood and made my way toward the door. I disliked this part of my new job. Teaching the kids in my classes was enjoyable, and many of their questions were even challenging, but disciplining misbehaving students was not fun. "Not my cup of tea," as my mother-in-law might say.

I stepped out the door, pulling it shut behind me. It turned out unruly students weren't the cause of the disturbance after all. A man and a woman around my age were weaving their way toward me, bouncing off the hallway lockers as they went.

"Go Bulldogs!" shouted the woman, her head tilted back, her long, dirty-blonde hair flying loose. She might have been good-looking, but today she was a bit of a mess, wearing a faded halter top over short, ripped jean shorts and ratty yellow flipflops.

"Woo, woo, woo!" The man joined the cheer, pumping a fist while his other arm was slung over the woman's shoulders. He wore heavily wrinkled work coveralls with the logo of some mechanic's shop on the front and had greasy, wild-looking hair.

"Hey," I called. "Be quiet."

They seemed surprised by my appearance, nearly tripping over each other and onto the floor.

Righting himself, the man turned bleary eyes at me. "Hey, dude, I know you."

I looked at him more carefully but confirmed that I'd never seen him before. "No, you don't, and you need to be quiet. We've got students taking finals."

"Finals." The woman snorted. "Finals are for losers!" She shouted that down the hall in case any students nearby hadn't already heard them. "You can't make us be quiet," she sneered.

"Christy Tomer," interrupted a familiar voice. "What are you doing back here?" Kelsey Wheeler, Elizabeth's best friend and the English teacher who taught in the room next door to me, had joined us in the hallway.

"It's our reunion, you geek. Time to party!" Christy pulled away from the man's embrace and started a one-woman celebration right in front of us, dancing around and raising the roof with her arms above her head.

"I know you too, man." The man pointed a finger unerringly at Kelsey despite eyes that didn't appear to be fully focused on anything.

"Rick Hoffman, are you drunk?" Kelsey glanced at her watch. "At nine in the morning?" She recoiled in disgust as he took a step in her direction.

"No, man. It's too early to get drunk." He and Christy exchanged looks before bursting into giggles. "We're high. Weed. It's the breakfast of champions," Rick answered. He high-fived Christy.

She continued to giggle. "Well, maybe we used too much. That's some strong stuff you've got, Rick."

Rick flexed. "That's right, baby. I'm strong."

When I moved toward them, Rick swayed from side to side. "Hey, man, you look familiar too." He reached up a hand to throw me a high five, but I sidestepped his disjointed effort and put a hand on his back.

"Nice to meet you, Rick. You better hurry. I heard they were starting the reunion this morning at the dock." I thrust him firmly down the hallway back in the direction they had come from.

"Cool," said Rick as my push gave him some much-needed momentum. As they staggered away, he looked back over his shoulder. "Come on, Christy. We don't want to miss the booze. Those cheapskates never buy enough for everyone."

Christy danced after him, offering us one final cheer. "Go Bull-dogs!"

Rick responded, "Who let the dogs out? Woo, woo." But they were both moving steadily toward the exit so it looked like they had enough forward motion to leave us in peace.

Kelsey watched them approach the exit before looking back at me with a smile and a thumbs up. Then her eyes narrowed as she glanced over my shoulder before raising an eyebrow at me.

I turned back to my classroom. A large clump of my students were crowded in the doorway, staring wide-eyed, evidently having watched the entire spectacle.

I clapped my hands twice and then winced slightly as the gesture reminded me of my mother-in-law. "Back to your desks. Show's over. You've got finals to finish!"

One of the students in the cluster asked, "Were they students here?"

I ushered them back into the classroom. "So I gather. Apparently they misgauged how much pot they were taking and hence that display of theirs. Remember, class, that's another problem that can happen when you don't get your units right."

Scattered groans and laughter greeted my commentary, but it succeeded in getting everyone settled back at their desks.

I returned to my desk, shaking my head at those idiots' antics. Ten years out of high school and still so immature.

Then, I sighed. That Christy was right about one thing, at least. I couldn't make them be quiet in the hallway. That was Lester Stapleton's job as principal, and one he was quite effective at. I grimaced, remembering this morning's events again. I was glad Lester wasn't hurt too badly. One dead person was more than I wanted to encounter today—or any day.

5

Wednesday Afternoon

Elizabeth

M y phone ringing jiggled me out of my focus on revisions for a client. I shook myself to return to the land of the living and answered.

"Elizabeth? Oh, thank goodness you answered. I didn't know who else to call," said a breathless Vanessa, tears in her voice.

"What happened? Is everything all right?" My thoughts of work fled as I heard her panic.

"They . . ." Her voice shook. "They arrested me."

"What? Why?" Anxiety flushed through me as her words brought back my own fearful memories of getting arrested a few months ago.

"I'm at the sheriff's office. I forgot my mother's out of town. I didn't know who else to try. Oh, Ella Mae, you'll help me, won't you?" Vanessa gasped for breath after she rushed to get all of that out.

"Yes! What can I do and who do I need to yell at?"

"Come on down and I'll explain everything," she said, her voice now down to a whisper. "You'll come, right?"

"Of course. I'll be right there," I said, yanking on my sneakers and grabbing my purse even before I hung up.

An ever hopeful Daisy jumped off the living room couch and beat me to the front door of my mother's house. "Not this time, Daisy. I'll be right back." Sheriff's offices were no place for a rambunctious dog.

The sheriff's office didn't look any more welcoming than it had the last time I'd been inside, but at least this time I was entering of my own volition. A woman huddled in on herself in the far right corner of the waiting room on one of the many red plastic chairs bolted to the ground. I felt a pang of pity for her but couldn't stop right now to see if I could help. I strode up to the clear plexiglass sliding window that separated me from the holding cells, office cubicles, and rooms that made up the bulk of the building.

"Hey, Lucas," I greeted the overweight officer sitting behind the desk. Even though I hadn't done anything wrong, I felt nervous being here. This place had that effect on me.

"Ella Mae!" Lucas hoisted himself to his feet, brushing crumbs from some former snack off the front of his uniform. His smile broadened. "What brings you here? Not that I'm not happy to see you, of course," he added quickly.

"I'm here for Vanessa Martini. She called me."

He nodded somberly. "Sho' nuff. They brought her in a while back."

"What for?" I demanded. Only a few hours had passed since we'd had breakfast. How could she have gotten herself into trouble with the law so quickly? She liked to talk a big game, but she wasn't the type to cause too much mischief herself, unless she'd drastically upped her game since high school.

"Well now." Lucas shook his head. "I can't rightly say."

"Can't or won't?" I snapped, and immediately regretted taking that tone with him. Lucas hadn't done anything wrong and was a big softie.

He hung his head. "Well now, Sheriff Tucker is pretty strict about us following proper protocol."

"I'm sorry, Lucas. I guess I'm just really nervous for her."

He glanced up at me, his grin back in place. "Now don't you worry none. Plenty of people have said much meaner things to me from across this desk."

We paused and looked at each other through the plexiglass as I considered how his job wasn't just about sitting around and snacking all day. After a long moment, I raised an eyebrow.

Lucas snapped into action. "Well, I reckon I should tell the sheriff that you're here." He made a quick call from his desk phone, keeping his voice too low for me to hear across the desk and barrier. Then he hung up and buzzed open the door beside his desk. "Sheriff'll be right out. He said it was fine for you to come on back here."

I walked into the back, trying not to feel claustrophobic as the heavy door clicked shut behind me. Maybe the sheriff felt more comfortable with me on this side of that heavy door.

Sheriff Tucker was walking toward me from the back hallway. Behind him was Vanessa, looking small and scared. Trent—Deputy Walker as I now needed to think of him, not as my former high school boyfriend—followed behind. As they left the narrow and poorly lit hallway, I noticed a small, extra person trailing closely behind Vanessa. It was Olivia, wearing the same backpack as this morning.

"Mrs. Trout," said the sheriff in greeting. He didn't smile or offer to shake my hand, but that was fine with me.

"Sheriff." I gave him just the briefest of acknowledgments before stepping forward to wrap Vanessa in a warm bear hug.

The sheriff stepped forward too, blocking my path to Vanessa as he put up a hand to stop me. "No touching the suspect."

Seriously, what was his problem. Did he think I was going to slip her a file to break out of her jail cell? The nail file in my purse was made of wood anyway. I glared at him. "Why did you arrest Vanessa? She didn't do anything wrong."

"Are you providing an alibi for her? You know providing false testimony is a crime," he said, eyes glinting dangerously.

"Sheriff, Lizzie, why don't we all calm down and go into the conference room to finish our discussion," said Trent.

I threw him a glare too just for good measure, but getting into an argument with the sheriff wasn't going to help the situation any, so I followed them into the nearby room. Deputy Hot-Shot Walker had been recently promoted to lead investigations in the town of Jenkins. Despite that lofty position, he still needed to stop calling me by that name. Having a pet name reserved only for his use was well and good when our high school romance was going hot and heavy, but not now for a respectable married woman like me.

The sheriff looked like he had regained his composure as we settled ourselves around the table. The presence of little Olivia and the out-of-place cuteness of her scooting herself in her chair closer to the table and then only barely being able to see over the edge probably helped us both calm down.

Before starting our discussion, the sheriff looked over at her. "Olivia, why don't you come with me and I'll find someone who can sit with you outside so the adults can talk in here for a few minutes." At her panicked expression, his tone softened. "Don't worry, you'll get to see your mother again in just a couple minutes."

Olivia seemed frozen to her seat and darted a questioning glance toward her mother, but she followed the sheriff out of the room when Vanessa nodded.

It wasn't that the sheriff was a bad man, or even a bad lawman. I just wasn't exactly his biggest fan. Not after he falsely accused me of murder and threw me in prison to rot. Sure, Trent had corrected me that it was just the county jail, and Jonas had bailed me out after only a few hours, but I felt like I'd been tried, sentenced, and served a lengthy term in the Big House. Having wild swings of emotion and overexaggerating things were all part of why we artsy types were given our very own license: artistic license.

After the sheriff returned by himself, Trent said, "Lizzie," before clearing his throat as he noticed both the sheriff and me stiffen in reaction. "Sorry. Mrs. Trout," he corrected. "Mrs. Martini here has been arrested for murder—"

"Murder!" I shouted in disbelief as I shoved myself away from the table. I wasn't quite clear on why I did that. It's not like I was on my way to lead a protest march or anything. Sitting back down, I remembered Sarah's comment this morning and added, "What happened? Was it Courtney Stanton? You know Vanessa wouldn't do that."

Sheriff Tucker's eyes narrowed. "How do you know the victim's name? Are you involved in this?" He did not look pleased by the prospect.

"The news is practically rolling through town," I replied with a smug smile that quickly disappeared as I thought about Courtney. Why did the sheriff think Vanessa had killed her? She wouldn't kill anyone. My older sister didn't do that sort of thing.

Ignoring my comment, the sheriff said stiffly, "Well, thank you for agreeing to help out. We have a little situation and Mrs. Martini felt you were the best option for assistance."

"Help out? Best option for what?" I knit my brows together in confusion. I didn't know anything about what had happened, and the sheriff would not want my help even if I did.

"It's on account of Olivia," Vanessa said in a quiet voice.

My head swung to her as my eyebrows twisted again. Did the sheriff think she was Vanessa's partner-in-crime? "What about her?"

"Would you please watch her tonight." Vanessa's face was pinched as she held back tears.

My mouth formed a circle before I consciously closed it. My concerns for Olivia immediately shifted. I knew nothing about taking care of children. "What about your mother?"

"She's not in town. She's on a cruise. It's her first vacation in years and I can't ruin it by telling her I was arrested for something I didn't do." Her eyes flashed with indignation as a little color returned to her cheeks.

"But—" I started.

"She'll be back tomorrow. It was a five-day cruise from South Padre Island. She docks back in Texas in the morning before flying home. She can take Olivia after school tomorrow."

I tried again. "But what about—"

Trent interrupted, "Olivia's father doesn't get home until Friday." His body stiffened as he added, "Our other option is calling Children and Family Services."

The suggestion startled me. Sending Olivia to stay with a stranger in foster care, even for one night, was just not right. Then I gulped. Of course, I was a stranger to her as well.

I paused for a moment as I recalled what that idiot at breakfast had said. Now that Olivia knew my name, we were no longer strangers, so all was good. Then I shook my head. It took far more than knowing someone's name to cross over the threshold from stranger to friend, especially for a child. Even though I had hung out with Olivia for longer than Giuseppe had, I was in no way qualified to take care of her. There were days I could barely manage to take care of myself.

But I took a deep breath. There was really no other choice. I nodded at Vanessa and gulped again.

In Mimi's words, things moved like greased lightning after that. The sheriff opened the conference room door and beckoned someone to send in Olivia. I kept a smile on my face, hoping it didn't waver too much as I greeted her. While Trent collected some paperwork that would allow me to take the girl home with me, Vanessa knelt on the ground and told Olivia to come over to her. She hugged her little girl tightly, eyes closed. Then she opened her eyes and whispered at length into Olivia's ear.

I signed and initialed the forms where Trent pointed without reading them, watching the tears rolling down Vanessa's cheeks.

"Understand, sweetie?" Vanessa asked as she finally pulled back from her embrace and looked her daughter in the eyes.

Olivia answered with a serious expression. "Yes, Mommy, I can do that." She glanced quickly at me and then back to her mother as she nodded.

"Okay, honey. Give me one more kiss and hug and then go with Aunt Elizabeth."

Aunt? I gulped again, my throat drier than a desert.

Olivia did as instructed and then scampered around the table to pick up her backpack. She settled it in place and looked up at me, her face still serious but ready.

At the sheriff's request, Trent ushered me and Olivia out of the room while Vanessa remained behind. That was another unexpectedly nice gesture on his part to keep Olivia from seeing her mother shackled and escorted back to a jail cell.

As we approached the waiting room door, I turned to Trent and hissed, "You better keep looking for the real killer. No way she did this."

Trent squeezed his lips together briefly and then whispered, "Lizzie, there's more to this than you know. Even if I was wrong this morning about some things, I was right about it being murder. She had motive and we can place her in the area at the right time."

"What? What do you know?" I stopped walking and turned to stare at him.

He gestured for me to keep it down and answered quietly, "Cameras. Now, you know I can't talk to you about the details." Noticing Olivia had stopped and was staring up at him too, he added, "Go on, take Olivia home and stay out of this." He placed a hand on my back and half-guided, half-thrust me out the heavy door to the waiting area.

He might not have said, "Don't worry your pretty little head about this," but that's what it felt like to me. I sensed my blood rising as my anger grew at being told what to do. I swiveled to tell Deputy Hot-Shot Walker what he could do with his attempt at bossing me around, but the metal door rattled the frame as it closed firmly behind me.

Fuming, I stepped over to the plexiglass window to remind him through the opening how I sounded when he made me mad, but the sliding window was closed and Trent had already skedaddled back to the conference room.

Deciding not to start shouting in the middle of the waiting room, I gained at least a little satisfaction that Trent had realized he shouldn't get bigger than his britches around me. He, of all people, should have remembered how much I really hated when men tried to tell me what to do.

I huffed out a breath, pulled my shoulders back, and marched out of there feeling like I had made my point without needing to make a scene. I'd call that character growth. Good on me.

When I opened the door and stepped into the parking lot, I took a deep breath to settle myself, closing my eyes as I turned my face up to the sun.

A small voice by my side surprised me. "I need to go to the bathroom," said Olivia.

My eyes flew open and I looked down at my new charge. We stood there staring at each other, eyes wide.

6

Wednesday After School

Jonas

W hen the final bell rang, students burst into the hallway with more excitement and noise than usual. They weren't just amped up from the relief that came from the end of finals but from the joy of starting their summer vacation.

We teachers weren't immune to the euphoria sweeping the building; our display was just a bit more restrained. Although I didn't see any fellow teachers giving each other high fives or emptying their lockers or desks onto the hallway floor, I certainly saw plenty of wide grins and dreamy expressions.

All of this hubbub served to lift my spirits as this morning's explosion and death still weighed heavily on me. I was glad I reached Lester during lunch and heard that he had been released from the hospital with nothing more serious than some cuts and bruises. Still on concussion protocol, the doctors had advised him to spend the rest of the day at home. Seeing this afternoon's chaos in the hallways, which undoubtedly would not have been a balm to Lester's spirits, I figured it was probably all for the best. If Lester had to suffer such a terrible accident, at least he received the consolation prize of not witnessing all of the rule infractions violating his hallowed halls of learning.

Elizabeth had also heard about this morning's explosion at the lake. She must have found out right around when classes began today. The speed of the rumor mill in this small town still amazed me. I heard her worried voicemail and had texted her after my first period that I was fine.

At lunch, I had called to give her the full story and update her on Lester's health situation. She seemed annoyed that I had called Lester before her. Elizabeth's long-held grudge against her high school principal sometimes got in the way of logic. My sequence made sense to me. She'd already known that I was fine from my text to her earlier in the morning. By calling Lester before her, I was able to give her a more complete update.

This whole newlywed relationship still required some fine-tuning. Parts of it I really enjoyed—even if we were living at her mother's place. But other parts—like guessing what she wanted without any clues and when applying logic to the situation was irrelevant—simply required more experience. I was sure that after a few more months, the rules of being married would make sense to me.

"Have a good summer, Mr. Trout," said Sydney as she walked past with some friends. After she had finished her final exam, Sydney had ceremoniously karate-chopped her foam-core cheat sheet, leaving the pieces barely fitting into the trash can in my classroom.

I chuckled again at her stunt as I waved goodbye. She'd turned the tables on me this time using my own lesson. Next year's students wouldn't catch me making that same mistake again.

Teachers were expected to work until the end of the week to finish grading and cleaning out the classrooms. I would not need long to accomplish these tasks as I'd applied my normal level of structured organization to my new role ever since taking over as the long-term substitute biology teacher in March.

Since I expected to finish submitting all of my students' grades by tomorrow, this afternoon also felt like the beginning of summer vacation to me. The feeling was probably boosted by all the unleashed teen hormones floating in the air around me.

As I wove around clumps of student clustered by their lockers on my way out of the building, the mayor's son caught my eye. Tyler asked, "See you Friday, right?"

"Definitely," I answered with enthusiasm. I was looking forward to this weekend. In addition to Elizabeth's reunion events, I was going camping on Friday night with Tyler and the rest of the students from the Outdoor Club, along with a few other chaperones. Except for next week's graduation, this was the last hurrah for the school year.

This summer would be the first real break I'd had since we got to Jenkins. With no preparation time, I'd jumped into substituting while also taking the required night teaching classes to earn my certificate.

All thoughts about our busy lives melted away when I stepped into the sunshine and beautiful spring weather. Pausing to close my eyes and soak in the sun, I enjoyed the warmth. Today's weather was great, without the excessive heat and humidity that everyone continued to warn me would hit us soon. "It's time for a run."

"Well, good for you, Mr. Trout," said a student as he brushed past my arm.

I flushed, not having meant to speak aloud. I walked the rest of the way to my car with my eyes open and stray thoughts kept to myself.

Just a few minutes later, I arrived home—well, actually my mother-in-law's house. A short commute was one of my favorite benefits of living in such a small town. "Elizabeth," I called as I opened the front door.

She didn't answer, but Daisy wiggled happily just inside the door as she greeted me. "Hi there, girl." I bent over to pet her. "Do you know where Elizabeth went? Did someone forget to put you in the backyard?"

Daisy didn't answer, but her enthusiastic tail wagging moved her whole body from side to side. If she had been stuck inside for long, she didn't appear to have suffered any lasting trauma as evidenced by her jumping off the ground in excitement.

"Okay, okay, you guessed right. We are going for a run." Not that it was such a huge leap of intelligence for my smart dog. We went running most afternoons.

Hearing the R word, Daisy bounded toward the drawer where we kept her leash.

I laughed. "Hold on, let me change first."

With Daisy egging me on, I was out the door with her in a jiffy. Elizabeth's work was scattered across her desk and spilling onto the floor, but that didn't give me any clues about her whereabouts.

If my desk had looked like that, someone ought to call the police and report a home invasion, violent struggle, and kidnapping. I'd once described Elizabeth's organizational approach as disarrayed pandemonium. She'd taken no offense, although she'd corrected that she viewed it more as a flurry of creativity. To manage my own need for order, I'd learned to mentally border off her work-space. For my sake, she'd adjusted her habits by constraining her creative flurries to mutually agreed upon areas. It was a workable solution that both of us were satisfied with.

Daisy and I ran toward the lake. When we reached Dale's Bait, Boat, and Float shop, Daisy became jittery and nearly tripped me when she darted across my path to switch to my other side, away from the water. Apparently she hadn't forgotten this morning's events either.

The dock area and waterfront looked empty. No police tape remained and no one moved along the dock. Just another random Wednesday afternoon in late May—except for the remnants of the earlier explosion. Was Deputy Walker right about this being a murder? He'd seemed pretty confident in his assessment.

Boats just didn't explode suddenly on their own. I'd heard of boats blowing up before, but all those stories seemed to involve someone fueling their boat and being foolish by smoking at the same time. That hadn't happened this morning. With everything so quiet on the lake, we would have heard the noise of the old gas pump working. And because the dock had been dark in the shadows from the hills, we'd have seen the light from a cigarette or match.

The only thing out of the ordinary that I remembered before the explosion was Daisy barking while we were out on the water. Had she seen something wrong? Had someone been trying to hurt her?

I mulled all this over as I followed the jogging trail next to the lakefront road. Now that we'd left the dock area, Daisy had calmed down and loped easily by my side.

Her doggie brain seemed to be past any worries about this morning, but not mine. I still wondered who would want to murder that poor woman—if that's what even happened.

Despite the traffic along parts of this run, I liked the trail because it curled and twisted through the woods by the water once I got beyond the beach.

We'd gone less than two miles when we reached the section where the trail shifted close to the road and the lake lapped right up against it. Normally, once I'd cleared the last few streets of Jenkins, I'd have a clear view to the far end of the lake. But today was different—an obstruction lay ahead of me.

A peacock blocked the road.

Not an actual peacock, but a man wearing a long-sleeve silk shirt with circles of bright teal surrounded by whirls of blues and grays. He stood on a boulder with a hand shading his eyes as he stared toward the far end of the lake. A large, imposing man in black stood next to the driver's door of a black Cadillac SUV, his arms crossed as he glared at the traffic trying to get past them.

A backup had formed as drivers waited their turn to scoot around the stopped car that blocked half the lane. Despite the mini after-school rush hour, no one seemed to complain. I'd gotten accustomed to folks around here not honking their horns, but it still seemed unusual for no one to holler out a window like I'd have expected back home in a big city. Even if folks wanted to protest, the daunting driver seemed to eliminate any of that simply by standing there.

I had to stop running when I reached them to avoid Daisy darting dangerously into traffic.

"Hey," I called to the peacock. "You're blocking the road. You know you can pull over right up there"—I pointed—"and walk back here to see the view."

"Yes, yes, we'll be leaving shortly." Mr. Peacock turned to glance at me. Dismissing me, he turned away again.

I watched him lift his phone and take pictures of the deserted fairgrounds at the other end of the lake.

Most visitors took pictures across the lake at the hills, not of the far side with its dusty old buildings, empty, packed-dirt parking lot, and weed-covered dunes beyond. A car honked, and I turned to see that the backup in the road had grown. People must have reached their breaking point. I couldn't remember when I'd last heard anyone in Jenkins break the tranquility by blaring their horn.

I frowned in annoyed agreement with the horn-blower and turned back to the peacock. "The lake's not going anywhere. You can take your pictures after you move the car." I stepped closer to him.

"Drosnic," said the man without turning.

The large fellow ambled over from his assigned post of scaring the drivers. He was taller and much bulkier than me. He glared as he scanned me.

My body reacted as well, telling my brain the best option was to leave right now. But I knew that was just my amygdala acting on its own, flooding my nervous system with stress hormones. The body's whole fight-or-flight system was fresh on my mind as I'd just finished testing my students on the autonomic chemical reactions of the human body.

It sounded complicated, but neither fight or flight was necessary at the moment. I only needed my frontal cortex to regain control. Just because a brawny, intimidating man was approaching didn't mean that I had to flee to survive.

Trying to stay calm, I took a breath. It was broad daylight with plenty of people around. I wasn't in danger even if this man was extremely large and muscular. I convinced myself to wait and reassess the situation as it developed.

"Mr. Lucchesi needs another minute. We'll be on our way after that," said Drosnic. Whether that was his first name or last wasn't clear. He stood so close to me that his deep, gravelly voice seemed to resonate within my own chest. He crossed his muscular arms and stared at me without expression. He had spoken calmly and without obvious threat, but his posture and self-endowed sense of authority only enhanced his intimidation factor.

I broke eye contact, realizing that continued engagement with this Drosnic fellow would serve no constructive purpose. All of this disruption had taken me out of my "zone" anyway. Once I stopped running, I found it hard to get back into that state of flow where I was fully immersed and felt a sort of energized focus.

I sighed and looked down at Daisy, dancing around at my side, clearly agitated by the interaction too. "Come on, Daisy, let's head home."

The peacock, Mr. Lucchesi, jumped down from the boulder, landing softly in his expensive leather shoes, his black hair full of so much product that it barely budged. "That's right. Y'all mosey on home now, ya hear, before you get yourself into a kerfuffle." His New York-area accent made a mockery of his attempt to speak like a local.

I ignored him and headed back, laboring more on the return than normal, probably because I was still annoyed at the men. I left the path a block earlier than normal and turned up a different street for variety's sake to try to shake the frustration out of my system.

As I approached Shear Heaven, the hair salon I'd been permanently banned from by my wife and mother-in-law, I noticed a large crowd gathering outside.

"Stop pushing, I haven't finished signing up," complained a stout woman who was leaning close to a sheet taped to the salon's window.

"Ladies, ladies, there's no need to panic." Suzanne Quentin was surrounded by a small crowd as she stood next to the signup sheet. "We've got plenty of spots and plenty more paper so's all y'all can sign up, no problem."

I stepped closer and leaned in to try to read the sign posted on the window. "What's going on?" I asked an older woman in a flowered dress.

"Oh it's so exciting." Her voice was giddy, her eyes alight with excitement as she turned to me. "They're filming a movie. Here. In Jenkins."

"Oh yeah," I responded, remembering Elizabeth had mentioned something when we spoke earlier about some movie scam she heard about in the restaurant this morning.

Apparently my voice lacked sufficient excitement because the woman's lips pulled back with distaste. She shook her head in silent reprimand at my lack of clear appreciation of the delicious magnitude of the opportunity. Then she stepped away from me, moving to close the newly-opened gap with the others. She tapped a taller woman on the far shoulder, causing her to look in that direction. Taking advantage of the momentary distraction, the older woman slid past her, disappearing farther into the crowd as she wormed her way closer to the front.

Suddenly I remembered the Oscar Wilde quote that Kelsey had repeated to me: "With age comes wisdom. But sometimes, age

comes alone." I smiled. Having an English teacher in the next classroom made for unusual discussions during our breaks.

Two sign-up sheets were posted. The one on the left read "Sign
up to be a Movie Extra." On the right, the sign advertised special
"Movie Try-Out 'Dos," with Shear Heaven as the exclusive venue
in Jenkins offering this service to prepare residents for all possibilities of participating in any local filming.

A wry smile slipped onto my face. I wasn't an expert on movie
production, but the timing and careful wording seemed like
another of Suzanne's clever marketing gimmicks—not that I would
ever mention that around Elizabeth. Suzanne was another of Elizabeth's high school classmates, but not a friend. Elizabeth referred
to her as "Susie Q, my nemesis." Sometimes she even included air
quotes for emphasis.

This was a clever ploy, though. Advertising an implied special
connection to a likely fake movie production in order to schedule
additional hair appointments was sneaky, as long as no one wondered how the salon would have gotten connected with some out-
of-town movie producer, or remembered that Shear Heaven was
the only place in Jenkins to get a haircut anyway. Not to mention
Suzanne would have to deal with disappointed clients if Elizabeth
was right that it was a scam.

Clicking my tongue to catch Daisy's attention, I walked away
without saying anything aloud. Angering this mob of women
didn't sound like a good conclusion to my already frustrating run.

Daisy and I walked the rest of the way back to Mary's house. I
got along with my mother-in-law fine, but living with her for the
last two and a half months hadn't been without its challenges. Elizabeth and Mary both had strong personalities, and living together
in a small house had caused plenty of friction between them. I was
looking forward to having our own place soon.

Upon reaching the porch, I stopped to stretch, but Daisy uncharacteristically whined at the door. Today had just not been easy on

her. When I opened the front door, she surged past me to the dining table.

A young girl with brown hair pulled up in hairbands sat on a chair, swinging her legs. She smiled up at me. "Hello, I'm Olivia."

7

Wednesday Late Afternoon

Elizabeth

"Oh, Jonas, you're home," I said as I entered the dining room. "This is Olivia." My voice trailed off as I considered how to explain her mother's predicament without scaring the girl.

"So I've learned," he replied dryly from a crouch where he had just finished high-fiving Olivia. He seemed so natural with kids—no awkward handshake with a little girl. He seemed to do well with the high school kids too. How had he mastered all that?

"My mom has to stay with the police. Because of the bomb," Olivia said.

My eyes widened at her matter-of-fact tone. For Jonas's sake, I added, "My friend Vanessa is her mother. I had breakfast with them this morning."

Jonas addressed Olivia. "I'm sorry you can't be with her right now, but I'm sure they'll figure everything out." Rising to his feet, he added, "What have you been doing with Elizabeth?"

"Aunt Elizabeth," she corrected.

You had to love the man; he didn't even raise an eyebrow at her assertion, even as my palms still got sweaty whenever she called me that.

"We got ice cream." Olivia's face brightened as she remembered the treat. "Chocolate."

I added, "After I collected her at the sheriff's. Then we came here and . . . I guess we just talked."

"Just talking," repeated Olivia with an exasperated little sigh as she laid her cheek on the table. "It's so boring here."

Meeting Jonas's glance, I tried to explain. "Well, it's not like . . . I mean my mother doesn't have any kids' toys anymore. What else is there to do?" I shrugged, holding my hands out to the sides. It wasn't my fault. I hadn't exactly planned on hosting a kid today by myself.

Jonas pursed his lips and looked at Olivia for a moment as she started kicking at the table leg again. "I think I have an idea of something you'll like," he said. "I'll be right back." He went down the hallway to our bedroom while Daisy bounded after him, eager to see his next surprise too.

Olivia stopped kicking the table and lifted her head, her eyebrows rising as she looked at me for explanation. I shrugged silently in response. I was just as clueless. Each of us had our strengths. Connecting with kids seemed to be an asset Jonas effortlessly brought to our marriage.

Daisy beat him back down the hall and into the room. She was clearly pleased with the outcome of the foray into the back of the house as she rushed over to Olivia's side and sat proudly next to her new friend, panting with her tongue lolling out of her mouth. Jonas followed more calmly, holding several sheets of printer paper and a fistful of my colored pencils.

Olivia's eyes widened in delight and her mouth formed into a circle. "Look at all those colors," she said, reaching out to accept Jonas's offering. She spread the pencils out on the table and then looked up expectantly at me. "What should I draw?"

"I . . . well . . . What do you want to draw?" I volleyed back.

Jonas stepped in again. "Why don't you draw a picture of you and your mom. I think she'll like it if you can give her a picture when you see her again, don't you?" After Olivia gave him a thoughtful nod and returned her focus to pencils, he added, "Elizabeth and I are going into the living room to talk for a little while."

Olivia didn't answer. She pulled a sheet of paper close and bit her lip as she picked up a pencil. Focusing on one's art was something I could respect.

When we had moved out of her hearing range, I explained, "Vanessa called me from the sheriff's. They arrested her for murder—of course she didn't do it—and she begged me to take Olivia. She was desperate." I snorted softly. "She'd have to be if she asked me." Then I finished, "It's just for one night. Vanessa's mother comes back to town tomorrow."

Jonas just took it in. He was good that way, not overreacting or interrupting. I definitely used up our allotment of drama all by myself, and probably for several years into the future. "Okay," he said after absorbing my words.

Before he could say anything else, I exclaimed, "It's ridiculous. Vanessa's not a killer."

Jonas cocked an eyebrow at me. "And you know this how?"

I flushed. "Because she's my friend—practically my sister. My friends don't kill people. She had no reason to kill that woman . . ." My voice trailed off as I remembered the snarky comment from that rollerblading Sarah Hill this morning.

"What?" asked Jonas, noticing my reaction.

"Well, Sarah Hill sort of accused Vanessa of wanting Courtney dead." I shook my head. The idea was even more ridiculous than Sarah's outfit.

"Who's Sarah Hill?" Jonas asked.

"Oh, she's this total skank. I wouldn't believe anything she said."

He tilted his head. "Don't tell me. You knew her from high school too?"

"Yeah." I shrugged. "But she's in between Vanessa's age and

mine. She graduated when I was a freshman. We weren't friends or anything."

Jonas stayed focused. "So, why did this Sarah think your friend killed Courtney Stanton by blowing up the *Full Throttle?*"

"Her boat was blown up?" I asked Jonas, surprised that I hadn't heard this detail yet.

When he nodded, I answered his question. "She was implying that Courtney and Adam were having an affair."

"Adam?" asked Jonas.

"Adam Martini, Vanessa's husband. Ex." I pointed to the other room where we had left the kid. "Olivia's father. He and Vanessa's divorce just finalized. That's why Vanessa was back in town this morning. She told me she got back their office downtown and half of their clients in the divorce settlement."

"What does Vanessa do?" asked Jonas.

"She's an accountant, same as Adam. They ran a small firm together. And from what Sarah said, I gathered that Courtney Stanton was an accountant too."

"Hmm," said Jonas.

"Vanessa's not a killer. She couldn't blow up a boat," I said, and then paused.

"What?" he asked again.

"It's nothing," I answered, my jaw tightening.

Jonas tilted his head and looked at me.

"Okay, so she was in the Marines and maybe had some explosives training—I think. But that doesn't mean she's a killer."

"Hmm."

"I mean it, Jonas. I know her. She's like my older sister. She's not a killer," I insisted, smacking him lightly on the arm for emphasis.

"Okay," said Jonas, not quite agreeing with me but also not arguing the point. "I'm sure the sheriffs will clear her." He shrugged, looking like he was done worrying about it.

I grabbed his other arm and stared into his gentle brown eyes. "Jonas, I'm worried. When I went to the sheriff's office for Olivia, Trent told me that they could place Vanessa at the scene this morning. Like with a security camera or something."

Jonas stiffened.

"What?" I asked him this time.

"There may have been someone on the docks before dawn near the boat that exploded. Daisy started barking but we couldn't see anything from the lake," said Jonas.

I grimaced as I remembered what Vanessa had told me during breakfast. Seeing Jonas's inquiring eyebrow lift, I explained, "Vanessa mentioned during breakfast that she had gone out walking really early in the morning while Olivia was still sleeping. That was why she was up and wanted to meet for breakfast earlier than we had planned."

Jonas seemed taken aback. "She went for a walk while Olivia was asleep?"

"She said they had a system. If Vanessa's out when Olivia wakes up, Olivia texts her and Vanessa calls the house right away. This is Arkansas. It's safe here, and this allows Vanessa to go for groceries or a walk."

"Or to plant a bomb on someone's boat." Jonas hesitated. "The timing could work. Vanessa might have walked down to the dock before dawn, installed the bomb, and detonated it when Courtney showed up."

We stared at each other in silence for a moment. Was this what had happened? Had Vanessa killed Courtney? What kind of evidence did Trent have on her anyway? Had she invited me early for breakfast just so she'd have an alibi?

Then I shook my head, making up my mind. Murder just wasn't in my sister's soul. Pranks, maybe, but not killing someone. She had been calm and engaged during breakfast. If she had just murdered someone, she would have been freaked out.

I certainly would have been.

But Vanessa hadn't acted at all cagey during our discussion. Even after Sarah Hill had surprised us and all but accused her of murder.

I nodded. I was right about this. "No way. She didn't do it. She just went through a tough divorce and now this. It's not fair." I almost stomped my foot.

"No," said Jonas softly.

"Why not?" I objected. "She's my friend—"

"I know, and I was agreeing with you that it wasn't fair."

"Oh."

"Hallooo," came a new voice from the front door. My mother, Dr. Mary Banks, the town doctor, school board member, and county commissioner, had returned home to grace us with her presence.

I chastised myself. That wasn't fair. Mom and I have gotten along much better than I'd expected after I returned with Jonas and decided to live in Jenkins. She'd been nice enough to let us live here too. It was what Mimi would have called a character-building challenge for me. To be honest, it couldn't have been easy for Mom either.

"Why hello there. Who might you be?" asked my mother as she moved into the dining room.

"I'm Olivia."

Jonas and I joined them. "Hi, Mom. You remember Vanessa, right?"

Mom snorted. "Of course I remember your babysitter."

"What?" I rocked back, angry at my mother for her insinuation that I had needed a babysitter in middle school. "She wasn't a babysitter. She was my friend, the older sister you never gave me."

From my side, Jonas cleared his throat. "What is that term you use to describe her?"

"My after-school buddy?" I asked, and then I heard myself and it clicked. "Mom!" I yelled. "Did you hire Vanessa to watch me after school?"

"Really? You're just figuring this out now?" She laughed—actually laughed—in my face.

Jonas put a hand on my shoulder, trying to stop me from exploding. "Elizabeth met Vanessa for breakfast this morning."

"And you kidnapped her daughter afterward?" My mother's eyes twinkled.

I took a deep breath, letting it out slowly while I tried not to start a fight with Olivia watching her "Aunt" Elizabeth. Mom usually wasn't this energetic by the late afternoon. She must have had a successful day of bossing around her patients or besting someone in her unending battles on the school board and county commission. Although I had found growing up as her daughter difficult, most people around here generally liked her. For the most part, my mother got along fine with folks—as long as they did what she wanted.

Back under control, I answered, "Vanessa was 'detained' by the sheriff because they think she's involved with this morning's 'incident.'" I purposely kept my language vague with Olivia sitting right here.

"The bomb?" asked Mom.

"Mom!" I glared at her. She should know better. Then, realizing she hadn't used the word "explosion," my curiosity got the better of me. "What did you hear?"

"I didn't 'hear' anything," lectured my mother. "I found some explosive residue indicating that."

Growing up, I'd wished my mother hadn't agreed to take on the extra, part-time position as the county's medical examiner. Other kids' parents didn't have such gruesome jobs. But, then again, I didn't know any other doctors nearby, so perhaps there weren't a lot of options and she did need the extra money.

Deciding not to probe further about her autopsy with Olivia

present, I returned to my explanation. "Vanessa needed me to have Olivia stay with us overnight while she tries to get things straightened out."

Mom scrunched her nose as she considered my words. Apparently deciding this was acceptable, she said slowly, "Okay, although I'd like to hear more details later." Then she smiled at Olivia. "This does explain why we are blessed with young Olivia's presence. But it doesn't explain why you're both standing around yakking and I don't smell any dinner cooking."

Jonas jumped in again before I could give her a piece of my mind. "I suppose we should get something going for dinner."

"How about steak?" proposed Mom.

"It's Jonas's turn to choose tonight, remember?" I spit out. If I let my mother have her way, she'd pick a meat dish every night, leaving my vegan husband to eat only the vegetable side dish or fend for himself.

"But we've got a guest," she protested, gesturing at little Olivia.

"I'm sure she can survive without steak. We'll figure out something she'll eat," said Jonas. He thought for a moment and then asked, "Olivia, do you like fried rice, like at Chinese restaurants?"

Olivia gave him a big smile. "Mmmm," she said, and rubbed her stomach.

Mom turned away, heading toward her bedroom to change out of her work clothes, but I could still hear her as she grumbled, "Fried rice needs chicken or pork, not more of that nonsense tofu." As she walked into her room, she added, "That does not qualify as actual food. Not in my book."

Jonas smiled at me. He'd overheard Mom's remarks too, but her commentary didn't faze him. "Why don't you sit down and help Olivia with her drawing and I'll make dinner."

I liked that plan. He was better at cooking anyway. I sat across from Olivia and looked at what she was drawing. She had sketched a basic house with two figures standing outside—one tall and one short, both holding hands.

I reached over and grabbed the dark gray, light gray, and brown pencils. Selecting the dark gray one first, I started sketching out some tree trunks upside down. It was a popular misconception that tree trunks were brown; when you really looked at them, most appeared more gray—

"You're drawing upside down." Olivia had stopped coloring and was staring at me like I was an alien.

Secretly pleased by how impressed she sounded, I shrugged. "Yeah, it just takes practice. If I have to do it, I try to picture the thing upside-down in my mind and then start drawing."

Olivia leaned forward, sticking her face right above my hand as I tried to draw without even seeing the pencil. "Can I try?" she asked after a few moments.

"Sure." I rotated the paper so it faced me. Handing her the yellow and orange pencils, I said, "Why don't you start with the sun? Drawing an upside-down circle is pretty easy."

"It's the same thing, silly." Olivia laughed as she started drawing. "Why did you give me both pencils?"

I looked up from working on some flowers to see her staring at me, her face barely above the table. "Because the sun isn't just yellow. It's kind of a blend between yellow and orange. Don't you think so?"

She squeezed her face together as she conjured an image of the sun in her mind's eye. "Yeah!" She became excited. "It is. Especially when the sun sets." She returned to drawing, making up for any gaps in skill with her enthusiasm.

I smiled to myself. I might not know how to introduce myself to a child, but at least hanging out with a kid who liked art was well within my wheelhouse.

I glanced up to catch Jonas standing in the doorway staring at me and Olivia with that goofy grin of his smeared all over his face.

Jeez, he's not going to have the 'let's have a baby' conversation with me again. Please not now. And certainly not with Mom nearby.

As Jonas opened his mouth, I jumped in before he could speak. "We've got to help Vanessa prove she wasn't the killer." Then, startled at my own words and that I'd slipped and said them in front of Olivia, I leaned back in my seat.

Fortunately Olivia didn't react, probably so accustomed to tuning out adult conversations that nothing registered unless her name was used. I could relate.

Jonas smiled, probably recognizing that I was only trying to distract him. "Isn't this the woman you've barely seen since high school until this morning?"

"She's still my friend—my sister, regardless of whether Mom gave her money. No way she did it." I took a breath and puffed it out. "No way," I repeated.

Helping Vanessa had started as only a spur-of-the-moment idea to distract Jonas, but it felt right. She was no killer. Deciding to double down, I grew serious. "We can do this. We're smart. We've got to help her. No one else will. We have to figure out who did it."

"Are you sure we should . . ." Jonas's voice trailed off as he caught sight of my special glare.

"She's my sister," I insisted. "We have to do this."

He gulped. "Okay, sure. We can at least try to help her out."

I relented on the glare. Too much of that powerful force could probably cause bodily damage anyway. "Thanks," I told him. "I believe in us. We can solve this."

After Jonas escaped to take a quick shower, I murmured more quietly, "Probably."

*****

When we started smelling the food cooking, Olivia helped me put away our art supplies and set the table for dinner.

Jonas had outdone himself. The fried rice was delicious. Even the tofu was good—stir-fried with some sesame oil into crunchy cubes of yumminess that mixed well with the vegetables, garlic, and rice. Not to mention whatever other secret spices he added.

I nodded toward Olivia, who was preoccupied with shoveling food into her mouth as fast as possible, and directed my words to the other adults at the table. "The, uh, paternal figure is in Sin City and doesn't return until TGIF." I continued to employ a form of code to keep Olivia from understanding that we were talking about her father.

"Are you trying to say Vegas and Friday?" asked Mom.

"Yes." I waved at her to stop being obstinate. She could certainly follow my cryptic conversation without being obtuse and revealing too much to Olivia. "My friend told me that the, uh, ex, loved to gamble. That was part of why the, uh, dissolution came about."

Mom pushed herself back from the table. "Olivia, honey, do you want seconds too?" At Olivia's nod, she took both plates back to the kitchen.

I looked at Jonas. "The ex would play poker with guys like Grody in the hidden bar."

Jonas set down his fork. "Okay, now you've got me totally confused. Who's Grody?"

I laughed. "Sorry, that wasn't code. It's a nickname for this guy we grew up with, Andrew Grady. His father owns the fairgrounds where we'll be going tomorrow night for the go-kart racing. They used to keep livestock there when I was young and he always seemed to come to school smelling like animals."

"And what hidden bar?" asked Jonas.

"The underground one." Seeing his incredulous look, I realized I'd neglected to give him the complete, off-the-beaten-path tour of Jenkins. "No, really, it's underground. There's this huge basement built under the kebab place over on Second Street."

"There's a kebab place on Second Street? Where? I've been down that street plenty of times and I've never seen a kebab restaurant."

"It's not really a restaurant. You know that old hardware store?" At his nod, I continued, "They sell kebabs out the back window when Mrs. Espinoza has time to make them."

He started shaking his head. "Now you're just trying to pull one over me."

I started laughing as I realized how silly it sounded. "No, really, it's true."

"Then how come you never took me there?" Jonas asked.

"They only serve meat," I explained.

"And the bar?" He still didn't believe me.

"I don't like going to bars."

"Since when? We used to go all the time."

"Those were nice places in Portland with good food and music. This is more of a hangout spot for high schoolers."

"A bar?"

"They only serve alcohol on Saturday nights when it's eighteen and older. Or they did. On a few other nights, they opened for pool and playing music too loud with some dancing."

Mom walked back inside with her and Olivia's plates refilled.

"Mom, tell Jonas I'm not lying about the underground bar and kebab shop."

"I'm not getting in the middle of something," she said as she sat down and took a bite.

Annoyed at her lack of support, I glared at her.

Jonas changed the subject. "I saw some unusual tourists today blocking the lake road out past the beach."

As he described them, I jumped in. "We saw them too. Remember, Olivia, those two men who were talking to us at breakfast this morning."

"They were funny," said Olivia.

"Why were they blocking the road?" I asked.

"One was taking pictures of the fairgrounds near the last few streets of homes where the lake comes in close to the road," explained Jonas.

"That's weird," I said. "They were telling people at the cafe that they're here to film a movie."

"Filming a movie here in Jenkins? Bah." My mother was never one to keep her opinions to herself. Her disbelief at the story was clear. Although I wouldn't admit it to her, she tended to be right more often than not, especially about happenings in Jenkins. My mother was pretty well-connected around here. If a movie company had planned to film in the area, she'd probably have known about it well in advance because they'd need permits.

"They're probably here scouting sites to build if we get awarded the last casino license being issued by the state," she said between bites.

"Casino? I was talking about Vegas before, not here in Jenkins," I explained. She must have gotten confused.

She rolled her eyes at me. "I'm not senile, you know. The state gaming commission is supposed to award the fourth and final casino location pretty soon, and it has to go somewhere in this part of the state." Seeing my confusion, she put her fork down for a moment. "You've heard the Arkansas legislature approved four casinos in the state, right? Everyone's been all abuzz about where the one for this region will go. I'm surprised you haven't heard about it."

I hadn't. I'd been so busy since getting back I must have been out of the loop.

Jonas said, "I've heard a bit at school from the teachers, and

Dale was talking about it this morning." He yawned as if just the reminder of his early start made him tired.

Mom snorted. "Oh, I'll bet he was. The mayor'll talk about that till the cows come home." She paused as she took a sip of water. "You know, I'll bet those guys you saw were mafia."

"Mafia?! Like in *The Sopranos*?" My mouth formed the shape of an O.

"Yes, dear," responded Mom. "They exist in real life too, not just shows."

"Seriously?" I put both hands flat on the table and stared at her as I demanded a straight response. "The mob is here in Jenkins?"

"Could be." She shrugged. Then, seeing my frown, she added, "Well, I'm always reading about the mafia showing up wherever there are casinos."

"Mom," I said, my voice practically dripping with scorn.

She crossed her arms in front of her chest. "Well, it's possible. They could be mafioso."

"You're acting prejudiced," I told her, and leaned back, crossing my own arms and watching her resume eating.

As nutty as she sounded, was she right? Was Mr. Fancy Shirt part of the mafia? Would that make the big guy a hitman? What kind of movie would they be making in Jenkins anyway? If they weren't here to film a movie, why did they draw so much attention to themselves and lie to everyone in the cafe? Finally, I shrugged. I could talk myself in circles if I wasn't careful.

Mom swallowed a bite. "Maybe they are mafia and they committed that—" She paused as she remembered Olivia sitting across the table and finished, "That heinous act."

"Mom!" I exclaimed. "You can't just accuse someone of doing that . . . that sort of nefarious deed without proof."

"Well, if it wasn't them, maybe it was the Cherokee," she said.

"What?" I exclaimed, louder this time. I couldn't believe her sometimes. She hadn't been this prejudiced when I was growing up, had she?

She looked at me unabashedly. "They're trying to win the casino too. They've got big casinos over in Oklahoma and have been itching to expand into Arkansas."

"That's a horrible thing to accuse them of. There's absolutely no proof that any Native American tribes were involved in that villainous act." I narrowed my eyes at her. "You know, Mom, being bigoted is not a good look on you. Especially for someone in your positions of authority."

Mom scoffed. "Don't get your feathers all ruffled. I'm not bigoted. I'm just hypothesizing from the comfort of my own home." Her voice lowered in pitch and became quieter as she grumbled, "What happened to the good old days when you could accuse someone of murder without getting into hot water with the PC police?"

I looked over at Jonas, but he stood up and headed for the kitchen, avoiding my eyes. Although that was probably the appropriate course of action considering we were house guests here, I'd never been known for my restraint. "Looks like you're enjoying Jonas's meal, huh Mom?" I asked her as Jonas brought in a chocolate chip cookie and handed it to an appreciative Olivia for dessert.

Mom grunted. "Not bad," she said as she finished the last bite—on her second plateful.

"I guess you like tofu more than you thought." I provoked her a bit more, figuring it was payback for her acting so intolerant. Besides, it had to be good for her heart to get her blood pumping. She didn't get any other exercise besides racing around to her meetings and patients.

My mother ignored me and turned to Olivia. "Young lady, have you had your bath today yet?"

Olivia looked down at her plate and shook her head. "No, ma'am. I don't have any pajamas here."

With my mother's well-deserved glare aimed in my direction, it was my turn to feel embarrassed. It hadn't crossed my mind to get some fresh clothes for Olivia. I stammered, "I didn't get keys to Vanessa's place."

"What did you do with her all afternoon?" she asked.

"We got ice cream," I answered. I had thought that was a masterful move to help distract Olivia as we left the sheriff's office.

As Olivia finished the cookie, Mom looked over at her and then gestured at her mouth.

Olivia reached for a napkin.

"Hmm," said my mother. "Ice cream *and* cookies today." She let her words hang out there long enough for me—as the responsible adult—to feel the sting of her disapproval. Then she clapped her hands twice in rapid succession. "Well, young lady, I think it's time for your bath. I'm sure we have some old clothes around here somewhere that can serve as pajamas for you. And while we're at it, we'll toss today's clothes into the washing machine so you'll have something clean to wear to school tomorrow."

I silently groaned. I hadn't thought about tomorrow.

Ugh, now I had to get up for school in the morning too. Oh, and start investigating a murder that I'd committed to solve.

8

Thursday Morning

Elizabeth

Figuring I could handle a seven-year-old girl by myself, I'd told Jonas he could have the morning to himself in honor of school ending.

I was wrong.

Fortunately, Mom was awake and around as it took her, me, and even Daisy to get Olivia in the car and us backing out of the driveway before eight. I had managed to keep everyone quiet so Jonas could sleep in and had just about enough time to get Olivia to school on time. I was even reasonably confident that most of her stuff had made it into her backpack, including the PB&J sandwich and apple that Mom remembered at the last minute to make for her lunch.

It seemed strange that the elementary school finished a week later than the high school, but then again, much of school had always seemed illogical to me.

Without asking for permission, Daisy had apparently decided to join us. I couldn't fault her for wanting to see this exciting change in our morning routine through to a conclusion. Normally she'd be begging to stick her nose out the window, but today she lay sprawled across Olivia's lap in the backseat. I didn't know if this position was more a show of possessiveness or protectiveness.

"So remember your grandmother will pick you up from school today," I reminded Olivia as I glanced at her through the rearview mirror. She sat quite low in the backseat without a booster seat. It had taken a small debate yesterday to convince Olivia that she was allowed to travel with me on short trips without her booster seat. I'd promised to drive slowly and swore a pinky promise that her mother would be okay with it, but I think the offer of ice cream had truly sealed the deal. Fortunately that precedent seemed to be holding.

"What about my diorama?" she blurted out as I stopped at a yellow light instead of squirting through like I normally would have done.

Proud of myself for such careful driving, I turned to look at her. "Your what?"

"I'm supposed to bring my diorama to school today," she said, and looked out the window. Her usual calm demeanor was now broken as her eyes glassed over with tears.

My breath caught in my throat as I mentally raced around my mother's house, wondering where she might have left something for school. "What diorama?"

"It's my ocean diorama." She kept her gaze out the window, as if trying to hide her tears.

"You didn't tell us you needed to make a diorama last night," I said, trying not to panic.

"It's already finished. Mom and I made it on Sunday." Her voice hitched on the word "Mom," and the tears dripped out of her eyes.

I started to tear up too. How sad to be all alone at age seven. Then a jolt ran through my body as I realized she wasn't all alone—I was supposed to be taking care of this sad little girl. How was I to do that? Eating ice cream from the container and watching sappy movies were my go-to tricks, but those didn't seem appropriate for a girl her age at eight in the morning.

Realizing how I might fix this, I made a sudden turn away from the school at the next corner. If I rushed over to Vanessa's apartment and managed to find the landlord to let us in, I could make it back here only a little late for school. Somehow I felt like I could hear my mother laughing at me from blocks away, but seriously, how much trouble could a kindergartner get into for arriving late?

I didn't know how to help Olivia feel better, but I could get her and her diorama to school. That would have to do until her grandmother collected her later today. She'd know what to do to make Olivia feel better. That's what grandmothers were for.

We jumped out of the car at Vanessa's new apartment and hurried to their unit as I scanned the area, searching for a manager or maintenance person. Of course, no one was in sight, and the two-story building with two apartments on each floor was too small for a live-in building manager.

"Well," I said, biting my lip while I considered my next move. Noticing the welcome mat in front of Vanessa's door, I knelt down and lifted it to retrieve the key that I assumed was there.

Nothing lay underneath.

"Shoot," I said as I stood up. Who didn't hide their spare key under the mat? I screwed up my face as I tried to put myself in Vanessa's shoes. She had to keep a spare key around somewhere. Looking over at Olivia, I said, "Sweetie, any idea where—" when I saw it.

Under one of Vanessa's windows a few steps away from her door sat a planter containing a large flowering bush. "Could she have . . ." I mused aloud as I stepped over to it.

"Oh yeah," remarked Olivia as we reached the planter.

I looked at her. "Oh yeah, what?"

"When she was saying goodbye, Mom wanted me to tell you to get the stick from here."

"The stick?" I asked as I leaned over and stuck my hand through the leaves to the surface of the dirt.

"Uh-huh, I think so." Olivia sucked in a shaky breath, tears still close to the surface.

Bingo! My hand brushed up against something metallic and small.

The dam broke and Olivia burst into tears. "I want my mom. Can we go see her now?"

Closing my hand around the hard object, I pulled my arm out and turned back to Olivia.

She stepped into me and wrapped her arms around my waist right as a police car pulled into the parking spot in front of us.

Busted! How did the cops know we were here?

My heart started racing until I saw it was only Trent.

"Lizzie?" he said as he popped out of the car. "What are you doing here?"

"Getting something Olivia needs for school." I awkwardly put an arm around Olivia as she bawled.

"What did you take from the planter?" he asked as he approached us, his eyes narrowing as he stared suspiciously at my hands.

"Nothing," I said, not even sure why I was lying to him, except that Vanessa had wanted Olivia to tell me about it. Not the sheriff, but me. I wasn't about to blow her secret—whatever it was. "I was looking for a key to her apartment." I straightened and met Trent's eyes as I patted Olivia on the back.

"Show me your hands," he instructed in a stern voice.

"How dare you!" I flushed with a mixture of embarrassment and anger. Realizing that I needed to convince him that I was really mad and not that he had caught me in the act of stealing something, I crossed my arms and glared. Pretending to be upset wasn't very difficult. It was rude to accuse me of taking something I shouldn't have, even though he knew me well enough to know that wouldn't stop me if I was doing what I thought was right.

Seeing him take another step toward me, I flipped each hand back and forth to show him they were empty.

"Thanks. Sorry about that," he said, now sounding abashed.

"I can't believe you, Trent Walker," I snapped, waving one hand dismissively at him as my other hand slipped the metal item from the planter into my jeans pocket. Then I gave silent thanks to Paw-paw for teaching me his sleight-of-hand magic tricks.

Maybe Trent Walker wouldn't want me to take the object if he had known, but he wasn't the boss of me. Besides, it didn't belong to him, and the sheriff's office was falsely accusing my friend of murder. If whatever I'd grabbed was nothing important, I'd return it later. Trent would never know. I was pretty good at lying to him by now.

Trent had stopped dead in his tracks, probably scared off by the combination of my anger and Olivia's sobbing. He held his sheriff's hat in his hands. "Hey, I said I was sorry, but we can't have you interfering with the investigation." He paused and tilted his head. "Why are you here again?"

I told him Olivia needed her diorama for school. He started to wring the brim of his hat and then shook his head with a chagrined look. "I'm sorry, but we can't let you inside or allow anything to leave the apartment until I'm done processing it. I searched Vanessa's office yesterday afternoon. I should be finished in a few hours at most."

That provoked a fresh round of sobbing from Olivia. "I have to have my diorama this morning."

"Seriously?" I stared daggers at Trent. "It's a kindergarten diorama."

He nodded helplessly, but his jaw was set. I knew once that had happened, he wouldn't change his mind without a big effort. Since when had Trent Walker become such a law-abiding citizen?

I shook my head. Obviously getting a degree and then a job in law enforcement had an impact on him. Both of us had changed a lot since high school.

I gave Olivia a squeeze. "It'll be fine, sweetie. Go get into the car. We'll skip school for today and go have some fun exploring up at my ranch." I was proud that I called it my place instead of my grandparents'.

She sniffed, wiped her nose on her sleeve, and trudged back to the car, but not before giving Trent a sour look. *Good for her!*

Trent waited until she closed the car door before looking at me sideways. "You're not taking her to school? Do I have to write you up for truancy?"

"Back off, Deputy Walker," I snapped. "You've got her mother locked up in prison and now you're going after her daughter?"

"It's jail," he said, his face threatening to break out into a smirk.

"What?!" I yelled at him. How dare he try to get cute with me?

Trent backed down. "Okay, okay, Lizzie. Don't have a cow."

I narrowed my eyes again. "I've told you not to call me that."

"Okay, jeez, I'm sorry. Just take her to school so she doesn't get into trouble."

I left him standing there as I walked off to my car, talking to myself out loud. "It's freaking kindergarten and I'll have a whole herd of cows if I want."

With Trent watching me leave, I headed away from Olivia's school, up the ridge. Maybe I wouldn't keep thinking of it as Mimi's ranch after our house was finished.

*****

As I drove, I wiggled the metal object I had pulled from Vanessa's planter out of my jeans pocket. Vanessa's "stick" was a USB flash drive. Why had she kept it outside of her apartment? And why had she secretly asked Olivia to tell me to grab it? Did it hold some incriminating evidence that tied Vanessa to the murder? Plans for blowing up Courtney's boat or details on how she'd remotely detonated the bomb?

I didn't believe Vanessa was capable of killing someone, but she sure had motive, opportunity, and probably the right skills. I started to sweat despite the cool temperature. Was keeping the USB drive a secret making me an accessory to murder? I certainly hadn't signed up for that. Clenching my jaw as I wound my way along the curvy road to the top of the ridge, I pondered my next steps.

Finally, as I turned onto the poorly paved road that led to Mimi's ranch, I came to a decision. I'd see what was on the flash drive before determining whether to bring it back to Trent or show it to Vanessa's lawyer—did she even have one yet? "Strategic flexibility," as Pawpaw used to say when he refused to make a choice. He seemed to always use this approach on important decisions, especially to avoid narrowing his selections. I remembered him using this phrase most often when Mimi asked him which pies she should make for Thanksgiving.

As my car rattled along the long, narrow driveway that served Mimi's ranch and our neighbor's place farther in from the county highway, I watched Olivia's head swiveling from side to side as she looked out the windows. The upper portion of the ranch now consisted mostly of meadows and clumps of trees that had sprouted close to the small "crick." Mimi's crick was a barely viable stream that petered out by the far corner of the property rather than any sort of actual river. Still, it had made the land good for small-scale cattle ranching back in the day. When I was growing up, the crick was my favorite part of the property.

I parked under the carport by Pawpaw's old converted workshop. As I got out of the car, I heard the workers finishing the framing of the roof and walls for our new house. I had inherited my grandparents' house, but when it burned down a few months ago, Jonas and I decided to stay and build a new house with the insurance money and our unexpected wealth from his last job.

Olivia's eyes went wide as she stared at the unfinished house. "Wow," she said as the sounds of nail guns and electric saws came from the back and inside of the house.

"Yeah, it's pretty cool to see them working. I'll show you around later, but first I want to see what's on your mother's stick," I said as I led her and Daisy to the workshop.

Opening the door released a wave of stinkiness. "Phew." I stepped back from the entrance to let the smell out. The odor wasn't from old tools, sweat, or spilled fluids from long-ago automobiles in this once-standalone garage. Something had died inside.

"Oh no," I said, realizing what must have happened and hurrying inside.

Olivia followed me and tapped on the glass walls of the tall, octagonal fish tank in the back corner. "Why is it so smelly?" she asked.

"I think one of the fish died," I said as I took off the light on top of the tank and pulled over the short stepladder to look inside. Jonas and I had found Mimi's old fish tank stashed in the barn when we were going through everything after the fire. It had looked to be in good shape, but I left it alone until we had cleared out most of Pawpaw's workshop.

We were planning to turn his old workshop into my art studio. By removing most of his old tools, replacing the single-pane windows with ones that were actually clean enough to allow light through, and painting the inside, we had made the old garage feel like a brand-new space. I loved it. I couldn't wait until I had time to dedicate to my art without workers hammering and sawing right outside the window. I just knew this newly designed space, attached to many loving memories of my Pawpaw, would allow me to be at my creative best.

Just this past weekend, I had finished cleaning and prepping the fish tank. I stocked it with some beautiful cichlids, and all had seemed well for the first few days. I came up here pretty much every day to work or deal with some question from the contractor about the house project. It was nice to have this little room set up to call my own while we waited for the construction to finish. Besides, watching the fish allowed me some peaceful meditative respite from all of the construction mayhem and a nice distraction from whatever project I was supposed to complete.

"Yup, here it is," I said as I used the net to scoop out the remains of a fish.

"Yuck." Olivia wrinkled her nose but followed me outside. "What was its name?"

"Well," I said as I dumped the fish into the trash can, "I guess I never got around to naming the fish." We walked back inside, but I left the door open. "We need to air this place out." I pulled the flash drive from my pocket again, hoping Pawpaw's ancient computer would work. Otherwise I'd have to wait until I returned home to use my computer. This little excursion hadn't been well planned.

As I sat down in front of his computer and pressed the power button, Olivia asked, "What should I do?"

"Hmm." I looked around the small room, searching for inspiration. What did seven-year-olds do? I latched onto the last idea that had worked with her. "Why don't you draw something again?" I pulled out some paper and colored pencils from a drawer and cleared a spot on my art desk.

"Isn't there something else to do?" she complained.

"Sorry, but we don't have any toys here. Draw for a bit and then I'll take you exploring, okay?"

She grudgingly agreed. "What should I color?" she asked as she climbed onto the chair.

I couldn't get away with using Jonas's exact suggestion again, so instead I proposed, "How about drawing a picture of something you did with your dad when you were with him last?" After I spoke, I felt guilty for betraying Vanessa, but I didn't want Olivia focusing on her mom again after her crying spree earlier this morning.

Olivia picked up a pencil and started drawing while I sat and waited for the computer to finish its laborious startup process. I laughed quietly to myself. This computer worked about as quickly as Pawpaw had moved, at least in his last few years.

I stuck the flash drive in a slot and brought up a window to view its contents. Dozens of files popped up on the screen, gradually filling the display as the old computer rattled its way through the directory as if pulling out each file from a drawer by hand.

"What do we have here?" Since I didn't expect Pawpaw's computer to answer, I scanned the list. Spreadsheets, photos, and saved emails cluttered the display. "Where should I start?" I mumbled before deciding. "Pictures, of course." Once a graphic artist, always a graphic artist.

I clicked on one of the picture files. A photo started appearing on screen almost line by line as the old computer formed the image on the display. A man wearing shorts and a blue shirt stood in a medium-sized motorboat, talking to someone out of the picture on the dock here in Jenkins.

As the rest of the picture filled in, another man kneeling with his back to us and wearing a gray and black flat cap became visible. On the hull right below the driver's seat where he was working I could make out the boat's name: *Full Throttle*. I gasped. That was the name—

"That's my dad," said a little voice by my elbow. Olivia was pointing at the man in shorts.

I looked closer. "Yes, it is." Adam Martini was older and a bit heavier, but he still looked like the guy I remembered Vanessa marrying. Why was he standing on Courtney Stanton's boat? And who had taken these telephoto pictures of him?

"Look, I drew the picture," she said, and thrust her picture in my face. She'd drawn a small figure holding hands with a tall person and another smaller adult on his other side also holding hands. I swallowed back some unexpected tears as I realized Olivia must have drawn a picture of herself with Adam and Vanessa, either remembering or wishing for happier times.

Her work wasn't half bad—my lips quirked as I noticed she had used a gray pencil for the tree trunks. I had to appreciate her willingness to learn. This wasn't the time to point out that her mother's hair wasn't that long or light. There was a proper time and place for critiques. Sometimes an artist just had to draw what they felt.

"You did a nice job," I said.

"Can we look at more pictures?" asked Olivia, pulling my attention back to the screen.

Had Vanessa been following her soon-to-be ex-husband? Had she hired a private eye? And to capture Adam doing what? I suddenly became concerned about what might show up on the other photos if I opened them with her daughter standing right here. "Not right now. I've got to look at the other files. They'll be boring. Go back and do more drawing," I told her. I'd have to check the other photos later in private. "Maybe add in more of the background and then start a picture of . . . say . . . your class at school."

Her shoulders slumped, but she returned to her chair. I clicked to open the first saved email message. Would these messages shed any light on why Vanessa had been spying on her ex-husband? Or what Adam had been doing standing at ease in the middle of the day on Courtney Stanton's boat?

The email was a fairly brief request to meet and discuss her providing accounting services to the small business—a dress shop in the next town. The client hadn't been interested. I opened another file to find pretty much the same thing. I opened five or six more with-

out finding anything too interesting. If this was all that was on the
flash drive, why had she hidden it in the planter?

Then I got excited when the next email contained a list of clients
that she had emailed to herself. Was she planning to go after them
once the divorce was final? Clever. Maybe Adam had found out
and gotten mad at her. Maybe, but what did that have to do with
Courtney Stanton's death?

Realizing I was reading the emails from oldest to newest, I
decided to switch approaches and opened up the newest email message. This one, a lengthy thread with an email user named DG24,
had much more back-and-forth than the others. Reading from the
newest email at the top of the file didn't make things clear, so I
paged to the bottom and started reading upward. Soon, I realized
what was going on. Vanessa was succeeding in convincing DG24
to hire her as the accountant for his or her business.

I frowned as I tried to figure out who DG24 was or what business they operated. Was Vanessa trying to grab a client that she
shared with Adam or was it a brand-new customer? Did any of this
relate to the explosion? "What are you doing here, Vanessa?" I said.

"Is that my mom's?" said an eager voice at my elbow again, holding a drawing in her hand. Olivia had moved to my side as silently
as a mouse.

"Olivia," I said, and then looked around the room, searching for
something that could keep her occupied for a little longer. Over in
the corner, one of the edges of the octagonal fish tank showed a
small trickle of water running down the glass. "Shoot," I said, hurrying over with Olivia hot on my heels.

"The tank's leaking," I explained.

"Are the fish going to escape?"

I smiled at the idea. "No. It's just a tiny leak. But if I don't fix it
soon, it could get worse and all the water will come out." I groaned
as I thought about the hassle of cleaning or replacing the carpet in
here on top of all the other work we had to do at the house.

"I don't want the fish to die. They can't live out of water. Can we glue it or something?" She started to sound anxious.

"I think we've got some time to fix it, but I'll have to get the right kind of glue from a store." I scanned the room and then grabbed a ragged towel to wipe the glass dry before pulling an old roll of duct tape from a shelf and ripping off several strips.

"There," I said as I carefully pressed the duct tape over the seams and reinforced them with several more rounds. "My Pawpaw used to tell me that duct tape can fix anything. At least temporarily." Olivia's eyes were focused on the handful of fish in the tank and her lips were pressed tightly together as if she were on guard duty to make sure they wouldn't die.

I knelt down and touched her arm. "Honey, I have a better idea for you. The fish need names. Why don't you draw a picture of each fish and make up its name?"

Her eyes brightened at the idea. "Yeah. I can name them after my friends, or . . ." She drifted back to pick up her pencils as she started thinking through the task.

Recognizing the signs of someone who was now caught up in their own project, I eased silently back to Pawpaw's old computer, pleased with myself.

As I read the more recent parts of the email thread, it looked like DG24 had asked Vanessa to review some spreadsheets and look for anything wrong. Reluctantly I opened the first spreadsheet file.

And immediately got a headache.

Numbers just weren't my thing. Artists did art, not math. Math was for . . . well, accountants. The spreadsheet contained a long list of entries, each with a brief title, category, amount, and accounting code. I knew that much because the column headers were written in English. Most of the entries were small and might have been supplies purchased from Walmart and some local hardware stores, but other entries had descriptions and codes that made no sense to me. Almost all the entries were for under a hundred dollars, but as I scrolled up and down the list, I found more than a few larger entries with vague titles and both positive and negative numbers. How would Vanessa figure out if something was wrong?

And what did that mean—something wrong? Spreadsheets did all the adding and subtracting for you. Was DG24 worried that someone was stealing?

I shook my head in frustration. All this searching had done was intensify my headache and remind me that I needed to find a new local accountant. It was hard to drop in to ask some questions of my current accountant when he lived over two thousand miles away in Portland.

Giving up on the spreadsheet, I returned to the file directory and opened another saved email. I'd gone through another dozen messages when the door suddenly banged shut.

I looked up in surprise.

A gust of wind must have blown it closed.

Then I noticed that the table where I'd set up Olivia was empty. I whipped around to check the fish tank, but it stood alone.

Olivia and Daisy were gone.

My heart lurched as I jumped to my feet.

When had they left the workshop?

I kicked myself mentally as I rushed to the door. How could I have gotten myself so involved that a dog and a kid could leave without my noticing?

They couldn't have gotten far. I couldn't bear telling Vanessa that her daughter was missing.

Throwing open the door, I heard the construction noise again.

But Olivia and Daisy were not in sight.

I started to run, but only managed one stride before a man from the main house yelled, "Watch out!"

A second later, something very heavy slammed to the ground, making it vibrate.

9

Thursday Mid-Morning

Jonas

Today was my first weekday without classes since I'd started substituting in March and I had intended to sleep in. The door slamming before eight o'clock put that dream to rest. Still, I was impressed that Elizabeth had gotten up and made it out the door with Olivia on time for school—quite the commitment for a woman who rarely woke before nine-thirty in the morning.

Unable to fall back asleep, I decided to go for a run. I had to laugh at myself when I picked up the leash from the drawer out of habit. Going without my running buddy felt strange. When I returned a little over an hour later, the house was still quiet, bringing with it a peaceful feeling. I took a leisurely shower, dressed, and lingered at the table over breakfast, waiting to see Elizabeth before leaving for school. I wouldn't need much time to finish the grades and close up my classroom, so I enjoyed this rare opportunity to have a quiet morning alone with my thoughts.

It was almost ten o'clock when I realized Elizabeth still hadn't returned. She wasn't expecting to meet me back here, so she must have gone to check on the construction or met someone for coffee. Slinging my backpack over my shoulder, I headed out.

The high school felt like a different place without the noise and energy of all the students. "Hello, Mrs. Crosby," I said as I walked into the main office. Her back was turned to the door as she filed papers in the large cabinets against the back wall. "Is—"

"He's in his office, Mr. Trout," she interrupted without turning around. "Sorry, there's no coffee to offer you as we finished the pot already."

"Okay, no problem." Glad I didn't have to decline her offer yet again, it occurred to me that perhaps next year, I'd buy an espresso machine for the main office just so we wouldn't have the same discussion every morning.

"Come in," called Lester after my knock.

"How are you feeling?" I asked as I looked at the bandage and marks on his head.

"A little battered and bruised but otherwise fine," he said, remaining seated behind his desk. That alone told me he wasn't fully recovered. Glancing down at his desk, he sighed. "Certainly better off than that poor woman."

I nodded, also thinking of the dead body I had glimpsed briefly. I swallowed and wondered if I should be ashamed for being glad Dale's berth was on the opposite end of the dock. Then, remembering my promise to help Elizabeth's friend Vanessa, I asked, "Did you know Courtney?"

He shook his head, his eyes downcast.

"How about Vanessa Martini? Did you hear she was arrested for murder?"

"Her I know. How do you know it was murder?" Lester looked up, eyes full of confusion.

"Heard it from someone."

He shook his head sadly. "Wouldn't have thought her to be a killer."

I latched onto his words. "So you didn't hear any talk about her getting into an argument with Courtney? They're both accountants, I hear." It was little to go on but the only connection we had come up with for the two women.

Lester stared at me for a moment. "What's this all about, Jonas? It isn't like you to gossip." He wagged a finger in my direction. "Is this Ella Mae's doing?" He scrunched his face and pressed his lips together before adding, "She has a habit of getting herself mixed up with the authorities in the wrong way. You're not going to let her drag you into trouble, are you?" He began to rise to emphasize his point, but then moved a hand to his side as if it was hurting and sat back down.

"No, we're not going to do anything that will get us in trouble." I clenched my jaw. Talking to either Lester or Elizabeth about the other was so difficult. They just wouldn't get over their past history even though ten years had passed. Elizabeth had matured over that time; she was no longer the high schooler that Lester remembered. But she also couldn't get past her view of Lester from the perspective of her less-disciplined teenage self. "It's just that Vanessa asked Elizabeth to care for her daughter, Olivia. The girl spent last night with us."

"Why am I not surprised that when there's trouble, Ella Mae isn't far away?" He clearly didn't want a response to his rhetorical question as he changed subjects. "I have to skip tomorrow night's campout with the Outdoor Club. I'm not up to it. I'd like to feel better by Saturday for the reunion dance. You know, those students started high school during my first year here as principal."

I forgot about the investigation as I considered how disappointed the students in the Outdoor Club would be. We'd had a hard time getting the second chaperone lined up. Losing Lester meant we'd have to cancel.

"Don't worry." Lester chuckled as he saw my crestfallen expression. "I've arranged for a suitable substitute. All will be fine." His voice turned serious. "Hey, thanks for caring about the kids so much. And for checking on me yesterday and this morning." As that was about as emotional as Lester got, he cleared his throat to mark its conclusion. "Now, get out of here and let me finish my end-of-year responsibilities. And I believe you have some grades to turn in today as well."

I nodded.

As I opened his office door, he repeated, "Thanks, Jonas," more quietly.

I smiled at him over my shoulder as I walked out.

Around the corner from the school office, I slowed to take in the crowd of adults that had gathered in one of the classrooms. They ranged in age from around my age to retirees, so I knew this wasn't another group of early-partying, misguided ten-year alums. Everyone seemed grim, with plenty of clenched arms and rigid bodies. This did not look like a group ready to party.

"What's going on?" I asked a woman who looked to be in her forties as she passed me on her way into the room.

"Emergency PTA meeting," came the response.

"At ten in the morning?" I asked, perplexed at why so many would be here on a weekday.

She stepped sideways, preparing to scoot past some folks in the doorway. "There's some missing money," she said before sliding inside.

I stopped outside the doorway and looked into the crowded room. A table had been pulled to the front, and a handful of people sat in chairs facing the audience. I could feel the tension in the room.

A woman with streaks of gray in her hair and a gavel in her hand was talking. ". . . First point of business—really our only point of business today—is about the money." She looked down the table at another woman. "Madame Treasurer, if you could explain what happened."

"Thank you, Madame President." A short woman about my age with close-cropped black hair shuddered out a breath. "I heard about Courtney's death yesterday evening." She gulped in another breath to steady herself. "After I got Jenny to bed, I decided to check the account. Just to be safe, you know." She paused for another gulp. "I freaked out. It showed our balance was zero." She placed both hands flat on the table before continuing, "I called, of course, but the bank was closed at that hour. Then I called you." She indicated the president.

"Yes, we know that much," said the president, her voice growing strident. "Go on."

"I just called again, but the bank said the balance is still zero." Then the treasurer's phone rang, its volume turned up high enough to startle her.

"Do you mind?" demanded the president when the treasurer pulled it out to look at the screen.

"I'm sorry." The treasurer stood up. "I've got to take this, it's from Jenny's school." Ignoring the dark looks from the others, she hurried toward the door as she answered, "Hello?"

"But!" interjected the president to no avail. Her mouth agape, she stared at the treasurer's back as she walked out of the room and past me into the hallway. The president turned to someone else at the table, but I didn't hear what she said.

The treasurer's voice suddenly sounded panicked. "She what?" Not waiting for a response, she added, "Is she okay? Can I talk to her?" She paced back and forth in the hallway as she listened. "Okay, okay. I understand. I'll be there right away." She hung up and darted back toward the room. I stepped out of the way as she scurried back to the table. "I'm sorry, I've got to go," she said in a breathless voice. "Jenny's had an accident."

"But . . ." stammered the president, the muscles along her throat tightening as she watched the treasurer grab her purse and race back out the door. The treasurer was gone before the president could speak again.

A hush swept over the room.

The man who sat next to the treasurer's now-empty chair asked, "Well, what should we do now?"

He seemed about to speak again when a hand clapped me on the shoulder. "Morning, Jonas," said Dale Cooper in a gruff voice as he slid past me into the room. I was surprised to see him show up for a PTA meeting, but maybe small-town rules allowed for the mayor to be involved in school business. Of course, his son was a student at this school too.

"Mayor!" cried several board members when they noticed his entry. They didn't look particularly pleased to see him, but his position always seemed to ensure special treatment. The president pointed him to the open chair at the front table, although whether Dale was pleased about this particular opportunity to become the center of attention wasn't clear since his back was facing me.

My grade book was calling, but I decided to hang around a bit to watch this live drama unfold. Maybe Lester had a point, and I was turning into a small-town gossip. I would need to do some self-reflection. Later.

The room had stilled, but the tension ran high below the surface. Could Dale's glad-handing style soothe the crowd's irritation? After knowing him for a few months, I had decided that Dale's friendly, positive attitude wasn't an act. It was simply Dale. That style also happened to serve him well as a politician looking to keep his constituents happy.

Holding an emergency daytime PTA meeting did seem like quite an overreaction. Many of the board members must have jobs, so this was a major time commitment to deal with some missing money. I would talk to Elizabeth later about making an anonymous donation to help make up for the lost few hundred dollars they must have earned from bake sales and other fundraising efforts.

The board member sitting next to Dale finished his quickly-whispered update to catch him up on the situation.

"Gone!?" Dale looked angrier than I'd ever seen him. "What

the devil happened to our money?" He quickly scanned the room. "Where's Beverly? Didn't I just see her in the hall?"

"She left. Got a call about her kid at school," said the PTA president. "Now hush—"

"In the middle of everything?" Dale shook his head in disbelief. "We need to know what happened to the money. How could it just disappear?"

Dale's anger was unusual, but he was never shy about showing his emotions in front of a crowd. Shy didn't describe him in any situation.

"We don't know," said the man sitting next to Dale in an exasperated tone. "We were just starting to talk about what to do."

Dale didn't let him continue. He slammed his hand against the table and muttered a few choice words. "Has anyone called the sheriff? The state police? The FBI?"

"Don't forget the UN," murmured a tall man in front of me who was resting against the wall with one foot propped up on the door jamb.

A couple others in the back row covered their mouths or coughed to hide their laughter. The folks near me didn't seem as stressed out as the rest of the room. Relaxing against the back wall, they seemed like they had come to watch the show instead of being truly invested in figuring out what had happened and solving it.

Seeing people shaking their heads around him, Dale slammed the table again. "We should contact the FBI."

Surprised at Dale's forcefulness, I wondered if yesterday's explosion hadn't traumatized him more than he had admitted. Calling the FBI to investigate lost funds from school bake sales or car washes seemed over the top, even for him.

"What are we going to do about the festival?" asked one of the other board members at the front table.

As Dale turned a withering look her way, I leaned forward. "What festival?" I whispered to the tall man near me.

Without taking his eyes from the front table, the tall man tilted his head to me and quietly replied, "It's the Annual Bean Fest and Great Ozarks Championship Outhouse Races."

I stared at him, sure I had misheard him. "Outhouse?"

"Yeah, they build these custom outhouses and race them." His face was expressionless, and I couldn't tell if he was pulling my leg.

Noticing my stunned silence, his eyebrows rose as he swallowed a chuckle. "They're on wheels—the outhouses, that is. It's like a go-kart race without engines. Two people push and one person . . . well . . . sits on the can."

I puckered my lips, fascinated at the unsavory concept. Here in the Ozarks, people would actually come watch outhouse races at a festival celebrating beans? It seemed more than a little odd, but no one in the room laughed at the mention of the festival. Was I really the only one who thought it peculiar? Normally, entire days would go by where Jenkins felt like a normal place. Then something like this would sneak up from out of the blue and blindside me with its weirdness.

Then I snorted as I remembered my previous home. Portland's most celebrated event was an annual Rose Festival, but they also held a very popular annual World Naked Bike Ride and hosted a UFO Festival that was second only in popularity to the one in Roswell, New Mexico. On reflection, I had to admit Jenkins didn't hold any patents on bizarre.

As if my momentary silence had merely been one of polite unfamiliarity, the tall man added, "They've got prizes for design and speed."

"Are you serious?" I asked, still wondering if he was taking advantage of the newcomer.

"Serious as a heart attack," he answered, and then turned his attention back to the spectacle in front of us.

". . . or maybe the Secret Service. Aren't they in charge of investigating shenanigans with money?" Dale swept his arms around as he asked these questions.

It sounded like I hadn't missed much of the conversation if Dale was still rattling off the names of different agencies to investigate the theft.

"Don't they protect the president?" asked a perplexed older man sitting near the front.

"I think they handle counterfeiting too," replied the woman next to him.

Dale interrupted, "Well, maybe that's involved here too. Let's get them on the horn." He surveyed the room again. "It seems awfully convenient that Beverly's not here. Are we sure she's not skipping town with our money?" He pounded on the table again for emphasis. "Come on, people! We've got to do something. Someone's stolen a hundred grand from us."

The room gasped.

"A hundred grand?" I repeated, thoroughly shocked. How did a small town's PTA raise that much money? How many pies had they sold? Who ate them all?

My comment went unheard by those at the front of the room as multiple people shouted at once. In a quieter voice, I asked the tall man, "How did they have so much money? And what were they doing with it?"

"They were bribing the town of Mountain View to let us hold this year's festival."

"Bribing?"

"I think they officially called it 'advanced royalties' for the right to hold the festival here in Jenkins." I could hear the air quotes around his words even though he didn't make any hand gestures.

"To be fair," said another nearby man from the side of his mouth, "Mountain View owns that festival."

A woman next to him spoke up. "But they had that tornado

damage so they couldn't rightly hold the festival till they fix things up."

"Still jes sounds like fancy talk for bribery to me," said the tall man. "And if they had too much damage to hold the festival, then why'd we need to bribe them in the first place?"

Still feeling a little shell-shocked from the revelation, I asked, "How big is this festival?"

"It's big. Like twenty-five thousand people come. They pay admission for the races and cook-off."

"Don't forget the music and craft show." The other man turned to look more closely at me. "Ain't your Ella Mae an artist? I'll bet she could get a pretty penny for some paintings there, her being a professional now and all."

"And cornbread," broke in the tall man. "There's some mighty fine cornbread along with the beans."

"I'm still confused. How'd the money get lost?" I asked them.

"Stolen," asserted the tall man.

I glanced back and forth between them. "Wait. What? How could that happen?"

The second man replied, "Dunno. That's why we're here. This ain't no ordinary PTA meeting. It's a far sight better'n that."

At his words, a few others standing nearby nodded in agreement.

"Y'all in the back, be quiet or leave," snapped the PTA president as she knocked the gavel on the table a few times.

"Us be quiet? Y'all be yelling this whole meeting," replied one of the men, but the front table ignored him as they continued talking over each other.

Dale raised his voice. ". . . it would have put us on the map and shown the gaming commission that Jenkins knows how to draw big crowds and have a good time."

The older woman in the front row objected. "There's plenty 'round here who don't want that casino here. The preacher tells us ev'ry Sunday that gambling's a sin." She pointed a finger at

Dale. "You would know that if you bothered showing your face in church once in a blue moon."

Dale's face turned red as his temper and frustration flared. "Stealing's a sin too. Can we focus on who stole all our money? How are we going to explain this to all the good people of Jenkins who donated their hard-earned money to bring that festival here."

One of the back row denizens blurted out, "The fairgrounds ain't even in Jenkins."

Dale snapped, "What are you, a land surveyor? I'll have you know that it's in unincorporated county land and we're the nearest big city."

I heard a few stifled laughs at his description of the town.

"Plus, don't forget the craft fair we planned along Main Street." Dale now sounded like he was pleading for their support.

At the laughter in the back, Dale clenched his jaw. Then he whirled around and jabbed a finger at the PTA president. "What was your role in all this? Only you and the treasurer have access to that account, right? You could have been part of the money going missing."

He didn't pause for confirmation before he shifted and pointed another accusing finger at a bald middle-aged man sitting at the far end of the table. "Or did you steal it, Ned? Mr. Past PTA President. I'm sure you still know the account's password."

"How dare you!" Ned roared, rising to his feet. "You can't just start accusing everyone of stealing."

Someone in the crowd spoke up. "Why not? You never wanted this festival here, Ned. Maybe you hid that money so we'd have to cancel it."

Dale gave an approving nod at the speaker.

"Courtney had access too," stated the man sitting next to Dale in a calmer tone.

Dale dismissed him. "Sure. Blame it on the dead woman." He shook his head. "No. I think we need a full-scale investigation start-

ing with everyone who opposed the festival. Ned and his support-
ers are the most likely ones to have sabotaged us."

"That's it. I resign," yelled Ned.

"You can't resign. You don't hold any office to resign," Dale
shouted back at him. Then he smirked. "In case your memory's
fading, you lost the last mayor's election, remember?"

Someone in the audience threw in a jab to everyone at the
front table. "Not planning to leave town all of a sudden, are any
of you?" That seemed to spark arguments all around the room as
some fought over the importance of holding the festival while others opposed it. Whether there were yet more sides to the debate
became unclear as the room dissolved into chaos.

As Ned flung the papers in front of him into the crowd, I backed
away, not wanting to get hit by any flying objects. This meeting
didn't look likely to turn productive anytime soon. With all the
accusations starting to fly, I figured heading to my classroom was
the best protection from getting accused of stealing money I hadn't
even known about. I wasn't too worried about this turning into
anything worse. Small-town PTA meetings didn't usually devolve
into riots. Of course, it was always possible that Mary had another
interesting bit of Jenkins history to share.

When I sat down to finish submitting the grades, I made sure
each set of class finals was neatly stacked side by side and distributed
evenly across the desk. Then I straightened a few stacks to make
sure my workspace was set up the way I needed it.

While getting things prepared, I couldn't help reflecting on what
I'd learned from the PTA meeting. Setting aside the details of the
festival itself to talk about with Elizabeth later, I mulled over one
of the comments someone had made about who took the money.
It seemed to me that Dale had dismissed his neighbor's remark too
quickly. Was Courtney Stanton's death somehow tied into this? I'd
have to talk that angle through with Elizabeth before getting distracted by a festival celebrating outhouses.

10

Thursday Afternoon

Elizabeth

E xhausted by the day's excitement, I was grateful to be heading home. Olivia's disappearance and the big crash this morning had freaked me out. I was so worried she had been hurt that I'd raced across the yard to our house. The dust was still blooming from where the sheaf of shingles had accidentally fallen off the roof. I'd yelled her name over and over while trying to lift the heavy shingles and find her. After a long moment of barely being able to breathe, I'd heard her voice calling, "Aunt Elizabeth," and Daisy barking.

She was safe.

Olivia had listened to my warnings after all and avoided the house construction. She and Daisy had gone exploring into the trees near the crick and were safe. I'd hugged her hard and tried to keep myself from crying in front of her. Then we spent the next few hours having fun until I'd gotten a call to let me know there would be an emergency meeting of the Juniors this afternoon and it was time to head back to town for lunch.

Today's just-finished meeting of the Jenkins Juniors—or, more accurately, the Jenkins chapter of the National Association of

Junior Auxiliaries—had been quite explosive with everyone yelling about Courtney and—

"Ella Mae," huffed Ethel as she trailed me out the door from the side room of the church building. "Wait up!" She was overweight and may have been slow on foot, but she was quick-witted and a professional-grade gossip. I slowed because despite my distaste for all the gossiping, she'd always been so kind and friendly to me. She caught me in the parking lot. "You've been neglecting me recently—you ain't hardly been by for a good how-do-you-do in ages."

I was still shocked by the news announced during the meeting and only wanted to go home, unhook my bra, and tell Jonas about all the hoopla while we relaxed. I was worried for Vanessa too, fearing the latest news would only add another nail in her coffin.

"Whew, Ethel, today has been a lot," I replied, scrambling to figure out what was safe to share with her. I couldn't very well tell her my day had started with Trent almost catching me stealing Vanessa's hidden USB stick from outside her apartment.

I continued, "You would not believe my crazy day. You know Olivia spent the night with us, right?" I paused to verify her rumor network was still as effective as ever.

"Of course, dear." Ethel gave me a look of slight reprimand for casting even a shadow of doubt on her gossip-collecting powers. "Yes, such a sweet dearie. She must be worried sick," she cooed encouragingly as she mopped her sweaty brow with a handkerchief.

Deciding to give her what she wanted, I shared some of my misadventures with Olivia. "I near about had a heart attack when Olivia snuck away from me at the ranch. Why, she was almost killed when those construction workers dropped a big ole batch of shingles from the roof right next to where our basement will be!" I was playing it up for Ethel's sake, knowing she always enjoyed a more dramatic tale.

I shivered just thinking of how terrible it would have been if Olivia had gotten hurt. She'd been busy creating a mini-dam with rocks and logs along the crick on my grandparents'. . . *my* land. Recognizing a kindred spirit at heart, I joined her in enjoying nature for a few hours. Daisy had joined too by stealing sticks from the dam to chew on and then shaking herself every time she got wet. It had been a fun morning.

"My goodness. We should count our lucky stars she narrowly escaped from that basement before it was too late," exclaimed Ethel, clearly already scheming to make the story more exciting.

"And on top of her near-death experience," I exclaimed, pushing to match Ethel's dramatic energy, "the poor girl's mother is still trapped in prison for a crime she didn't commit. It's straight out of one of those TV dramas. Olivia'll be safe with her grandma for now, but who knows what happens next?"

I'd been surprised to have felt mixed emotions when I dropped Olivia off at her grandma's place. Relieved to deliver her safe and sound, having discharged my duty to Vanessa, I still felt a pang of sadness as I waved goodbye to my new little friend. Hurrying to get to the Juniors meeting, I had driven away before things got too sentimental—or, more importantly, before her grandma could ask me why Olivia was all muddy and hadn't gone to school today.

"Poor baby," agreed Ethel. Although her focus for the meetings appeared to be her endless quest for good gossip, the group actually met regularly to volunteer on projects to help the community. I'd decided to join to reconnect with more women in the area, and because my mother wasn't a member, it gave me some much-needed time away from her.

"I've already eaten my emergency chocolate and I've still got . . ." My voice trailed off as I suddenly remembered the rest of today's schedule. I gasped, "Omigosh! I've still got the reunion thing tonight. I've gotta run."

"You be sure to stop by for a right decent gossip session real soon now, ya hear?"

Without promising anything specific, I waved goodbye while I hurried off to my car.

Between dealing with Olivia and then the news from the meeting, I was in a tizzy. And the reunion hadn't even started yet! At least we might get some useful digging done about Vanessa, Adam, and Courtney at tonight's shindig.

I broke a few land-speed records for the short trip back to my mother's house and burst into our room only to find Jonas calmly sitting on our bed with his shoes off, reading a book and rubbing Daisy. We'd be late if he didn't get a move on and get dressed. "I've got to jump in the shower," I said, bending over and kissing him while peeling off my clothes.

When he hadn't started moving by the time I reached the bathroom door, I said, "Snap, snap. We've got to hurry and get ready."

This would be the first time I'd seen many of my high school classmates since I left town ten years ago. Although many had moved away from Jenkins, most hadn't left Arkansas. I felt both excited and nervous, not completely convinced I really wanted to make an appearance at my reunion but also eager to see what everyone looked like after ten years.

From the shower, I called out through the open door, "In a million years, you'll never guess what I heard at the Juniors meeting." When he didn't respond, I said, "Come on, guess!"

"What?" he asked finally.

I frowned as I rinsed off the shampoo. He wasn't even trying. I rubbed conditioner into my hair. "You're supposed to guess."

"You told me I'd never guess in a million years and we've got to be at the reunion kickoff event in only thirty minutes. I figured I didn't have time," he answered.

I loved this man but he had to learn to play along. Being so practical interfered with my storytelling mojo. "Guess what big event the Juniors were going to help hold in Jenkins this year?" But since this really wasn't a fair contest, I answered my own question. "It was the Bean Festival and—"

"Outhouse Races," he finished, to my surprise.

Startled, I asked, "How'd you hear that?" Instinctively, I had turned in his direction to hear his response. Unfortunately this meant I got sprayed in the face, so I blew water out of my mouth and added, "Oh, of course. Bet they were talking about it in the teachers' lounge."

I finished my shower and grabbed a towel. Leaning out the bathroom door, I saw he hadn't changed and was simply tying his shoes. "Wait, is that what you're planning to wear?"

He looked up and paused, apparently more interested in the view of my dripping wet body than his shoes. "I could, uh, take my clothes off if you'd like," he offered as a sly smile spread across his face.

"Stop it," I replied, but my own smile disagreed with my words. As he stood up, I stepped back and wrapped the towel tightly around myself, then shooed him away. "I want to get to the event on time." Turning to face the bathroom mirror, I added, "Go put on something nicer."

He hesitated, and I ignored the warm feeling I was getting from him staring at me as I pulled out the hair dryer. If I didn't do something to disrupt the atmosphere he was brewing with all his staring, we'd be late, so I closed the bathroom door.

When I opened the door a few minutes later, Jonas had changed clothes and had returned to sitting on the bed petting Daisy. She certainly seemed happy with the attention.

His eyes trailed me across the room but he didn't interfere as I removed the towel and took my time selecting the right bra and panties for my outfit. I put them on, perhaps striking a few unnecessarily provocative poses along the way, but why disappoint an admiring audience? We were still newlyweds, after all.

"You'll never guess what's gone wrong," I said, eyeing his outfit and scrunching my nose.

"Missing money," he said calmly as he scratched Daisy behind her ears. "Next question."

"Very funny, mister." I pulled out my fancy jeans, the tight ones that fit just right with the sequins on the back pockets. "Good guess. Did you hear how much is gone?"

"A hundred thousand," he answered nonchalantly.

Annoyed that my big news wasn't a surprise, my eyes narrowed at his lack of emotion. Then I saw his eyes flick up from Daisy to look for my reaction and I knew he was teasing me.

Playing along, I stomped my foot. "Stop it. You don't get to steal my thunder."

"Sorry. I heard about it from—"

"Nope," I interrupted. "You broke the rule. I get the best gossip in Jenkins, not Johnny Newcomer."

He cocked his head and smiled. "Johnny's new to town. How would he know that's the rule?"

"Because I make *all* the rules, silly," I answered. Then I stepped close and kissed him to soften the blow of this revelation, which really couldn't have been a surprise by this point in our relationship. I caressed his smooth cheek. "You are really cute in that blazer."

I sat down next to him to pull on my dress cowboy boots. "Now, go change again. This time into that blue silk shirt and your black jeans. This isn't a blazer kind of event."

He threw up his arms in mock dismay but went to the closet. I knew he didn't care what he wore and I wanted to show off my boy-toy in all his splendor to my friends.

"By the way, Mr. Hot Shot Gossip Guy, it was fifty grand, not a hundred."

Standing at the closet, he turned and frowned. Then, in a more serious tone, he said, "No, they were pretty clear at the PTA meeting this morning that a hundred thousand was gone."

I furrowed my brow as I remembered the discussion from the Juniors meeting. Slowly shaking my head, I pinched my lips together. "Nope. The Juniors only lost fifty thousand. Their festival account was empty." I looked over at him.

"The PTA folks were talking about a PTA account." His eyes widened. "Two accounts are empty?"

I gasped. "A hundred and fifty thousand dollars missing from two accounts?" Suddenly chilled, I wrapped my arms around myself. "What are the odds of that happening at the same time?"

11

Thursday Evening

Elizabeth

S omehow, we made it right at the scheduled start time. As we
approached the check-in desk, I peered past it, looking inside
the room for old classmates. I suddenly worried about how much I
had changed since graduation. First, I'd bolted out of Jenkins like
nobody's business, and then returned married ten years later, ready
to live here—at least for now. Would my old friends still like me?
Had I made a mistake dragging my newlywed, urban-loving husband here and deciding to build a house up in the hills? I froze in
place as I reconsidered whether even attending the reunion was a
good idea.

Jonas squeezed my arm. "It'll be fun," he said gently, and then
added, "Well, at least it'll be interesting."

I laughed with him and my pulse calmed.

Sure, my life had really changed, but I was still the same. I
snorted softly at that thought, wondering how my friends back
in Portland would react if they knew my ten-year high school
reunion kickoff mixer was taking place at the fairgrounds just outside a small town's city limits. I tried not to consider what it meant
that I started to feel excited again and was looking forward to a
night of go-karting.

Remembering the rest of our discussion at my mother's house, I promised myself that I wouldn't drink too much or get too distracted by friends. At least not until I'd done something useful to help out Vanessa. If she hadn't been arrested, she'd be home now with her daughter. And what about the missing hundred and fifty thousand dollars? Surely that had to be connected to Courtney Stanton's death. Someone here had to know something.

Taking a deep breath, I set my shoulders back. I was on Team Vanessa this evening. With all these people gathering, a good number of them still living in or around Jenkins, I could surely learn something useful that could help her. It was the least I could do for my sister, for a friend who had trusted me with her daughter, even if that trust was somewhat misplaced. Asking a few questions wasn't much to make up for temporarily losing her daughter, failing to properly bathe her, not even managing to get her to school, and wasting all her work on the ocean panorama.

"Why, it's Ella Mae," exclaimed the overweight man with thinning hair and a comb-over who sat behind the table with his pen at the ready and an array of name tags spread before him.

I didn't recognize him so I relied on his nametag. "Daniel. How good to see you again." I couldn't remember if he had been one of my teachers, or perhaps he worked at the fairgrounds and remembered me from long-ago visits. Instead, I pasted a large fake smile on my face and looked around the room as if the decorations completely fascinated me.

"Surely you remember me—from marching band!" he said as he handed us our badges.

I managed not to gasp. He looked super old—in his forties, even! "Of course, Daniel from marching band," I gushed, even though he was still a stranger to me.

Daniel nodded happily and flipped through his papers as I scrutinized his features. Whoever he was, he had aged poorly. Technically I had been part of the marching band, but only because cheerleaders performed in front of it. We certainly didn't associate with the band. The football players were far better-looking and held better parties.

Marking off our names on his checklist, Daniel explained the plan. "The bar's in the back—beer and wine only. They'll be bringing out food and some cocktails shortly. In the meantime, enjoy all our decorations and don't forget to go grab some *puke* punch." Giggling like a kid, he pointed at the large clear bowl full of hot pink liquid with blobs of white and green floating on a table prominently located in the middle of the room. "It's like from those school dances. Remember that one time at Halloween when—"

I interrupted, "That's great. You did a great job of decorating." I glanced around again at the limp streamers taped to the ceiling with clumps of balloons hanging dejectedly down as if they had already given up on tonight. "Really great." My voice petered out.

"It's spiked. I made it myself." He sat back in his seat, proud of his work. "And we won't get in trouble with any chaperones now."

"No, we won't," agreed Jonas smoothly as my mouth refused to continue this discussion. As Jonas caught sight of a lonely couple entering behind us, he added, "It looks like you'll be busy handling the crowd, Daniel. You and Elizabeth will have to catch up later."

I pulled myself together enough to flash Daniel another decent fake smile as Jonas took my elbow and guided me away.

When we reached the bar across the room—and far from the pink puke punch—Jonas looked at me, eyes twinkling. "So that was your friend Daniel," he said archly. "Daniel who, again?"

I grabbed a glass of white wine. "Daniel from marching band," I snapped, and then gulped down the contents.

Fortified with a little liquid courage, I pulled Jonas so we could stroll around the nearly empty room and pretend we didn't look so pathetic for arriving too early. What had I been thinking getting here right on time? Maybe there was somewhere to hide while we waited to blend in. A steady stream of cars pulling into the parking lot gave me hope that it wouldn't be too long before a critical mass arrived.

"Ella Mae!" said a voice that didn't sound at all embarrassed to be here so early. It was Grody. He halted in front of me, holding a pile of paper forms. He was tan and thin, probably from spending time helping out around the fairgrounds, and wore his hair longer than I liked for men, but that was his problem.

I smiled a greeting. We'd never been all that friendly back in the day, but I was grateful not to feel so awkward standing here by ourselves. Mentally reminding myself to use his correct name, I said, "Jonas, this is Andrew Grady. He graduated with me too and his father owns these fairgrounds." He had an excuse to be here at the reunion early.

Turning back to Grody, I said, "This is Jonas." But then I remembered I'd already mentioned his name so that made me flustered. "He and I . . . we got married not long ago." I flushed at how silly I sounded.

Jonas jumped in. "Nice place you've got here, Andrew." He gestured at the old building around us.

"Thanks, bruh," said Grody enthusiastically. "Looks great tonight, doesn't it?" Without waiting for our opinion, he added, "Business has been good and I've pretty much convinced my dad to tackle some big new plans."

"Really?" All I ever knew that happened here was the annual county fair, the go-kart racing, and regular swap meets. "What kind of plans?"

His smile spread. "Well, most of it is still confidential, of course." He rocked back, smug as the cat that caught the canary. "But I can tell you that we're planning to bring the rodeo back to Jenkins." He paused, watching for our reaction.

He looked like he expected us to be excited, but rodeos had never been my thing. After a moment too long, I responded, "That's great."

His shoulders slumped, and suddenly I regretted my lack of enthusiasm, but then he explained, "Well, the plans may be put on hold on account of the festival. I assume you've heard about the missing money?"

"Yes," said Jonas as I realized that by this point, the whole town must know about it.

"Gotta have money to make things happen. My grandpappy said that a long time ago when the stands burned down and the rodeo couldn't come to town."

"Of course, insurance probably helped," said my ever-sensible husband.

For some reason, this comment made Grody's boot start rat-a-tat-tatting on the ground in excitement. He leaned forward and asked, "Can you get insurance for that? For losing money, I mean?"

Jonas shrugged. "Sure, but not after the fact, of course."

"Well, it's a fact I lost money," Grody blurted.

"Are you still talking about your grandpappy's fire or yourself?" Jonas sounded as confused as I felt.

Grody's foot stopped tapping and his watery blue eyes blinked rapidly before he answered, "I meant them. It's such a shame the PTA lost all that money for the schools and kids. That's a fact, ain't it?"

"Yes," answered Jonas slowly.

With Vanessa unfairly rotting in prison, I had no patience for this nonsense. Grody was just being selfish; he didn't care about the PTA. "I don't remember you being all school-spirited or anything. Aren't you just thinking about yourself now that the fairgrounds won't make money on the festival?"

Grody's eyes flashed with annoyance. "Well, I don't know where you get off saying something like that. You ain't been in town long. You don't know what's what anymore."

A quick glance at Jonas revealed that he seemed taken aback as well. I'd been impatient and hadn't meant to be rude. "I'm sorry."

"Apology accepted," Grody said. Then he took a breath. "Well, maybe you're right. We really need the money that festival would have brought in. I wouldn't have mentioned it, but seeing Beverly just reminded me again."

"Wait! She's here?" I rotated my head from side to side, looking for her.

Grody gestured behind me. "Passed her heading over that way last I saw her."

I made some inane excuse to leave and promised we'd catch up with him later. Jonas and I had to locate and talk to Beverly before this place filled up.

On the far side of a wide pillar wrapped with more sad streamers, I found her. Beverly stood with one fist clenched across her chest while she held a full wine glass with the other as she pretended to have accidentally paused in the exact location where people entering the room couldn't see her.

Out of the side of my mouth, I whispered, "That woman in front of us looking out the windows, in the red skirt, that's Beverly Wong, the PTA treasurer." Before Jonas could respond, we reached the pillar. "Beverly, it's good to see you again."

Although we hadn't snuck up on her, she jumped a little in surprise and spilled some of her wine onto her hand.

"Thanks," she said as Jonas handed her a napkin. "Hi, Ella—" she started, and then noticed my name tag and finished, "Elizabeth. Is that what you're going by these days?"

"Yes, I decided to use my actual name when I left for college. This is my husband—" I paused briefly to savor that strange and delightful word before continuing, "Jonas." I touched his arm and then realized she didn't need my help to identify which man I meant when he was the only one nearby. Despite her obvious tension, she pointedly looked at my hand, slowly stroking Jonas's arm without my awareness, and quirked her lips. "That's right, I heard you recently got married. Congratulations."

I flushed and pulled my hand away. "Thanks. And, how's, uh . . ." I scrambled to come up with her husband's name while also trying to figure out what to do with my now-awkward hand floating out in space.

"Michael," we both said at the same time, and then laughed.

That seemed to relax her a bit as some of the tension left her body. "Fine," she said as my hand started to feel normal hanging by my side again.

"How's your daughter doing?" asked Jonas.

Beverly darted a look at him and frowned as she tensed again. "How did you know I had a daughter?"

I looked at Jonas, curious as well. It wasn't like him to have stalked my classmates and memorized personal details about them before the reunion started. Between the two of us, that was more likely my style.

"I saw you at the high school this morning," he explained. When she clenched her jaw, he added, "I'm a teacher there and just walked by when I heard you on the phone before you needed to race out of there. Is everything all right?"

She scanned his face and saw only his polite expression of concern, which caused her to relax the tiniest fraction. "Yes. Well, Jenny's fine now. She broke her arm but it's in a cast and she's home now resting with Michael." She sighed and let a wry chuckle escape. "Broke her arm skipping from her classroom to the school library. Can you believe that?"

I couldn't. I didn't remember being particularly fragile as a child. I'd fall and get scraped up all the time but never broke anything. Pawpaw or Mimi would slap a bandage on me, hand me a popsicle, and kick me back outside to go play. Of course, as I thought back, Kelsey had broken her foot one day late in the summer just by jumping off a curb. A curb! That was only like four inches off the ground. If kids were so fragile, how did they ever survive to adult-hood?

Jonas murmured sympathetically, "Sounds like you had a really tough day."

I quickly piled on with some supportive noises.

"Horrible," Beverly answered, and then sighed heavily. "Whole month has been tough, really."

"Month?" I blurted out without meaning to interrupt. I wanted to get her to talk about the money and Vanessa, not delve into what happened last month. Finding out how the money had been lost might explain if Courtney had been involved and help me clear Vanessa's name. This wasn't the time to sidetrack into a discussion on Beverly's hard life.

I glanced around. A few more people were now milling around us. If I could learn something useful quickly, I could find my old friends and start enjoying tonight.

Beverly started to wave her hands but remembered her drink just in time and took a sip instead. "The whole month, I've been run-ning up and back to Mountain View, getting dragged into doing all these ridiculous errands, and then . . ." Her voice trailed off and she sniffed.

"Why were you going up to Mountain View? Was it for meet-ings about taking over the Bean Festival?" I was proud of myself for steering us back to the festival and the money.

"Oh, I wish," she said. "First, it was bringing up some clothing donations we had collected to help after the tornado, then I spent a whole weekend working on a community cleanup project, and then a bake sale." She paused. "Then they started making even more outrageous demands."

"Who was making demands? And why?" asked Jonas.

I frowned. He was taking our interrogation off-track. Blah-blah-blah, I got it—she worked hard. I glanced sideways at Jonas, trying to signal him to stop derailing us from talking about the money, but he hadn't learned to read all my signals yet.

"Mountain View's mayor and the rest of the festival board. They're impossible," Beverly complained. "They refused to commit fully to giving us the festival. Russellville was bidding against Jenkins and those Mountain View folks were playing us against each other. I was spending all my spare time sucking up to those old farts. Can you believe I even had to rent a big pickup and drive a load of ammonium nitrate up there for some old coot's farm?"

The growing noise nearby made me glance around again. The handful of people near us had expanded. People were whispering and seemed to be looking in our direction. I flicked my eyes down at my blouse, but I hadn't spilled anything on myself. Jonas looked good too—in fact, I thought with a smile, he looked pretty hot in his jeans and shirt. I made a note to buy him some dress boots.

"This was certainly not part of my plan," Beverly concluded.

"Sounds annoying," I agreed, and then tried again. "I heard there's been some financial mishap—"

"Oh gosh, you too?" she interrupted. "I thought I'd come here for a quick visit to see some old friends and then head out in time to get Jenny into bed." She drank a big gulp of her wine. "I'm so done with today. Everyone's been on me about the money."

"Yeah, I heard. Sounded pretty rough," said Jonas, his voice calm enough to soothe a rattlesnake back into its hole.

I recognized his tone from when he talked me out of sending some particularly forceful response to a client's unrealistic requests. It usually worked on me—and I hadn't lost a client from my graphic design business in months. He was about to follow up with a question, hopefully about Vanessa's role in all this, but his calming effect didn't last.

Beverly burst out, "All I wanted was to hold a successful event. We'd have a huge crowd, make a bunch of money for the schools, and that would get me elected to the school board this fall. A year or two of that would set me up to beat that old fool mayor of ours. I mean, how hard would winning an election against him be?" A disparaging snort showed what she thought of Dale Cooper.

Before we could respond, Beverly continued her rant. "With another high-profile event or two like the festival, I'd win the support of businesses around the area, and that would fuel a run for governor of Arkansas. If I played my cards right, that could all happen before I turned thirty-five. Maybe senator by forty. And then who knows what could happen next?" Her voice trailed off as she stared out into space, her eyes misting over. "All gone now." Another pause, and then, "It could have happened," she whispered, reaching out her free hand as if to touch her dream before it wisped away with the setting sun.

I wondered how many glasses of wine she had drunk before the one in her hand. Then my eyes narrowed. If she was after world domination by age fifty, had the lure of all that money pulled her in another direction? Had she killed her accountant and stolen the money to fuel a run for political office ahead of schedule?

"I thought teaching was tiring, but being a successful politician sounds exhausting," Jonas said sympathetically.

But I was suspicious now and done acting patient. "What about Vanessa Martini? Did you set her up?"

My words startled Beverly out of her self-pitying reverie. "What?" She shook herself back to earth.

But before she could answer my all-important question, someone else interrupted us. "You have a lot of nerve showing your face here." We looked up to find Susie Q standing there with a hand resting on her jutting hip. She wore a form-fitting, light blue mini dress that shimmered in the fading light. Her bright red lips puffed up as she turned a scornful expression in Beverly's direction.

"Hey, leave us alone," I protested, even though I had just been accusing Beverly myself. Susie Q and I were like two magnets whose ends repelled each other. No matter what she did or said, I always instinctively jumped to do or defend the opposite.

"Well bless your heart, Ella Mae, for being so totally consistent. Figures you'd be hanging out with Jenkins's newest crook." Susie Q rolled her eyes so far back, she almost fell over.

Beverly stammered, "I'm . . . I'm not a crook." It was a good effort, but I wasn't yet buying her performance.

"What'd you do with the money, Beverly?" accused a voice behind me that I couldn't identify. The people gathering around us murmured in agreement, their tone growing increasingly negative.

Beverly looked around, taking in the angry crowd glaring back at her. She announced, "I've got to go." Then she ducked her head and pushed past the onlookers, heading to the exit without meeting anyone's eyes.

"Loser," exclaimed a woman standing just behind Susie Q who was dressed in even worse taste. Her black leather, skintight mini dress had a deep V neckline that stretched most of the way down to her belly button, and her hair extensions nearly went down as far in back. And if that didn't get the message across, her black leather lace-up high-heel ankle boots with the cut-out front shouted, "I'm a tramp." Of course, Christy Tomer would be hanging out with Susie Q during our reunion. She must have cleaned up from how Jonas described her looking this morning at the school.

While the crowd still chattered about Beverly, Christy looked back and forth between me and Jonas. "Didn't I see you at the high school today?" She pointed at Jonas. Then, pretending she'd just noticed me, she stuck her nose in the air. "Why if it isn't Ella Mae with all her highfalutin dreams." She sniffed dismissively. "I heard you're back home in Jenkins, living in your mama's house, married to a substitute teacher, and ain't even working for nobody." Pausing for effect, she jeered, "Another loser!"

Susie Q snorted and then dramatically slapped a hand over her mouth, drawing even more attention to her giggling reaction.

Jonas held my arm snugly when he heard me start to growl, but he was right—Susie Q and Christy weren't worth it. I didn't want to spoil the evening by engaging with them.

Pleased with her put-down and my apparent inability to formulate a decent comeback, Christy flicked her artificially long hair over her shoulder with a bejeweled wrist and swiveled away from us while her skanky date—the same Rick Hoffman she had been dating back in high school days—let out a long wolf whistle as he watched her walk away. Susie Q hurried after her so she could regain her position as the queen bee of that clique.

I held my reaction in check long enough for them to get out of earshot and the crowd to lose interest in me. "Oh, I can't believe them," I said, spinning to face Jonas.

He put his hands on my hips and leaned forward to kiss me before pulling back to look at me.

The distraction had his desired effect as I started to calm again.

Still keeping his hands on my hips, he said, "Who cares what they think? Technically, she wasn't wrong anyway." When I stiffened, he added with a slight grin, "Technically, of course. I mean, we are staying with your mother until our house is built. I am a substitute this school year. And you're self-employed so you don't have a boss." He chuckled, ignoring the fact that he was anything but a loser. In fact, we were now wealthy—from the buyout of the company where he had started working after college as one of their early employees. It was so Jonas that he wasn't at all concerned about her comments.

I fought a smile. He was right, as usual. It didn't matter what they thought of us. "Did you meet Christy already?"

"Not exactly," answered Jonas without further explanation.

"Well, I still don't like her. Or Susie Q." My lip lifted into a sneer just thinking of her again. We had despised each other in high school and our relationship hadn't improved since then, especially after what happened when Jonas and I first came to Jenkins.

"Just think," Jonas said, "there's no way either of them will be able to get into go-karts tonight wearing those outfits. It's just not a slinky dress kind of event." He winked as he tossed my earlier blazer comment back at me.

I chuckled and then relaxed, leaning forward into his arms and closing my eyes for a moment. Then my eyes snapped open as I pushed away from him. "Beverly never answered us about Vanessa. I wish we'd had a little more time to ask her some questions. We didn't get anything useful." I pouted my lips and then frowned again at Susie Q and Christy's interruption.

"What about that bit about the ammonium nitrate?" asked Jonas.

My brows knitted together. "What about it?"

"That can be used for explosions, like that big one in Beirut a while back and in Oklahoma City long ago," he explained.

"Really?" I cocked my head. Art degrees didn't tend to give people useful backgrounds in chemistry. "I've only heard of it being used as fertilizer. Pawpaw used to get some delivered each year back when he tried to start doing organic farming. We should ask Mom if the explosive residue she found was ammonium nitrate." I went silent as I considered whether Beverly really had blown up Courtney, stolen the money, framed Vanessa, and then turned up here to garner sympathy before running for office. That would be cold. Really cold.

Breaking the silence, Jonas pondered aloud, "I wonder if they turn the results from an Outhouse Festival into fertilizer."

"Gross." But I laughed at what I thought was a joke and lightly swatted him on the arm, causing him to almost spill his wine. I rested my hand there to help him balance. He did have a nice arm.

"Do you think she was telling the truth?" he asked.

"About her grand scheme to run the world? Yes. About the money or killing Courtney? I don't know. She didn't really answer.

Just like a good politician, though, wasn't she? Managed not to answer a direct question and disappeared during a distraction." I rolled the possibility around in my head. "It is awfully convenient that she had access to a lot of bomb-making material shortly before an explosion."

Jonas's mouth tightened into a thin line as he nodded thoughtfully at me.

But before we could speak again, a loudspeaker squawked to life. "Ladies and gentlemen! Start your engines!" It was Colton Buck, or CB, as he was called, because he talked more than the radio. That loudmouth codger had somehow charmed his way into becoming the football announcer for the Jenkins High School home games. "The go-kart circuit is now open."

Everyone seemed to swarm toward the track.

CB ignored the chaos to give us instructions. "Don't worry, food and drinks will circulate. Up to four can race at once, so form a group or just stand in line and we'll get you on the track as soon as possible. I'll be your handy-dandy race announcer this evening, keeping everyone posted on the standings, track records, and, of course, adding color commentary along the way."

Without pausing to take a breath, and changing his tone as if the broadcast had just begun, CB continued, "Yessiree, we've got a beautiful evening here at the Jenkins Fairgrounds International Rodeo and Raceway. Light winds from the southeast don't look like they'll impact the race times at all, so we're hoping to see some track records fall tonight, folks. First up, it looks like we've got ourselves quite the racing group matchup. It's the battle of the varsity versus junior varsity alums, duking it out once again for all the honor. In the red car—"

Yup. CB could talk until the cows came home.

Jonas chuckled as he took my hand and strolled with me toward the line that already snaked back and forth behind ropes to the track. "This is going to be interesting. Give a bunch of people too much to drink, let them race around a track in an open go-kart against others who've also had too much to drink. Then let them all drive home. What could possibly go wrong?"

12

Thursday Night

Jonas

"After-party at the secret underground bar below the hidden kebab shop." I laughed overly loudly at the ridiculousness of my own statement. "Who'd have expected so much excitement from a night out in Jenkins?" Part of me realized that I must have had a little too much to drink if I thought it was so funny. I followed Elizabeth down the wooden steps at the back of the old hardware store on Second Street. I'd seen the staircase before when I'd stopped in the store for something, but I had always assumed it led to a basement storage room.

Elizabeth only tittered in response, grabbing my arm tightly as we made our way down the dimly lit stairs. She'd probably had too much to drink too. With a silly grin on her face, she pushed open the thick door at the bottom, revealing a blast of light and noise from the crowd inside.

One end of the room had a small plywood stage with large speakers facing the audience from each corner. A jukebox pushed against the back wall must have served as the entertainment option for nights like this when a live band wasn't playing. Across the room, a grungy-looking bar decorated with Christmas lights strung up as a permanent display—or so I assumed, since this was

May—dominated that half of the room. The women looked to have split off into multiple groups scattered around the room while most of the men were clustered by the bar. Men didn't seem to worry about cliques when alcohol was an option.

A bit surprised that this was actually real, I stopped right inside the door next to Elizabeth. "Honestly, I thought you were just trying to pull a fast one over me about this place."

Her eyebrows leapt in mock astonishment. "Why good sir, what an utterly preposterous idea!" She pressed both hands against my chest, leaned in with a wink, and kissed me. "If I were going to trick you, you wouldn't have figured it out so quickly."

Before I could come to grips with the implications of that comment, she focused a bit and her face grew serious. "Don't forget to ask folks about accountants. Maybe we'll get lucky and hear something to help Vanessa."

Her reminder wasn't necessary as it was all we had discussed since leaving the go-kart track. We'd even sat in the car for a few minutes, going over our brief discussion with Beverly Wong while much of the crowd had peeled out of the parking lot—some fishtailing like they were still in the go-karts. I was content to carry on our conversation until the coast was clear.

Elizabeth's face brightened as she gestured at a nearby group of women. "I'm gonna catch up on gossip with the girls over there. No need to hang on to my apron strings and eavesdrop. Go on now and talk with the guys. Besides, you need to make some friends out here."

"I have friends," I protested. Just because she hadn't been awake early didn't mean my morning fishing trip on Wednesday hadn't taken place.

"Guys your own age," she said firmly. "Dale and Stapleton are too old for you to hang out with all the time."

"I know people my own age," I said, perhaps a little too defensively.

"Talking to that guy, Bill, in the teachers' lounge is a good start, but you don't do anything with him outside of school. Now go." She made a shooing motion with both hands. "Go play nice." She rubbed my back as she gently shoved me toward the bar before walking off to join her former classmates.

I shook my head. After that little demonstration, Elizabeth's worries about her ability to be someone's mother could safely be laid to rest. I took a deep breath, deciding to keep that summary to myself, and wandered forward, feeling self-conscious about interacting with the other men. Nothing that a good drink wouldn't solve.

Before going to the bar, I stopped in the restroom. An old piece of graffiti high on the wall above the mirror caught my eye: "EMB knows the truth about DK." I stood looking at it for a moment as another man walked in. EMB was how Elizabeth signed her old paintings. It stood for Ella Mae Banks. That piqued my curiosity. Who, or what, was DK? And what was the truth? I'd have to ask her.

Back in the beer line, I made sure to talk to some guys, as instructed. But idle chatter with a group of strangers wasn't a core strength of mine. Soon, I found myself standing alone in the middle of the group of men while conversations raged around me. "Bruh" this and "bruh" that—it just wasn't my thing.

I decided to check on Elizabeth. Turning, I found myself unexpectedly face to face with Deputy Walker. We exchanged the normal polite greetings.

Then he said, "I, uh, guess that I'll be seeing you tomorrow night," and shifted from foot to foot uncomfortably.

I wasn't sure what he meant because I wasn't going to any reunion events tomorrow. Friday night's reunion schedule was focused on school clubs. Surprisingly for a small high school, there had been over twenty active clubs while Elizabeth was a student and even more now. She planned to bounce between multiple club reunion gatherings tomorrow night while I went camping with the current Outdoor Club kids. We'd go together to the final event, the dance, on Saturday night. That I was looking forward to. Elizabeth was a fun dance partner.

The deputy must have noticed my puzzled expression. "I'm, uh, well, I've agreed to take Principal Stapleton's place for tomorrow's campout."

"Oh," I said, and nodded. "That was nice of you. I guess we'll see each other tomorrow night, then." My voice trailed off with nothing else to discuss coming to mind. He and I had never spent any time together and he seemed to make Elizabeth uncomfortable. I certainly wasn't interested in asking him questions about his dating experience ten years ago with my wife. The only other things we had in common were the last two murders that had hit Jenkins, and bringing that up at a party didn't seem appropriate.

Conversation topics now exhausted, we stared at each other silently for a moment as the jukebox switched to some quieter '80s ballad. I started to make an excuse to move on. "Well, I, uh—"

"Hey, Trent," interrupted a tipsy guy I hadn't met yet, "heard you're in charge of a murder investigation now. Pretty wild, man. You catch the killer yet?"

With the noise level in the bar lower, two other guys standing nearby heard and turned to listen.

"Sorry, Rex, I can't talk about it," the deputy answered, and took a small sip of his beer.

One of the new guys nearby slapped him on the back. "Dude, it's just us. We won't tell the sheriff. Tell us about the crime scene or something. Was it all gory or what?"

More of the men stepped closer.

"Yeah, I heard that woman blew her top." The speaker snorted at his own attempted humor.

Despite the poor taste, several others tried to top him. One raised his beer bottle and countered, "Yeah, that story just exploded around town."

"Stop, stop. It's not funny," said the deputy. "The poor woman died."

The snickering quieted but didn't disappear completely. "Come on, Deputy Dog, tell us something. I'll buy you another drink. You've been nursing that one all night," cajoled Rex.

"Nah, thanks, I'm good," said the deputy.

"Go ahead and drink up, bruh. Who's gonna stop you for drunk driving?" asked Andrew, the son of the fairgrounds owner.

The guy who had wandered around the hallways high during finals stood behind him and stared intently at Trent and me.

"Thanks, Andrew, I'm fine." The deputy's jaw tightened, but then he forced a smile and added, "That go-karting tonight sure was awesome. Did I hear right that you won the whole thing? That's awesome, dude. Just like old times!"

The guys around us all cheered as Andrew raised his bottle in acknowledgement. As guys banged Andrew on the back for his victory and pulled him closer to the bar for another round, he completely forgot he was in the middle of teasing the deputy.

I smothered a smile at how easily the deputy had handled them. It must have been tough to shift from being an ultimate insider, a star on his high school football team and one of the popular boys, to this new role where he'd always be a bit of an outsider amongst the general public. People never quite knew how to handle themselves around cops—even if they weren't doing anything illegal or if the cop was off-duty and at his high school reunion.

"Hey, you're Ella Mae's husband, right?" A short guy with beady little eyes turned his sights on me.

"Yeah, I'm Jonas. Jonas Trout," I answered, but then felt self-conscious again. It wasn't as if only James Bond could introduce himself that way. I took a sip, trying not to feel awkward.

"I heard you were at the docks too, weren't you?" the man demanded.

I nodded, feeling like a deer in the headlights as more guys shifted their attention to me.

His buddy jutted out his chin. "Bruh, you're not a cop. Tell us about it."

I stole a quick glance at the deputy. His eyes caught mine and he gave a minute shake of his head, sending me the clear signal not to reveal anything.

My eyes flickered around. Many of the men were now listening to this conversation. "Well . . ." I hesitated as I tried to think of how to "play nice" while not getting the deputy upset at me. "It was really early in the morning. I didn't really see all that much of the explosion because I had to dive into the lake to rescue my dog, Daisy." My throat suddenly felt dry so I took another sip.

"Hey, that's right." The short guy's buddy put down his drink. "I heard a dog was hurt. How is she?"

"Oh man, how bad was she hurt?" asked the short guy, suddenly turning solicitous.

I was taken aback as the crowd started murmuring their concern for Daisy, but at least they'd stopped asking for gory details. "No. She's fine," I answered. "She was just out of sorts that morning. She was even barking earlier when we were out fishing and she never barks. I looked back to the dock and—"

A new voice jumped in. "Who cares? I've gotta take a leak. Jump ahead to the dead woman already."

I swallowed and then said, "I really can't." Before they could challenge me on whether I meant "can't" or "won't," I added, "Daisy jumped into the water before the explosion so I had dived in to rescue her . . ." My voice trailed off as I struggled to figure out how to thread this conversational needle.

Fortunately the first guy bailed me out. "Yeah, man, dogs get spooked easily. My dog still startles easily ever since that car nearly ran him over last month." He turned to his neighbor. "You remember, bruh? It missed him by this much." He held out his hands a few feet apart.

The mention of his dog sparked a new question to me from the other side. "Did you have to take her to the vet?"

Without waiting for my answer, someone else said, "Bet they have some pretty powerful drugs there with all them farm animals they have to treat. Mebbe they gave you some extra samples?" The short man opened his mouth eagerly as he peered up at me, searching my face for a sign that I'd hook him up with some illegal drugs—right in front of the deputy sheriff.

My eyes flicked back to the deputy. Now he merely raised an eyebrow of amusement at me.

Suddenly a loud feminine voice interrupted. "Come on, Rick, let's blow this popsicle stand!" It was Christy, the woman who had been high with Rick at school yesterday. Her slinky black dress barely reached her thighs. "If they're going to play these loser tunes, we're bugging out. Let's go to a real bar and have some fun." She tottered unsteadily on her pointy ankle boots. "You guys coming with, or sticking around this dump?"

A loud chorus of agreement answered, so Christy swiveled, nearly stumbling on her stilettos. Grabbing Rick's shoulder and planting a loud, sloppy kiss on his lips, she then stuck her nose up high and strutted away as her boyfriend stayed behind to watch her depart. He then tripped over himself to catch up. Most of the men's eyes followed her for a moment before they lumbered after Christy, bouncing off each other and the walls as they climbed the stairs unsteadily.

I caught the deputy's eyes again and raised a questioning eyebrow toward the stream of people who were heading out to their cars and clearly not in proper condition to drive safely.

"Off-duty," he mouthed at me, and then took a step closer and spoke quietly. "Besides, there's a sobriety check-point right where

Main Street merges onto the county highway." He winked. "I'd suggest you take side streets back to Mary's house to avoid a major traffic backup tonight."

I chuckled and gave him a thumbs-up before he walked away.

I was about to find Elizabeth when she surprised me by wrapping her arms around me from behind. "Hey, sweetie, ready to go?"

"Sure," I said, putting my half-finished beer on the bar and turning to leave. "Hey, I saw an interesting message in the men's bathroom. It said, 'EMB knows the truth about—'"

"Yeah, yeah, old news." Elizabeth blushed as she grabbed my hand. "But that's a story for another time. Let's go home." When we were halfway up the stairs, she sighed. "That was fun. I haven't been here since . . . forever." She looked back over her shoulder. "But that was enough. I don't think we need to come back." She sniffed. "The place smells, and it's really just a teenage hangout."

Others on the stairs around us agreed. When we exited the hardware store—now dark except for one row of lights that led to the front door—she called, "See you tomorrow," and waved to friends as we all split up.

As soon as we turned away from the others, Elizabeth leaned in close and quietly crowed, "I got something!" Then she released my hand and started one of her little happy dances at my side. "Brooke told me that Adam Martini was gambling a lot. Sounds like he was doing it more than Vanessa even knew."

"How'd you learn that?" I asked, mostly to keep her talking and see if she'd keep dancing.

Elizabeth caught me staring at her and stopped wiggling around. "Brooke told me. Her husband—I don't know him, but apparently he used to play poker with Adam and some other guys. She said the stakes had gotten too big for her husband. They're saving up to buy a bigger house. They're hoping to have a kid soon." She threw her hands into the air. "I can't believe I hadn't heard she'd bought a place. She's coming to lunch tomorrow but I'm going to have to pay a visit out to Ft. Smith to see her. Oh, maybe we can go together and have dinner at that place we liked. You know—that place . . ."

"The Green Papaya," I supplied. "But how does this help Vanessa? Adam was in Las Vegas on Wednesday. In fact, I thought he doesn't get home until tomorrow night. So he's not the killer."

Elizabeth deflated a bit, but two steps later she snapped her fingers. "I've got it. Maybe he's in debt and those mafia guys came out here to collect and got the wrong person."

"Pretty far-fetched." I laughed. "And now you think your mother is right?" After Mary had thrown out that line about the mob coming to town, Elizabeth had been quoting old mob movies to me and chortling ever since.

"Who knows?" Elizabeth shrugged.

"Doesn't make much sense that the mob would fly two guys halfway across the country just to settle a poker debt. And why would they pretend they're making a movie?"

Elizabeth ignored my skepticism as she glanced around us before she spoke. "What if it was really big and he couldn't pay? They'd fly out their muscle to whack him and send a message to their other deadbeats. You know, 'Pay us back or you'll swim with the fishes.' That big guy could be the hit man." She gasped at her own words as her eyes grew large.

I laughed. "Still sounds like you've been watching too much TV. So why kill Courtney instead?"

"Hmph!" Elizabeth stopped just short of the passenger door and may have even stomped her foot. "Well, Mr. Debbie Downer, at least I'm brainstorming here. No dumb ideas when you're brainstorming, remember? I don't see you doing much to help my friend."

"Okay, okay," I conceded. Then, trying to make up for laughing at her, I said, "Maybe you're right. Maybe those guys are part of the mafia." This wasn't enough to convince her of my support for her

cockamamie idea, so I continued, "Maybe they found out Courtney and Adam were together and they killed her after he wouldn't
pay up. In fact, I'll bet he's dead too and his decapitated head will
probably turn up someday in the desert outside of Las Vegas."

Elizabeth narrowed her eyes at me, clearly skeptical that my sudden re-engagement in this game of "who can come up with the
most ridiculous idea" was anything but an attempt to enhance my
chances with her tonight.

She would have been correct in guessing my motivation.

I opened her door for her, but when she didn't acknowledge the
gesture or make a move to get inside, I decided to come clean.
"Okay, I'm sorry. I didn't mean to laugh at you."

Elizabeth's face softened. "Thank you," she said, and leaned in to
kiss me.

I continued, "Maybe Adam and his gambling did get tied up
with the mafia. He is in Las Vegas, after all. And there is a hundred
and fifty thousand dollars missing and Adam's new girlfriend,
Courtney, seems to be the accountant for it all. In the morning,
let's do more brainstorming on what to do next." Then I foolishly
added, "You do have to admit, your idea did sound a little silly,
kind of out there."

She paused for a moment but then flipped her hair over her
shoulder and turned to get into the car. "I don't have to admit anything. I'm allowed to be silly." She blew a kiss at me as I closed her
door. "That's in the rules too."

As I started the car, Elizabeth asked, "Toward the end it looked
like you were in the middle of things at the bar. Did you learn anything useful?"

Other than recommending her friend Vanessa might look to
other towns for any future dating plans, I couldn't think of anything, so I merely shook my head.

Elizabeth tilted her head and placed a hand on my arm. "Well,
did you have fun? Who were you talking to?"

"It was fine. A few typical loudmouths but I chatted with some guys who seemed okay." Noticing her about to pile on, I added, "Yes, I'll talk to them more on Saturday at the dance. Oh, and that Deputy Walker seems like a decent guy."

Elizabeth crinkled her brow. "Who? Trent?"

"Yeah, I've only really talked to him before when you were ar—" Then, remembering she didn't like to discuss her arrest for murder a few months ago, I quickly edited my comment midstream. "—around."

Her hand on my arm tightened.

I explained, "The others were giving him a hard time about not drinking and not talking about the murder. I was impressed how he kept his cool and redirected the discussion."

"Wait!" She twisted in her seat to face me. "You can't become friends with Trent."

"What?" I shrugged as I glanced over to check how worked up she had become. "We're not friends. I just talked to him a little."

"One question." She breathed in hard. "Why were you talking to him? What did you talk about? Were you talking about me?" She pointed her finger and glared. "I don't want you talking about me with Trent, do you understand?"

I made sure to come to a complete stop at the stop sign just in case more deputies were randomly canvassing the neighborhood streets. "You know that was more than one question, don't you?"

"Don't try to change the subject!"

Before she could get too annoyed at me for only doing what she'd requested by talking to some of the other guys, I said, "He just told me he's taking Lester's place as a chaperone at the campout tomorrow night. We barely said two sentences before the others bombarded us with questions about Courtney's murder. We didn't talk about you." I stopped there, hoping that would preserve her good mood.

She chewed on her bottom lip in that cute way of hers for a few moments as I let out my breath quietly and drove to Mary's house. Then she crossed her arms and looked at me again. "Why didn't you talk about me?"

13

Friday Late Morning

Elizabeth

With the spring weather having not yet turned miserably hot, sticky, and buggy for the summer, I'd decided to walk the short distance downtown to my lunch date with my high school besties. Once our new home was finished, it would be too far to walk to the shopping district. But the view from up on the ridge would more than make up for that minor inconvenience.

"Besides, if I give up driving altogether, my car will get too lonely." I laughed at myself as I realized I had spoken out loud and then quickly looked around to see if anyone was close enough to overhear me. Talking to myself was a habit caused by working alone. Jonas liked to tease me about it. I smiled to myself, thinking about how wonderful our lives had turned out. Well, maybe except for the living with my mother part.

I sobered up as I remembered Vanessa. Her life had just taken a turn for the worse. With her divorce finally over, she was just restarting her life here in Jenkins. Instead of joining us for lunch today, she was locked up in prison. When Olivia realized I was dropping her off at her grandmother's and her mother was still not free, her sad expression had just about broken my heart. I had to do more to help, not only for my friend but also for Olivia. We artists and nature lovers had to stick together.

"Ouch." I slapped my arm, killing the mosquito that had bitten me. Automatically, I reached to wipe my hand on the back of my jeans but then paused, remembering I had noticed a tissue in my purse earlier this morning. Being that prepared wasn't like me, but Jonas must have stashed one there for some reason.

I pulled it out, grateful that at least chigger season hadn't yet struck. By the time that got bad here, I hoped to be living up on the ridge where the breeze would help disperse those swarms of mean-spirited, biting insects. As I wiped my hand, I glanced up at the store window in front of me.

"Oh, look how cute that is," I said as I caught sight of the pretty blouse on display. "I might like that for my birthday next month."

The idea appealed to me, so I tilted my head from side to side as I considered it more carefully.

"Yes. I would." I tried to quiet the urge to keep talking to myself, but since the voice in my head kept agreeing with me, who was I to argue? Before making a final decision, I checked my watch. "I've still got time." We weren't meeting for another fifteen minutes, and Kelsey would be at least ten minutes late, as always.

The blouse on the mannequin called to me again. "I really should take care of that for Jonas. It might be gone by the time he gets around to shopping for my birthday." I frowned when I noticed the store wasn't yet open. Thwarted in my attempt to do a good deed for my husband.

Realizing the city hall building was right next door and they had a trash can in the lobby, I walked over. If I was quiet, I could get in and out of the building without Ethel hearing me. If she waylaid me, I'd turn into the headline story for her lunchtime edition of the Jenkins rumor mill.

Pulling the door open quietly, I tiptoed into the lobby, my eyes focused on the half-opened door to the town offices while I prayed Ethel wouldn't choose this moment to leave her office.

"Ella Mae!" exclaimed Dale Cooper as he descended the remaining few steps from the second-floor staircase. "Have you heard the good news? These charming gentlemen are considering filming a movie here in Jenkins. How fortunate I ran into them!"

My mouth dropped open as I saw who was following him—the peacock and his assistant/bodyguard from the diner.

"A movie! In Jenkins!" Dale repeated, practically bouncing with excitement. "They are so fortunate I heard them wandering around lost upstairs. Now I can give them a proper Jenkins welcome. Luckily, I can clear my schedule for the whole day. I'm taking them to the club for a special lunch and then I'll give them a tour of all the best locations in Jenkins."

He turned to wink at his VIPs. "Maybe even get them out on the water. You know, hold them hostage on the lake and not bring them back to the Hampton Inn until the deal is sealed." He let loose a hearty laugh while his eyes gleamed greedily at the prospect of landing this big fish for the benefit of Jenkins as well as his own reputation.

I winced at Dale's volume. He turned on his unnecessarily booming voice, not to mention adding the pompous tone, whenever he was performing in his mayoral role.

Giuseppe stepped forward. Today, he wore a different garish, yet actually stylish, shirt, covered with colorful vertical stripes that had an almost graffiti-like brush stroke. I had to admit it looked good on him. Fashion was fashion, despite the wearer. Sadly, the brimmed straw hat on his head ruined the overall effect. He looked like he was trying to play the Southern gentleman, not realizing that Arkansas had its own version of Southern style and no one in their right mind would be caught dead wearing a hat like that around here.

Giuseppe smiled back at Dale, although it looked a bit forced to me. "Yes, yes, very fortunate you found us. The real estate office appears to be closed today, so we would have been wandering around on our own without your most gracious assistance."

Turning his attention to me, Giuseppe doffed his hat. "And to add to our good fortune. It is so wonderful to see you again, lovely Liza." He paused as his face turned quizzical. "Or do you prefer Ella Mae?" He tsked at the very sound of this nickname, shaking his head to rid himself of such an unpleasant sensation. "No," he concluded without any input from me. "That does not suit such a beautiful woman. To me you will always be Liza. It will be just our little secret," he finished with a wink.

As he leaned over to execute a sweeping bow, silly hat held out to the side, I tried my best to ignore him and frowned. What had they been doing upstairs? I'd seen them with the realtor on Wednesday. She certainly would have told them she didn't work on Fridays. The only other office up there was Vanessa's accounting firm. Was Giuseppe trying to break in to look for her memory stick? Mentally kicking myself for forgetting to ask Jonas to check out the files this morning, I realized we'd have to go through the rest of it later.

Rising from his bow, Giuseppe asked, "And where is your lovely friend, um, Valerie, wasn't it?"

"Vanessa," I said through clenched teeth.

"Yes, yes, of course. I hope she is well too." He showed his pearly white teeth as he smoothly rolled the hat back onto his head.

My eyes narrowed. Was this clown toying with me? Could my mother be right that he was part of the mafia? I considered it only for a second before shaking my head. That was nuts. Besides, he looked too ridiculous to run an organized crime gang and survive the vicious turf wars they were so well known for. Even if he was somehow involved with the mafia, why would he come to Jenkins, kill Courtney, and frame Vanessa for the murder?

Then my eyes flicked to Drosnic, his enforcer, looming behind

Giuseppe and Dale. Maybe Giuseppe had sent Drosnic to do the dirty work while he flirted with silly women around Jenkins, telling them fantasies about making movies.

Movie!? I blew out a puff of disgust at what had to be a lie. No one would travel to Jenkins to make a movie. But, then, thanks to Dale's big mouth, an idea struck me. Smiling to myself, I concluded it was well-nigh one of my most brilliant ones this week. While these guys were out gallivanting all day with Dale, I would see what I could learn about them at the Hampton Inn. I'd heard last night that Laila, one of the girls I had been friendly with back in high school, had just been promoted to assistant manager at the hotel. This afternoon would be an excellent opportunity to visit her at work and see what I could dig up on these guys.

Noticing the men were still looking at me, I realized my continued smiling and nodding must have seemed a bit strange. Feeling pleased that I hadn't spoken any of my thoughts out loud, I said, "Well, you gentlemen have a good afternoon. I've got a lunch of my own to get to."

Giving them a quick wave goodbye, I stepped to the side, barely remembering my original task in time, and tossed my tissue in the trash. As the building's door was swinging shut behind me, I picked up my pace as I heard a woman's voice. "Ella Mae, you're not forgetting to visit good ole Ethel, are you?"

*****

The five of us were given a table for six outside on the sidewalk next to a low guardrail. I pressed my lips together as the waiter removed the empty chair that Vanessa wouldn't need today, annoyed at him through no fault of his own. She would have enjoyed meeting these women now that our age difference wasn't a big deal. Then I scooted all the way over to take the seat closest to the sidewalk as Kelsey scrambled in next to me and the others sat across from us.

Angela, Brooke, and Carlita—the "ABC" girls—were in town for the reunion. Back in the day we all used to hang out together, but I hadn't seen them in years. I laughed, happy to see them again as we placed our lunch orders and started chattering over each other.

"Do you remember"—a lot of my discussions since Wednesday evening had started this way—"we used to tease Kelsey to get her to change her name so we could be the 'ABCDE' girls?"

Everyone burst out laughing, and then, without thinking about it or coordinating, the others shouted out options: "Diana," "Deborah," "Daphne." Angela blew the paper from her straw at Kelsey to punctuate her choice.

"I kinda like Daphne." Kelsey laughed, then shook her head to avoid raising any hopes before picking up her iced tea.

I noticed that all our drinks were non-alcoholic. There had been a time we'd have been trying to scam or flirt the waiter into giving us something alcoholic. Amazing how times had changed. We had all overindulged last night, and at twenty-eight years old, we seemed to know our limits.

The thought startled me. When did we start acting so mature? Or was this the real deal and we weren't just pretending to be adults? That almost made me sad.

Carlita raised her glass. "To us!"

Before everyone took a sip, I quickly threw in an additional toast. "And to Vanessa! May she join us soon."

"Here, here!" they cried.

"How's her daughter handling all this?" asked Angela. Of course, she'd ask after Olivia. She was always the most sensitive, plus she had a toddler of her own.

"She was okay, I guess," I answered. "She stayed with me on

Wednesday night and then I dropped her at her grandmother's yesterday afternoon."

"You?" came a chorus of surprised voices from around the table.

"Why are you all acting so surprised?" I couldn't keep the hurt out of my voice.

"Sorry. I forgot your mother still lives here to help you." Before I could respond, Angela added, "I'll bet Vanessa really appreciated you being such a darling and supporting her."

"Where was her husband?" asked Carlita. "What's his name?"

"Adam's an ex now. I heard he was out of town," said Kelsey.

Where had she heard that? How much gossip about Vanessa had spread throughout Jenkins already? And why was everyone so shocked that I had taken care of Olivia? If I wanted to take care of a kid, I reckon I knew how to handle one just fine, thank you very much.

"You know I saw him with Courtney out for dinner at this place in Ft. Smith," said Carlita.

"Adam?" asked Kelsey.

"Wait, what?" I'd been distracted. If Adam and Courtney were actually dating, this put Courtney's death in a whole different light. Had Vanessa been jealous?

Seeing my shocked expression, Brooke waved a hand at me. "It's no big deal." She shrugged as if that could dismiss the problem. "Vanessa and Adam have been separated for over a year and their divorce is final, isn't it?" She glanced around the table. "I think it's too soon for him to start dating again, but isn't that just like a man?"

The other women agreed, but I didn't let it go. I didn't care whether Adam had started dating, only that he'd been dating the woman who was killed. The woman Vanessa was now accused of murdering. My stomach clenched. This could make things even worse for my friend. I started to panic a little. Carlita must have been mistaken. Many of the rumors around town were wrong, after all.

"Are you sure they were *together* together? Not just talking business?" I asked, remembering that Courtney had also been an accountant.

"Honey, I think I'd know when two people are out on a date—she was practically sitting on his lap, and I imagine they only needed one fork between the two of them, the way they kept feeding each other. They were so into each other, they never noticed me in the restaurant. Let me tell you, any business they were talking about was funny business, if you know what I mean."

The others laughed at Carlita's colorful description, but I stayed quiet, worrying about Vanessa while the conversation moved on to other topics. A few times I started to raise the topic again, to point out how this was bad news for Vanessa, but I just couldn't bring myself to rain on everyone else's parade. I didn't want to be the party pooper.

Our lunches came quickly. Probably the chef could hear us from all the way inside the kitchen and prioritized our food so we'd leave faster and the restaurant could regain some peace and quiet.

While we ate, the other women compared notes on the classmates we'd seen last night. I was only half paying attention to all the "he's doing this," "she's done that," and "can you believe she said" comments when something caught my ear.

"Wait. Are you talking about Grody?" I asked.

"Yeah. Carlita said Andrew was being squirrelly, well even more squirrelly than normal." Brooke laughed.

"Of course, he has always been a little odd. That's why he was called Grody, right?" agreed Carlita. The laughter grew louder, making my head hurt. The sun seemed too bright also. Whose idea had it been to meet for lunch today?

"I spoke to him right at the beginning. He didn't sound off to me," I said, trying to remember all the way back to the beginning of last night's reception.

"Like I said, he's always odd," said Carlita. "But last night, he was downright twitchy."

"There was definitely something up his craw," agreed Brooke.

"Was it something specific?" I asked, but no one had anything useful to contribute so the conversation moved on. There was certainly no shortage of oddballs at our reunion to gossip about.

A minute later I finally remembered Grody's odd comments about the lost PTA money and pursed my lips. Was he involved somehow? He wasn't even married, let alone had a school-aged child that would cause him to join the PTA. I'd need to talk to Jonas about this.

"What?" asked Angela from across the table as I grimaced involuntarily, but this time not because of anything involving Vanessa, Grody, or Courtney.

I pointed my chin behind her as I noticed Susie Q and her posse of three women sashaying side by side down the sidewalk toward us.

"Aw, shut the front door. Really? They had to show up right as we're trying to have a nice lunch and enjoy some time together?" Carlita twisted in her seat to look behind her.

I saw it happen almost in slow motion, but how that forkful of salad spilled all over my blouse remains a mystery. I've used utensils since I was a toddler, more or less successfully, thousands of times. Why would my hand-eye coordination decide to go on the fritz right as Susie Q approached with three of her followers? She was a bringer of curses to my life. A bane of my existence. *Ugh.*

Quickly I dipped my napkin into my water glass and swiped at the yellow stain spreading across my white top. Of course I had worn white today. All that achieved was making the stain even more glaringly obvious, as the napkin dissolved into a million tiny pieces, all sticking to the honey mustard dressing mess on my blouse. *Delightful.* About the only thing left would be for some bees to come investigate the scene.

At about the same time I realized my blouse was beyond repair, Susie Q reached our group. Placing her hands on the rail alongside our table, she craned her head to get a better look at the mess I'd made on myself. "Nice look, Ella Mae. Took the time to get all gussied up, I see," she purred.

Nearly whacking me in the head with her purse, Christy Tomer pushed in next to Susie. "Howdy, girls. We'd love to join you for lunch—"

"But you're not invited," whispered Kelsey into my ear.

Christy didn't seem to hear her and continued, "But we can't."

"Well I declare, what a shame that is," said Brooke in her sweetest voice.

Susie Q narrowed her eyes for a moment before plastering on her fake smile. "Well, bless your welcoming heart. Brooke, I can tell you still have the warm manners your mama taught you. And thank you kindly for the lovely invitation—"

"It wasn't an invitation," murmured Kelsey.

Christy broke in, "We can't because we're off to do some serious damage, shopping for dresses over in Ft. Smith." Just the thought was enough to cause her to raise her arms and conduct a little celebratory jiggle right there on the sidewalk. One of the other women joined in. I didn't remember her name because I generally tried to forget the names of people I never wanted to see again. Too bad that strategy hadn't succeeded with Susie Q.

"Rick liked my outfit last night so much—"

"What little there was of it," whispered Kelsey again, this time making me snort.

This time Christy must have heard her as she threw us a pouty glance. Her Botoxed lips so close to us made her pout appear as if a bright red football had landed on her mouth. I moved my hand up to cover my mouth, clamping my lips in an effort to stop the giggles.

Pretending to ignore us, Christy looked away from Kelsey and me as she continued, "He gave me money to go buy another outfit to make myself into a 'hot tamale' again for the dance tomorrow night." She tittered in delight and turned to Susie Q. "Did I tell you that he was talking about having something special for me on Saturday?" She squealed, "Ooh, I'm so excited. I think he's finally gonna propose."

The four women squealed and clumped together for a jumping group hug. After far too much of their theatrics, Susie Q declared, "Time to get this show on the road."

She pointed at Christy. "We've got to buy that dress and then get you a tune-up at Shear Heaven so you'll be picture-perfect. In fact, maybe we should all go for a little touch-up if we're going to appear in any photos commemorating your engagement."

She headed off but then realized the others were still wriggling in excitement for Christy. Susie Q reached back and grabbed Christy's arm. "Come on," she said, and dragged her along, causing the others to follow behind. Thankfully, they'd already completely forgotten about us as they started throwing out wedding ideas while moving away.

Sitting there silently in their wake, we watched the spectacle move down the street. Then Kelsey said, "Well, buh-bye to y'all. So good to see you gone!"

The rest of us cheered low enough that Susie Q wouldn't notice.

Brooke said, "I'll bet Christy needs a tune-up. She probably used up all her oil extracting herself from that skintight leather thing she wore last night."

Carlita joked, "Maybe she should go buy the missing half of last night's outfit."

"It was a miracle that she didn't catch a cold last night with all that exposed flesh," said Angela. By far the nicest of our group, she always struggled to come up with good insults.

"No, the miracle must have been how she managed to get in and out of the car without exposing even more flesh," Brooke added.

"And what does Rick Hoffman or Christy Tomer know about tamales, anyway? Looks to me like I'm the only hot tamale around here." Carlita raised her hands alongside her face, creating a picture frame effect to show off her Latina heritage.

"Well, how about that Suzanne Quentin. Ain't she as pleasant as a porcupine wrapped in rattlesnakes?" Brooke raised her voice to make herself heard over our laughter.

I smiled in appreciation, but noticed people at the other outside tables throwing dirty looks in our direction. Still, I couldn't resist piling on. "Is it me or does Susie Q always seem to manage to squeeze in a mention of how a visit to her salon will save the day?"

"Why bless her heart." Angela blinked her eyelashes with exaggerated innocence. "Always so kind and generous in helping her fellow women—and for only a slight fee."

Amidst the laughter, I put down my drink before I spilled it all over myself to join the honey mustard dressing.

"Christy Tomer and Rick Hoffman getting hitched? Oh my!" Brooke returned her attention to the newest rumor of the day.

"I think it's a case of sleaze attracting sleaze," declared Kelsey.

Approval of her comment caused everyone at our table to cheer and high-five each other. No wiggling, jiggling celebrations for us. We were far too dignified for that.

I grinned, finally enjoying this lunch in the sun with my old friends. When the waiter turned to look at us again, I called him over to order two slices of key lime pie to go.

When he delivered them, I had to slap Kelsey's hand away. "It's for Laila." She could order her own slice; this one would make the perfect congratulations gift to bring on my visit to Laila at the Hampton Inn.

14

Friday After Lunch

Jonas

Finished with my packing for tonight's camping trip, I'd barely lain down on the couch for a nice nap when Elizabeth breezed in.

"Good, there you are. I was hoping to catch you," she said as she whooshed into the living room. She leaned down to give me a kiss and then gave attention to the squirming Daisy.

"What happened to your shirt?" I pointed at the yellowish splotch all over her front that still had shreds of what must have once been a paper napkin sticking to it.

"Nothing to worry about. I'm going to change, then head over to meet my friend Laila."

I pointed to the plastic container she had set down on the side table next to the armchair. "Is that for me?"

"Never mind that either. It's for Laila." She paused and blew me an air kiss. "I've got something else for you."

I sat up and grinned. It was okay if the box wasn't for me, I liked everything else she could possibly offer.

"You could go to the fairgrounds and talk to Andrew Grady."

"You sure you don't have something for me?" I raised an eyebrow in case she hadn't caught my drift.

"It's more of an idea of something you can go do. It's part of helping Vanessa. Everyone thinks something's up with Grody."

I settled back down into a prone position for my nap. "I've got that campout."

"That's not until late afternoon, right?"

I nodded.

"Did you finish packing yet?"

Reluctantly, I nodded again, concerned where this was going and that I was running out of excuses.

"See! You've got time after all." She gave Daisy a squeeze and me another kiss before walking away.

I stood up to follow her. "Why Andrew? What am I going to do there?"

She headed down the hall to our bedroom. "The girls were talking about how weird he was acting last night."

"Lots of people were acting weird. It's a reunion." I wasn't relishing the idea of trying to fool some strangers and pry into their business. "What would I even tell them?" But as soon as the words had left my mouth, I realized my mistake. For Elizabeth, inventing a cover story was as easy as sliding off a greasy log backward.

I stopped dead in my tracks in the hallway, shocked that my thoughts had started sounding Southern. Maybe Elizabeth was right that I needed more friends my own age. Hanging out with the likes of Dale Cooper, Colton Buck, and Lester Stapleton was messing with my mind and my vocabulary.

From our bedroom, Elizabeth answered, "You could tell him you're thinking about investing some of your money. See if you can figure out what's up with Grody and listen for any gossip about Vanessa. Oh, and while you're talking, ask for a recommendation for a local accountant. It'd be good to have someone local for my business."

I stood in the doorway and focused on the crazy part of her idea. "Investment in the fairgrounds?"

She pulled on another blouse. "I don't know. Tell him you like go-karts and horse shows and—"

I interrupted, "Right, and swap meets?"

Elizabeth stopped with one arm in and one out, looking surprised. I think my cutting her off made her realize that this planned escapade had zoomed right over the edge of my comfort zone. She finished putting on the shirt, her voice turning soft. "It's just a little lie."

"I don't lie," I said simply. It had started back in a college orientation activity when someone called me out in front of the group and accused me of lying about a time I'd faced hardship. The fact that he'd been correct hadn't improved things. I had hated the feeling of embarrassment and vowed never to lie again. After all these years, my commitment had grown into a matter of pride. Not even for a good reason.

"No, you don't," she said as she wrapped her arms around me and nestled her head on my chest. "And I love that about you. But you are also good at not blabbing out everything you know." She stepped back and raised her eyebrow, as if reminding me of some significant example, but I had no idea what she was talking about. Not understanding her was not a new sensation, so I let her comment slide past. When I didn't respond, she sighed. "So don't mention horse shows and swap meets, but you did like the go-karts, right? And we are trying to figure out what to invest all that money in, right?"

I thought about it for a moment. "Okay. I can do that as long as I don't have to actually tell him I want to invest in the fairgrounds."

She walked past me down the hallway and I followed her again. "How about you tell him you had a good time last night and need something to do in the summer. Maybe you'd want to work there a little."

"Like repairing go-karts?" I snorted. The summer was for outdoor activities and relaxing, not fixing mechanical things inside a hot repair shop.

"Or something. You told me you used to love state fairs back in Oregon."

"That was when I was a kid," I protested.

"Don't forget that carnival last year," she pointed out, bending over to tie her shoe.

"That's because you were there."

"That's sweet. See how good you are with improvising." She swooped up to kiss my cheek as she grabbed the food container off the side table. "Just imagine I'm with you today. Now come on, let's get you into your car."

She gave Daisy a treat, put her outside, and then hooked her arm through mine as she dragged me outside. I wasn't exactly resisting, but I wasn't enthusiastic about the whole idea either. As we walked out the front door, I saw she had pie inside the box. I wondered if any place in the area sold vegan pie. Or cake. Cake would do in a pinch.

*****

The fairgrounds parking lot was practically empty today. I pulled in next to a nondescript door with small letters reading, "Office," around which several other cars were clustered. Last night, I hadn't noticed this door, but Elizabeth had been so nervous about encountering her former classmates again that I had stayed focused on her.

I opened the office door and found myself inside a tiny, windowless reception area with four closed doors taking up most of the remaining wall space. A miserable-looking woman sat working behind a desk close to the entrance.

"What?" yelled a hidden voice barely muffled by the thin wood door separating us.

I stood there for a moment, feeling stupid, wondering why I had agreed to come here. Then I reminded myself of little Olivia. She had seemed so sad and scared sitting all by herself in the dining room at Mary's house. I took a breath, grounding myself. I would do this for her.

"May I help you?" asked the woman at the desk.

"Oh, she was a real piece of work," exclaimed another hidden voice. At least two men must have been arguing in the room and not realizing, or possibly not caring, that their assistant could hear everything.

Little dots of red colored the assistant's cheeks as she pretended she couldn't hear them.

"I'm here and hoping to talk—"

The first voice interrupted, "How would you know? She always acted professional when she was here."

The second voice boomed, "Oh yeah, well you never saw her on a Saturday night. The way she handled those truckers, whew!"

The assistant's eyes flicked back and forth between me and the closed door.

"—to Mr. Grady," I said. "About the fairgrounds. Maybe."

I stuttered to a halt, not even sounding coherent to myself, as the first voice responded, "When did you spend time with her on a Saturday night? I didn't know you were seeing her."

"I wasn't seeing her, Dad, not in that way," the second voice scoffed. "She ran the best game in town. Come on, everybody knew that."

The first voice got louder. "No, not everybody. Whose idiotic idea was it to play poker?"

"Bruh—" started the second voice.

"I'm not your brother," shouted the first voice, and a hand

slapped against a wood surface. "Wait, is that why you're always hitting me up for money? Because of your—"

"Excuse me," mumbled the assistant as she quickly pushed away from the desk. In two quick strides, she reached the door and slipped inside, sliding it shut behind her.

"What?" demanded the first voice, but I couldn't hear the woman's answer.

She must have told them they had company because the door flew open and Andrew Grady stalked out, slamming the door shut behind him. "Oh, it's you," he said by way of greeting. "You're Ella Mae's husband, right?"

"Jonas," I supplied.

"Okay," he answered, visibly trying to calm down as he opened a door revealing another office.

"I'm . . . I'm here to talk about a possible investment," I said, this time making my purpose clear.

"Investment?" Andrew scoffed, but then added, "You'll have to talk to my father. This is still his place." Apparently changing his mind, he pulled his office door closed and stalked past me, out of the building.

"Mr. Grady will see you now." The woman returned to the reception area, her face still red as she avoided my eyes, even though she had no reason to feel embarrassed. She wasn't the one yelling at her son.

"Thank you," I said, and stepped past her into a surprisingly luxurious office that was larger than the entire reception area.

An older man with close-cropped black hair seasoned with gray stood beside the desk, drinking from a chipped coffee mug. He stared blankly at the bookcase along the wall, his features anguished.

"Mr. Grady?" I asked, looking at the sad man lost in his own world. When he didn't answer, I added, "Is everything okay? Should I come back another time?"

My words startled him. He jostled some of his coffee and then swore softly before setting the mug on his desk and wiping his hand with a napkin. He hadn't yet looked directly at me, and I wasn't sure if he remembered he'd told his assistant that it was okay for me to come in.

He dropped heavily into his desk chair and slumped his shoulders. "No. No, I'm not," he said, finally meeting my eyes as he sighed. "I owe a lot of money and now I've lost the town's goodwill. I could lose the whole business."

I didn't know what to do with this information. Who did he owe money to? How had he lost the town's goodwill? Would any of this help Vanessa? I struggled to come up with the right response. I couldn't very well ask him if he had killed Courtney Stanton as my opening question before we'd even sat down, but neither could I just ignore his comments. What would Elizabeth say next? "I'm sorry," was the best I could come up with.

Mr. Grady furrowed his brow. "Why was it that you wanted to meet with me?"

After his admission, I felt silly answering. Who in their right mind would still want to continue this discussion now? But I'd promised Elizabeth, and nothing better came to mind, so I kept to the script I'd planned on the ride over. "I'm considering possible investments and wanted to learn more about the fairgrounds business."

"Oh," he said, his mouth forming a circle as his eyes widened. He clanged his coffee mug onto his desk and practically leapt to his feet. "Sorry about all that doom and gloom. I'm just having a bad day. Call me David," he said, grabbing my hand and shaking it vigorously. "The money problems I mentioned are not because this place isn't profitable. No, quite the contrary. That was more of, um, more of a personal thing. I'm sorry you had to witness that."

"You want some coffee?" He turned back to the bookcase where a small pot of coffee was percolating.

"No, thanks," I said, eyeing the old pot with suspicion.

"So, have you been here before? What brings you to Jenkins? It's a nice town, but a bit off the beaten track."

"I was here last night for the reunion—"

"Ah, one of Andrew's classmates returning to take a victory lap around your old stomping grounds, eh?"

I tried to correct him, but he had switched on a bit of manic energy now. He reached for a business card. "Here you go—in case you need to reach me with any questions. You know, we could go over the books, but I always find it's best to get the lay of the land first, don't you?"

I opened my mouth, but he didn't wait for a response before continuing, "In fact, why don't I show you around the whole place, especially the parts you didn't see last night."

Putting one hand on my shoulder and gripping it as if to make sure not to let go of the goose that would lay him some golden eggs, Mr. Grady escorted me out of his office. "It's just through this door," he explained as he opened a heavier door that led into the large event space where last night's mixer had taken place. A couple of older men were moving slowly around the room, pulling down the decorations and cleaning up the place.

For the next fifteen minutes, Mr. Grady raced me around the complex, waving his hands and showing me where he hoped to add a baseball field—"Minor League Baseball brings in a steady crowd and they spend a lot of money on beer and food"—repair the grandstands—"Bigger crowds mean bigger events, and that means more profits"—and on and on. All the while, he pumped me for information on how much I might want to invest, how quickly I would decide, and which of his ideas I wanted to support the most. I hemmed and hawed my way through it, pretending interest and trying to avoid committing to something I didn't actually want to do. With him doing nearly all the talking, it wasn't hard to avoid outright lies.

"I'll send you the books and then you can meet with my lawyer. Heck, bring your own if you have one around here and we can negotiate the finer points."

I started to remind him that I hadn't committed to anything yet but he grabbed my hand while patting me on the shoulder. "I'm really looking forward to this. Yes sir, this could be the start of a whole new chapter for us." After a final handshake at the door, he bustled back toward his office, leaving me alone in the sudden quiet.

During that entire conversation, I'd felt like a fraud and learned exactly nothing useful. I hadn't even gotten a chance to ask for a recommendation for a local accountant. The only time I managed to mention Vanessa's name, Mr. Grady had only said that it was a shame about her arrest.

I took a deep breath and walked outside—only to hear a different voice yelling into a phone.

"It's been one screwup after another! You gotta fix this asap." Andrew waved his free hand as he paced away from the door. Pivoting, his eyes went wide when he caught sight of me standing by the entrance to the event hall. "Bruh, I've gotta go," he said into the phone, and then added, "Call ya later," before hanging up.

"Uh, sorry about that," said Andrew. Then he puffed out his chest and pulled back his shoulders. "How'd the tour go? Can I answer any questions for you?" Evidently picking up his father's habits, he clapped me on the shoulder. "So, you're gonna invest with us? That's a wise choice. We've got a lot of great plans here. Did my dad share them with you? Maybe I should tell you more about the best ones myself since they were my ideas anyway."

I tried to tell him no thanks, but he was off to the races. It took me another ten minutes to extract myself before he'd finally finished shaking my hand and walked me to my car.

I sat in my car decompressing as I thought about what to do next. I didn't enjoy this sleuthing business. Of the two of us, Elizabeth was the more natural detective, better at dissimulating. Whereas I got quiet when I wasn't sure what to do in a new situation, Elizabeth tended to become more brash. She was nosier and liked to gossip with others, like all those friends she had met for lunch today and the one she was heading out to visit. Come to think of it, although she wouldn't care to admit it, she was much like her mother.

Finally I decided what to do next. My mind made up, I started the engine. Before heading home, I was going to find myself a piece of pie. Or cake, in a pinch.

15

Friday Early Afternoon

Elizabeth

A fter I made sure Jonas had left for the fairgrounds, I hopped in my car to visit Laila at the Hampton Inn. When I started the engine, a thought struck me. Because Vanessa had told me Adam was away in Vegas for the whole week, I hadn't even considered him as a suspect. But then, during lunch today, Brooke had mentioned that he had been seeing Courtney. What if they had a falling out and he killed her? Maybe that missing money was the cause, and Adam killed Courtney and took it to Vegas. Had he been playing us for fools all along?

Chewing on my cheek, I turned off the engine and went back inside. I flipped open my laptop and started searching for flights. I needed to find out if my idea was even possible. As I navigated through the airline sites, I started daydreaming about a nice vacation with Jonas, away from my mother and all the decisions we had to make for the house. Finally, I sighed and turned back to my computer. Relaxing on a beach somewhere wouldn't feel right while Vanessa was rotting away in that cell.

In the meantime, the computer had found some options. One more click got me the answers. *Yes!* There were plenty of options for the first flight of a round-trip. But then I realized that direction wasn't the key issue. I reversed the search to check for a return flight. Trailing my finger down the list, I gasped and nearly fell off my chair before grabbing my phone.

I made the call, hoping to catch him.

"Hi, Lizzie. I mean Elizabeth. Or are you insisting I call you Mrs. Trout now?" Trent's tone was friendly at first but had grown snarky by the end of his greeting.

"Oh, stop," I said, clamping my lips together to cut off my next comment about him acting like a baby. Provoking him would be counterproductive. As much as I hated to admit it, I needed his help.

"You know how Vanessa told us Adam was in Las Vegas all week?"

"Lizzie—" warned Trent. All snark and friendliness had disappeared from his voice.

"No, wait, hear me out," I said. "What if Adam flew back to Arkansas without telling anyone, killed Courtney, and then flew back to Vegas?" Trent's silence was a clear sign of encouragement, so I continued, "I just checked the flights. Adam could have taken a flight at eight-thirty on Wednesday morning from Little Rock and been back to Las Vegas by one-thirty our time. I assume you called him at some point to tell him his girlfriend died. What time did you speak to him?"

"I can't—"

"What time?" I insisted.

He groaned. "Middle of the afternoon. I'd have to go check my notes—"

"See!" I exclaimed, then realized I'd been interrupting him. "Sorry, but you see it's possible. He could have flown here anytime on Tuesday. I found a flight that got in around midnight so no one would have seen him—and oh, he could have stayed in a hotel instead of his own place to really throw everyone off his trail." I could tell Trent was about to speak, so I talked even more rapidly before he could cut me off. "Then he could have set up the explosion and gone back to Vegas, pretended he was sleeping in and waking up late if someone had called him before his flight landed."

"Hmm. I see. And how did an accountant learn to construct and detonate an explosion remotely?"

I breathed in sharply. Although I suspected he meant his question to be rhetorical, Trent had accidentally confirmed that Courtney had been murdered using some remote control thingy. I started to panic as I wondered if he knew about Vanessa's experience with explosives in the Marines and whether this meant she was in even more trouble.

Realizing his error, Trent babbled, "That's not what . . . I meant as a purely hypothetical." Finally, with more than a little pleading in his voice, he said, "Lizzie, you can't talk about this."

"I'm not one of the town gossips," I snapped.

"And," he added, his voice returning to his deputy tone. "You can't get involved in a murder investigation."

"I only want to help my friend, and you're a sheriff—"

"Deputy," he corrected me.

"Well, Deputy," I said, emphasizing his title while still trying to keep a friendly tone, "how about you do the investigating and call the airlines to see if Adam flew out of Little Rock on Wednesday morning? Or I guess you should also check Ft. Smith. I didn't have time to look at those flights, but that's also a possibility."

"Ooh," I gasped as a new thought struck me before he could respond. "Maybe he never even went to Las Vegas. Have you checked with his hotel to verify he was there?" Another thought tumbled out. "He could have a fake ID and used that for the flights. Maybe you should call TAA, or does the FAA handle that? Can't they run some sort of facial recognition software to see if he was in the airport on Wednesday? Or would that be CIA or FBI?" I was getting excited. With the right assistance, we'd be able to nail Adam in no time.

"Now you're starting to sound all crazy-like," Trent said with a reluctant chuckle.

Resisting the urge to reach through the phone lines and slap him, I took a breath. In my head I re-heard what he'd just said and smiled. "Well, I guess that must mean you believe everything else."

"Lizzie, don't go twisting my words. In fact." He paused and then lost the whine in his voice as the highly trained law enforcement officer regained self-control. "I can't talk to you about the investigation at all."

I ignored this silliness. "But you said 'now.'"

"Huh?"

"As in *now* I'm sounding crazy. Meaning *before* everything I said made sense to you." I was hopeful I had convinced him—either the Trent I knew from high school or this newfangled professional guy on the phone. If this panned out, Vanessa would be off the hook for sure.

"Now you're sounding crazy again."

Aargh. "But you'll check?"

His response was a curt, "We'll see."

I knew a lot of different ways to skin a cat, but Trent remained wily, and no matter what I said, he wouldn't get trapped into committing to follow through on my theory.

After he hung up a few minutes later, I paced the room, pondering. If Adam was the killer, then Vanessa would go free. But Olivia would lose her father to prison. I was torn—sad for her but happy for her mother, my friend. Of course, if he was a scumbag murderer, then Olivia was better off without him around. But it was also possible Adam wasn't the killer. Who then? And what should I do about it?

I couldn't just wait around for Trent to look into Adam's alibi. Despite his lack of firm commitment, I felt confident he'd do it. He'd never been good at resisting pressure from me. In the meantime, I'd go check out that Giuseppe fellow and his thug while they were away from their hotel for the day. Maybe despite all previous experience, my mother was right with her cockamamie theory and they were in the mafia. But why would they kill Courtney? What would an accountant have that the mafia would want? Pretty spreadsheets?

With no answer popping into my mind, I hurried out to my car. Before I could start the engine, my phone rang. "Hi, long time no see," I said to Carlita. Almost ten years had gone by since I'd seen her and now she was calling me an hour after we had lunch together.

"You were talking about the Gradys at lunch, right?" she asked without preamble.

"Yes." I was surprised because she hadn't appeared to have been paying much attention.

"Well, I just got off the phone with your Trent."

"He's not *my Trent*. I'm married now," I said, perhaps a bit more indignantly than deserved.

"Well, good," she declared. "Because he's cute. Maybe he'll call me again for another consultation. In fact, maybe I should call him this time."

"Wait. What are you talking about? *I* just got off the phone with Trent, not five minutes ago. How did you *just* get off the phone with him?"

"Are you jealous? I thought you said he wasn't *your* Trent?" she teased.

"He's not!" She was getting annoying.

"Well, good," she repeated. "Just wanted to make sure."

"Carlita," I fussed. "I ain't got no time for this."

"Okay, okay. I'm just messin' with you," she said. "Although I really will call Trent. He called me about twenty minutes ago. You remember I said I was a supervisor at Guardian Security?"

I nodded and then remembered we were on the phone. "Yeah. You mentioned it at lunch."

"Well, Trent called to tell me that the sheriff's department didn't need us to segregate the security camera footage anymore."

When she paused, I asked, "What are you talking about?"

"The footage from the Gradys' home," she explained. "The sheriff's department subpoenaed it for their investigation—"

"And you didn't say something at lunch?" I interrupted, annoyed that she'd let me prattle on about how I was helping Vanessa when she was sitting on information about a key suspect. Or at least one of the suspects Jonas and I had identified so far.

"Ella Mae, I couldn't. I could lose my job if I talk about an active investigation involving our clients."

I harrumphed, but I understood. "Why are you able to tell me now?" Before she could answer, I added, "What did they learn about the Gradys?"

Carlita said, "We have to segregate the footage whenever there's a criminal investigation. Then when the authorities tell us they're done, we can remove it from our special processes for handling legal situations." When I didn't respond, Carlita said, "Don't you get it? This means they're no longer looking at the Gradys as suspects in Courtney's murder."

"What else did Trent say?"

"Are you asking if he talked to me about you?" She laughed. When I growled, she quickly said, "I know, I know. You're an old married lady now." Her tone grew serious as she finally got around to telling me the news. "Apparently their techs reviewed the footage. No one came or left the Gradys' house from midnight when Andrew stumbled in to just before eight in the morning when Mr. Grady left the house."

"Huh," was all I could muster. Jonas and I hadn't placed any bets, but I had thought Andrew was a likely suspect. His gambling problem, the general squirrellyness others had reported about him, and just—I don't know—something about him made me suspicious. Of course, I had just finished deciding Adam had killed Courtney too. Perhaps I was too suspicious about everyone this week.

"Anyway." Carlita drawled out the word after I hadn't spoken for a while. "I've got to get back to work. Please don't tell anyone I told you this. I don't want to get into trouble. But now that they've released the footage, I figured you should know before you go accusing the Gradys of killing Courtney."

I gulped as I thought of how embarrassing that would be, especially when Trent could immediately tell me how wrong I was. "Thanks, Carlita. Thanks for having my back."

Hanging up, I sat in the car. That was really nice of Carlita to risk her job for me—well, really for Vanessa. Even though I was alone, I pinched my thumb and forefinger together, pulled them across my lips to zip them closed, and promised not to rat her out.

Eliminating the Gradys as suspects might be good for them, but it wasn't good for Vanessa. If the Gradys were innocent, then it was time to pin down which of our other suspects had killed Courtney. After considering them again, I finally shrugged. No one was the obvious killer. But if I was going to check into the two guys claiming to be movie producers, I definitely didn't want them around while I did so. Besides, I had to go to the hotel anyway. Laila would eventually hear that I'd bought a slice of key lime pie intended for her and it would be rude if I didn't bring it to her. Whatever information I picked up while there would be a bonus.

16

Friday Mid-Afternoon

Elizabeth

W hen I walked into the lobby of the Hampton Inn, I was startled to see a familiar figure laughing by the front desk. I hadn't invited Kelsey along. She always bumbled our plans during high school and got us caught. She could never keep a straight face and she'd make me start to giggle. Then she'd start to giggle, and I'd laugh, and then she'd start to belly laugh, and then I'd laugh so hard I'd have to pee, and whatever scheme we'd been working would be totally busted.

Having Kelsey here was a problem. I was annoyed at me and my big mouth for mentioning Laila at lunch. Kelsey was going to make her suspicious and mess this all up.

I gave Laila a warm smile. "Hey, Laila, how are you doing?" Then I threw Kelsey the stink eye and added, "Long time no see."

Kelsey smiled at me, looking for all the world as if she was supposed to be there. Laila came around the counter to give me a tight squeeze. "Ella Mae. It's so good to see you. Wow, it's like a convention in here, what with the reunion and now you two stopping by. Kelsey was just telling me you'd be here soon." She returned to sit behind the counter, wearing her company polo shirt, thin as ever. Her sculpted cheekbones made her face look angled and sharp with her straight brown hair cut short and parted in the middle. She looked at me, clearly curious about why we had descended into her workplace at the same time, out of the blue, in the middle of a workday.

More prepared for this than I'd have been during our high school days, I had my cover story ready. Pulling two boxes out of the paper bag I carried, I set them on the counter. "We just had lunch with the old 'ABC' gang and your name came up. Congratulations on the big promotion to assistant manager!"

Laila's hand unconsciously went up to her name tag where "Assistant Manager" appeared under her name as she bobbed her head in acknowledgement.

I continued, "I realized I hadn't seen you since I've been back in town, so I decided we should celebrate." Opening one of the boxes, I brandished the slice. "With a piece of key lime pie."

"Ooh." Laila stood up to reach for the pie and plastic fork, my gift smoothing over any lingering suspicions she might have had. In my experience, pie had that sort of effect most of the time. It definitely worked on Jonas.

Kelsey leaned over the bag and dug out a second fork. "Oh, yummy. There's a second piece too." She turned a bright, fake smile toward me as she fluttered her eyelashes in Betty Boop fashion.

I would have snatched the fork out of her hands but I didn't want to ruin my chances of learning something from Laila. As soon as I noticed a third fork lying in the bottom of the bag, I calmed, grabbed it, and poked Kelsey's fork out of the way so I could get a bite out of *my* slice.

"How have you been doing? Sounds like work's gone really well?" I asked Laila while trying to ignore Kelsey's rapid consumption of my pie.

Before Laila could respond, Kelsey jumped in, speaking with

her mouth full. "Oh, before you got here, we were just talking about—"

I elbowed her to be quiet, but she swayed her hips out of the way and continued, "—all the excitement in town with those movie producers around." She threw me one of our eyebrow signals. Many years had passed since I had seen one of those, but we had spent hours developing and practicing our very own secret code during childhood. Once learned, who could forget that?

Her message received, I stopped trying to elbow her and listened.

"Laila told me those guys are such bigshots that they reserved the big two-bedroom family suite. You know, the expensive one on the fourth floor." Kelsey smiled sweetly at Laila and then turned to me, self-satisfaction shining through her bright eyes.

All I managed in response was an impressed, "Oh." Kelsey had scoped out the whole situation before I'd even arrived on the scene.

"And they've been driving all over the place looking at sites and talking to people in the lobby about their movie," she added.

"Oh." Then, realizing I was acting suspicious by being so amazed at Kelsey's success, I fumbled for something to say to Laila. "Oh, hey, we missed you at the mixer last night. Are you going to make it to any of the events tonight or tomorrow's dance?"

"I can't make tonight. We've been so busy with the hotel completely full for the reunion that I've had to work extra shifts. But it's been okay. I've gotten to see all the alums who are staying here for the weekend."

"Oh, I'm so glad you've been able to chat with folks even though you're working. I have to introduce you to my husband Jonas. He'll be at the dance with me."

"Mmm, that sure was a great key lime pie, wasn't it?" Kelsey held up her fork in my face before licking it clean.

I looked down. That nuisance! Sure, she had been helpful in learning where the guys were staying, but it was downright ornery of her to eat all my pie. I'd only managed to get one bite.

Before I could snarl at her, Laila said, "Oh yes, that was very good. Thanks so much for bringing me a treat."

I attempted to steer the conversation back to those guys to see what else Laila knew about them, but some guests picked that moment to exit the elevator and approach the desk.

Laila gave us an apologetic smile. "I better help these folks."

"No worries. You talk to them and then we'll—Hey!" I protested as Kelsey pulled me away from the counter.

"We'll spend more time with you on Saturday night," I said. Kelsey and I scooted away from the counter and the other couple moved forward while I tried to think of the next step.

The guests pounced on Laila while I considered choking Kelsey. When Laila left the desk to get something from the back room, Kelsey pulled my arm again. "Come on!" she urged as she hurried us to the elevators.

Reluctantly, I allowed myself to get pulled away. "What are you doing here?" I hissed as the doors closed and she jabbed the button for the fourth floor.

"Shouldn't you be saying thank you?" Kelsey stuck out her tongue at me. "I found out what room they're in."

"Okay, thank you. But what good is that?" My appreciation was laced with vinegar as I crossed my arms and asked, "And why are you here?"

"Hmpf." She moved her hands to her hips. "Do you think you're Vanessa's only friend? At lunch, you were talking all about how you'd done this and you're doing that. All to help prove Vanessa's innocence. You never asked if anyone else wanted to help." Her eyes took on a mischievous glint as she narrowed them at me. "You practically exploded when Angela talked about Laila and then you ordered pie for her and you. Only two slices! What kind of friend are you?"

I squirmed as I recognized she was right about how selfish I'd been. But then I absorbed everything she'd said and realized she had cracked my plans to come here this afternoon just from my pie order. Hmm, that girl had skills. I hugged her. "You're totally right and I'm sorry. But, dang! You didn't have to eat all my pie."

"If you had bought a slice for me like you should have in the first place, you wouldn't be in this position." She nodded in self-righteous agreement and stepped out as the elevator doors opened on the fourth floor.

I had to laugh at this new, forceful side of Kelsey. Her students didn't stand a chance of outfoxing her. I followed her into the quiet hallway. "Goofball," I said softly, and then had to stop suddenly to avoid running into Kelsey as she stopped dead in her tracks.

Right in front of the sign pointing to the room numbers, she turned to me, eyes wide. "What do we do now?"

I gulped. I hadn't really expected to get anywhere with Laila beyond perhaps a brief discussion about the guys staying in her hotel and hopefully learning if some movie studio had paid for their rooms or sent them any packages. Now that we knew what room they were staying in, what were we supposed to do next?

Pushing forward and putting up a good front for as long as possible was my only thought at the moment. I threw back my shoulders and said, "Come on," before marching down the hallway to the only suite in the hotel. "Fake it till you make it," was something Mimi always used to tell me when I'd get nervous about performing in an upcoming play. I ignored the little voice in my head pointing out she'd told me this when I was in middle school and had never intended it as advice before trying to break into the hotel room of potentially dangerous criminals.

As we turned the corner to where the suite was located, I could hear Kelsey slowing down. "I . . . I don't want to get in trouble," she stammered. "That was all just fun and games, but breaking into a room—Eliza, I can't do that."

When Kelsey got stressed, she reverted to calling me by the nickname she had bestowed upon me during our English Honors class in junior year. Remembering how she'd tricked me into reading *Pride and Prejudice* just so she'd have a study partner for the test made me smile. I was just about to admit that I didn't have any idea how to break into a hotel room either when I saw the suite's door was ajar.

I stopped so abruptly that Kelsey ran into me this time. "What happened? Are we going back? What are you doing?" she asked as she disentangled from me.

"Look," I whispered, pointing at the door propped open and blocked by a maintenance cart. I snapped my fingers as an idea struck me. "Come on." I grabbed her and pulled her back around the corner.

Kelsey allowed herself to be dragged along but scrunched up her eyebrows when I stopped right by the corner and poked my ear out. "What are you—"

"Shh!" I interrupted, raising a finger to my lips as I strained to hear around the corner.

She started to speak again, but I flicked our hand signal to be quiet without looking at her. Then I heard the squeak I was waiting for. Someone had moved the maintenance cart so they could leave the suite.

"Follow my lead," I hissed, and strode confidently around the bend.

A muscular-looking young man with a shock of wiry black hair was leaving the suite. He wore a gray-blue work uniform.

When I came within a few steps, I recognized him. "Roger Newman, as I live and breathe! How are you?" Roger was the kid brother of one of our friends from school. Whenever Kelsey and I were over at her house, he always managed to hang around outside his sister's room, looking like a puppy dog with his tongue hanging out, drooling over me.

Startled, he looked up from where he was replacing his tools in the maintenance cart. As a kid, Roger had always seemed to be chomping on some bubblegum and getting bits of it stuck to his face when his bubbles popped. As he also didn't seem to shower often, the sticky remnants had attracted dirt so his face looked dirty despite his clean clothes.

I noticed Roger hadn't yet removed the wedge on the floor that kept the door to the suite from closing. Score one for my timing. But minus a million because Roger stood there chomping gum and looking sweaty and dirty. And I couldn't place it, but there was an extra smell of an overwhelming men's body spray surrounding him.

"Ella Mae?" he asked, but then he caught sight of who was with me. His whole demeanor changed as his surprised expression morphed into eagerness. "Kelsey Wheeler," he breathed.

Briefly I wondered how to bedazzle him enough to make him walk away while forgetting the wedge that held open the suite's door. Deciding the mission was worth it, I threw away my pride and thrust my chest forward and shoulders back to distract him. "What are you up to these days?"

Roger blinked as if he'd somehow forgotten I was there before glancing at me. "I work here in maintenance. Got my HVAC certificate after high school and I've been working ever since." He returned his attention to Kelsey and smiled. "Make pretty good money too," he told her proudly.

When I made an encouraging sound, the noise seemed to startle him. His brows knit together in confusion as he looked down the hallway behind us. "What are you doing here? The elevator is the other way."

I jumped to respond since I'd come up with a brilliant idea and hadn't had the chance to inform Kelsey. "We were visiting a friend who's here for the reunion." I giggled for effect. That, along with sticking out my chest, had always worked to distract guys in the past. "I guess we just got turned all upside down when we left her room and wound up here by mistake." I giggled again since I'm cute when I giggle. Jonas has confirmed this, but I already knew.

Roger only half listened to me as he stared at Kelsey. "You know, you still look just as pretty as a peach." He blushed scarlet and briefly looked away.

My mouth dropped open as the situation finally became clear. He liked Kelsey, not me. Had that always been the case and I'd missed the signs? I started to feel a pang of jealousy before shaking my head slightly. That was stupid. I had Jonas, and Roger was . . . sorta icky.

Kelsey's eyes flickered to mine before returning to Roger. "Oh, Roger, aren't you sweet."

While Roger stood there with his face flaming and mind clearly racing for something else to say, I figured out how to get inside the suite.

"Ooh, I've really gotta go." I danced, trying to look like a sudden pee emergency had just struck. "Do you mind if I go in there?" I inclined my head to the still-open door.

He hesitated. "Can't you go back to your friend's room?"

"She was jumping into the shower," I said, proud of how fast I'd come up with that one.

He started to frown. "Downstairs, there's a public—"

"Oh, please. It's urgent!" I interrupted, making a whole production out of it, as if I were seven and couldn't hold it in. My recent time spent with Olivia had sharpened these mimicry skills.

Kelsey leaned forward and touched his arm, making him jump halfway out of his skin. "You and I can stay here and catch up while she goes. You know, I've been thinking about you, Roger," she cooed, tilting her head and raising her eyebrows suggestively.

I thought Kelsey looked ridiculous. Any idiot could tell she was only putting on a show.

But Roger was a guy, so he was hooked. Swallowing audibly, he told me, "Go on then," his eyes never leaving Kelsey's face.

I was in! Kelsey was a trooper for throwing herself into the breach. I paused for a second, suddenly concerned about whether my mother was right and those guys really were part of the mob. What would happen to me if they found out I was snooping around their stuff?

Kelsey looked decidedly uncomfortable standing with her hand on Roger's arm. But the way she kept glancing down the hallway told me she was more worried about someone she knew seeing her talking to Roger. She was safe out here in the hallway with Roger for the short time I'd need to search the room. Probably.

Kelsey kept her voice syrupy as she said, "You go on, honey. I reckon ole Rog and I have plenty to catch up on." But when Kelsey swiveled her head to look at me, her eyes burned like twin lasers, sending me the clear message to get her out of here pronto.

I squeezed past them, wrinkling my nose as I got a whiff of Roger in passing. Accidentally on purpose, I kicked the doorstop out of the way so the suite door could close and Roger wouldn't notice that I didn't head into the bathroom that was right by the door.

The suite was nothing special—this was the Hampton Inn in Jenkins, Arkansas, after all. A basic lounge area with a couch, coffee table, and chair facing a large-screen TV greeted me. The lounge area was empty save for some empty beer cans toppled on the coffee table and the sports section of the *Little Rock Gazette* crumpled on the couch. A painting mounted on the wall was so wrong it made me pause. The colors didn't go with the rest of the room, the landscape wasn't from anywhere near Arkansas, and the perspective was skewed. I had drawn better pictures in middle school. No wonder hotel artwork was safe from theft.

I strode into the first bedroom, eyes scanning the room quickly. I was looking for something—anything—that might be a clue. What would movie producers have lying around their hotel room? Or mafia members, for that matter? I shivered even though the suite was empty and told myself it was just my body reacting to yet another ugly painting.

The room must have been Drosnic's. It was small and contained only an unmade bed, nightstand, and small closet. He had a few sets of boring dark clothes hanging in the closet and a small suitcase on the stand. Not wanting to rummage through a strange man's underwear, I merely held the zippered part open and looked in the suitcase. No gun, but I assumed Drosnic carried it with him, if he had one. Otherwise, what would be the point of being a body-guard?

Worrying about how much time I had, I trotted to the next bedroom, which had to be Giuseppe's, unsure what to expect. Wouldn't a movie producer's suite have headshots and movie scripts scattered around? Or perhaps the remains of room service champagne and chocolate-covered strawberries? Maybe that was just my silly preconception from some movie or another. In fact, did the Jenkins Hampton Inn even serve champagne, let alone chocolate-covered strawberries?

But then what would a mobster's room look like? I envisioned a scene out of *The Sopranos,* but years had passed since I'd watched, so all I could bring up was a noir scene of some dimly lit backroom in an Italian restaurant with cards and poker chips scattered around a dead body slumped over a table.

Neither scenario greeted me. Aside from the ugly geometric painting hanging on the wall that didn't even match the others in the suite, Giuseppe's room was neat, but much larger, with a built-in bathroom, king-size bed, and his very own TV resting on a dresser. There were no poker chips, and the large window letting in the afternoon sunshine made it obvious at a glance that there was no dead body.

I scanned the room again and noticed a thick folder peeking

out from behind the TV. Quickly crossing the room, I flipped open the folder, half-expecting headshots of models and actors. But instead I found photos of empty land, derelict buildings, and the fairgrounds, along with a county map. Unfolding the map, I saw a large red circle around the fairgrounds and the neighboring Clearwater Cove, and another circle around a lakefront ranch on the southern part of Lake Capitola, almost as far south from Jenkins as the fairgrounds lay to the north.

Kelsey's laugh rang out through the suite door, sounding somewhat desperate. My time here had to end soon. Whipping out my phone, I snapped a picture of the map and another of the photos of the fairgrounds. What this all meant was beyond me, but maybe the men were telling the truth about scouting locations. The only question was—for what?

I scurried back to the suite door and took a breath to compose myself before opening it. "Whew, much better," I said, and then strolled back into the hallway, remembering at the last second to hold my breath as I passed Roger.

"Eliza!" Kelsey latched onto my arm and practically yanked me in between her and Roger. "Remember that thing? We've got to hurry if we're going to make it on time." She turned to leave, pulled me again, and, over her shoulder, said, "Nice talking to you, Roger."

"Maybe . . . do you think we could . . ." Roger sputtered.

Kelsey didn't slow down as she answered, "We'll see. Bye."

She had us up to a trot by the time we turned the corner. Kelsey jabbed at the elevator button half a dozen times until it finally dinged and opened on our floor. As the elevator doors closed with just the two of us inside, Kelsey took a big gasp of air. "Geez, you sure took long enough. I thought I was gonna puke. He must swim in that body spray."

I snorted. "Same brand from forever ago?"

"Possibly." Kelsey laughed. "Think his mother still buys it for him?"

Kelsey always could make me laugh. By the time we reached the ground floor, we were both laughing so hard we were gasping for air. As we stumbled back into the lobby, I hollered at Laila, "See you on Saturday!" She looked plenty busy handling a customer having a meltdown while several more grumpy-looking guests waited in line.

Outside the hotel, Kelsey asked, "Did you find anything?"

I bit my lip and shook my head. "Nothing definitive. They could be movie producers or part of the mafia." I shrugged. "Or real estate developers or just about anything." I explained what little I'd found in their suite.

"Well, that's a disappointing denouement to our little spying expedition." Kelsey couldn't hide her chosen path as an English teacher any more than I could stop noticing art.

Suddenly I felt tired as the adrenalin rush wore off. I'd dared to break the law, risked death by a mob hitman, thrown my best friend out as a sacrifice to a horny, icky maintenance man, not to mention gave up a slice of key lime pie, and all for nothing. I had no more proof about what Giuseppe and Drosnic were doing in Jenkins than I'd had this morning. Nothing to report to Trent so he'd arrest them and release Vanessa. Annoying as it was to admit, my mother might still be right about them. And worst of all, none of it helped Vanessa.

"Are you heading home now?" asked Kelsey, noticing my slump.

"Yes." I hugged her goodbye. She'd turned out to be helpful after all despite showing up unexpectedly and eating my pie. "But first, I think I'll swing by the restaurant. I need my very own slice of key lime pie and then a nap."

17

Friday Late Afternoon

Jonas

Entering the house, I paused to pet Daisy as she met me with her usual exuberance at the front door. Then I walked toward the voices in the dining room. "Hi," I greeted Elizabeth and Mary. I was surprised by the unusual sight of them playing cards at the table. Mary was usually too tired to play cards during the week.

"Hi! Were you out at the fairgrounds this whole time? What did you do—buy the place?" Elizabeth teased.

Mary glanced up from her cards with a concerned look laced with reprimand. "You bought the fairgrounds?"

"No." I laughed. "That would not have been a wise decision."

Elizabeth chuckled. "Come on, Mother. You've been living with Jonas for several months now. Have you ever known him to be impulsive like that?"

Next to Mary rested the remains of a slice of pie—key lime by the color staining the plate. "That was nice of you to bring a slice of pie home for your mother," I said to Elizabeth.

Elizabeth threw an annoyed look at her mother, who didn't notice. "Sure. Let's go with that." She tilted her head quizzically. "Seriously, where were you for all this time?"

"I . . ." My neck started feeling warm. It seemed silly, but then again, I was officially on vacation today so I was entitled to a little silly. "That pie you had earlier looked so good, I decided I wanted some for myself. I went to get some." Before she could tease me further, I asked, "Did you learn anything from your friend?"

"What friend?" Mary glanced between us as she tried to catch up.

"Laila. She just got promoted to assistant manager at the Hampton Inn." Elizabeth put on the angelic smile that was her clear tell that she was holding something back.

Mary was an old hand at reading Elizabeth. Her face narrowed with suspicion. "What were you doing there? Trying to learn what?" She watched Elizabeth for a moment before placing a card onto the table.

"Congratulating Laila, of course." Elizabeth's smile didn't quaver, but she quickly turned her attention to me before Mary could dig further. "What kind of pie did you get?"

Offering her a smile of my own, I bailed out Elizabeth from her mother's inquisition. "Strawberry rhubarb. The chef said those fruits are in season now and it was her best vegan pie available. I don't know about her others, but this was just about worth the trip." I shook my head—a two-hour roundtrip for a piece of pie sounded ridiculous in hindsight, but I'd really had, in a term I'd learned from Mary, a hankering for pie.

"Where did you go?" asked Mary as she picked up a card that Elizabeth had discarded.

Sheepishly, I looked down as I mumbled, "Conway."

"Conway! Do you have your head full of stump water? What in tarnation could have possessed you to drive all the way over to Conway for a slice of pie?" She stared at me as if I'd suddenly grown an extra head.

Elizabeth's eyes twinkled and I could tell this wouldn't be the last I heard of it, but she returned my favor of trying to divert Mary's attention and mercifully changed the subject. "What did you learn at the fairgrounds?" She drew a card.

I smiled. We did make quite the team. "I overhead father and son arguing about money."

"What kind of arguing?" Elizabeth discarded another card.

"They were yelling at each other from inside an office when I walked into the reception area," I explained as I sat down at the table.

Elizabeth looked intrigued. "Anything specific?"

"Something about a woman and money." I paused, remembering the shouting. "Does Andrew have a sister or brother?"

Elizabeth thought for a moment and then shook her head. "No, it's just been him and his dad for as long as I've known him."

From the other side of the table, Mary mumbled to herself before slapping a card onto the table.

I shrugged. "Well, it definitely sounded like Andrew was gambling at some woman's poker table and lost money."

"Really?" Elizabeth raised an eyebrow.

"They both seemed to know who she was but they didn't mention a name."

"You think it was Courtney?" asked Elizabeth as she read my face.

"Yes. Well, probably." I shrugged again. I hadn't thought of a way to confirm my suspicions during my tour. I couldn't very well ask Mr. Grady, "Oh, this is a nice place, but could you please tell me the name of the woman I overheard you yelling about through the closed door in a private meeting when I walked in unannounced?"

Elizabeth put her cards face down on the table. "Wait. So you think Grody killed her?"

"Who's Grody?" interjected Mary, and then tapped the table a few times to indicate Elizabeth should pick up her cards.

"Andrew Grady," answered Elizabeth.

"And you call him Grody? What are you, twelve?" Mary rarely pulled her punches.

"We were fifteen when we started calling him that."

"Oh. That pleases me to know how much more mature you were by then." Mary shook her head and shifted a card into a different spot in her hand.

Elizabeth's face showed her struggle to keep her temper from flaring. "Mother," she said, teeth clenched, "have you ever heard anything like this about Andrew?"

"Well, no one ever calls him Grody that I've heard," said Mary without looking up from scrutinizing her cards. Then, finished making biting remarks for at least the moment, she added, "You know there's always some talk. I never pay it no mind. Are you conceding?"

Elizabeth's whole face screwed up into a glare, but she made a visible effort to calm herself as she picked up her cards and placed one down. "Do you remember hearing anything about gambling?"

Mary interjected, "Ha!" She grabbed the discarded card and said, "People are always yapping their trap about something. You know I don't go for that sort of thing."

Elizabeth snorted but didn't meet her mother's eyes when Mary glanced sharply at her.

"What did you learn?" I asked Elizabeth before another argument could break out.

"Just about Laila and her promotion," she said, her expression turning angelic again.

I threw her a puzzled look, wondering why she was holding back. She acknowledged me with a flick of her head toward her mother and replied, "I told Mom she got a promotion so I went to congratulate her."

Mary set her cards down. "I'll be right back and I'm not conceding. Jonas, please watch my cards. I've got a winning hand here."

I nodded and jutted my chin out, staring at Elizabeth to emphasize I'd accepted my responsibilities as Mary's watchdog and intended to honor them. Mary gave me a suspicious but approving "Harrumph" and went to the restroom.

As soon as she was gone, Elizabeth sighed. "How much longer before we can move into our house?"

"The contractor said only a few months more. We could be in by early July if everything goes well. The bonus we offered helps." I paused. "Why the hotel? Do you want to move there?"

"No, I wanted to check out those guys who are claiming to be movie producers."

"What did you do?" I asked, curious to hear now that she'd obviously survived this poor decision without injury or arrest. I never liked to criticize decisions when it was too late to make a difference.

Blithely, she didn't answer my question. "I don't believe they're movie producers."

"How do you know?"

"I searched their room."

"You what?" Despite myself, I half-stood from the chair before sinking back down. Her deed was already done, nothing to worry about now.

"Oh, don't worry. I knew they were out for the afternoon. I ran into them snooping around Vanessa's accounting office before lunch. Good ole Dale had latched onto them like white on rice. They were off for a whole afternoon tour of the Jenkins area."

I paused, thinking of how crazy Dale could drive someone when he switched into his huckster pitch as the leading Jenkins city promoter. Fortunately he had stopped using his used-car sales persona around me and I'd gotten to know him as a decent man behind all his boosterism. Those two men were in for a ride. If they were trying to pull something over on Dale, they'd have to put up with his full Jenkins dog and pony show first. It only seemed fair.

Focusing back on the issue at hand, I asked Elizabeth, "If they're not movie producers, then what are they?"

"I'm . . . I'm not sure." Elizabeth paused. "They might be mafia looking for their next casino. Or even real estate developers."

"So you think your mother might be right?"

"Of course her mother is right," answered Mary as she returned at precisely the opportune moment.

I wondered if she had paused just outside the room, listening to us. But that would be unlike her. She tended to blaze ahead, making her own path and expecting others to react to her, not the other way around.

She sat down. "Anything specific I'm right about this time?"

"Life. Life in general, Mom," said Elizabeth, her voice full of sarcasm.

Mary harrumphed again but didn't complain about the backhanded compliment. She scrutinized her cards. "I'm just gonna romance this card," she said as she picked up an eight of clubs from a pile in front of her, put it in her hand, and studied her cards for a bit. Removing a card from her hand, she then returned the same eight of clubs to the table and drew a face-down card from the stack for her actual move.

Elizabeth squinted at her mother. "So you were just test-taking that card?"

"Yes," answered Mary curtly as she swapped around a few cards in her hand.

I still hadn't fully grasped all the rules for card games with Mary. There were your normal rules of gin rummy, which I'd already known from years of playing cards with my own family. Then there were all the extra Mimi-inspired rules from Elizabeth's grandmother, most of which felt like some form of near-cheating. "Testtaking" was only one of the odd Banks family card rules. There was this whole "May I?" set of rules surrounding what happened with the discarded cards. As often as Mary and Elizabeth explained them to me, it still felt like they made new ones up every time we played.

Elizabeth quirked her lips. "You know you've got a funny concept of romance. Maybe that's why you've been single for so long."

She clearly was feeling braver than me. I leaned away from the table.

Mary snapped, "Don't be rude, missy."

Elizabeth's phone rang. When she looked at the screen, she snatched it up. "Hello!" she said quickly, and then paused to listen. "You're kidding!" She leapt to her feet, nearly knocking over her chair. "I'll be right over."

Elizabeth threw her cards onto the table. Daisy jumped to her feet and started barking. None of us knew what was happening, but Daisy understand it was clearly time to act excited. "That was Vanessa. She's home!" Elizabeth was so excited she was jiggling.

"They already found the killer?" Mary sounded skeptical.

Elizabeth lost some of the bounce in her step. "No, Mother. She said she's still under investigation." Regaining some of her previous enthusiasm, she added, "But she gets to go home to Olivia! This must mean the sheriffs are looking seriously at some other suspects. I'll bet my tip to Trent about Adam Martini paid off."

"What tip?" asked Mary with an edge to her voice.

"I'll have to tell you more about it later. I'm going to Vanessa's place to see her now." Elizabeth rushed over to me and hugged me. Not to be left out, Daisy bounded into me and knocked us both sideways. As we laughed, I recovered my balance and used the momentum to dip Elizabeth into one of those movie dance swoons before pulling her up and kissing her goodbye.

"Mr. Romantic," grumbled Mary, but she had a smile tugging at her lips.

Elizabeth caught her breath and then said, "Have fun at your campout. Try to get some sleep so we can have fun at the dance tomorrow. Oh!" She clapped her hands together. "Maybe you'll come meet her this weekend."

Daisy took her clap as an invitation to keep playing and jumped up on Elizabeth's side. "Okay, okay," laughed Elizabeth. "Come on, girl, you can come say hi to Vanessa and Olivia too."

While I resolved to look into dog trainers in the area, Daisy didn't need a second invitation. She dropped to her paws and raced over to the front door. She stood there impatiently, whining and waiting for her slower human to follow her and open the door.

In the sudden quiet after Elizabeth left, Mary looked at me, then nodded to the cards on the table. "You want to take over Ella Mae's hand?"

I smiled politely but shook my head. "I better get going for the campout."

Mary reached over, picked up Elizabeth's cards, and scrutinized them. As I left the dining room to get my camping gear, she concluded, "Yup, I would have won."

18

Friday Evening

Jonas

I knelt in the forest behind the rock and called, "ah-oo-gah" as instructed while I held the top of the thick canvas sack open just in case anyone was close enough to watch me. In the distance, I heard others echoing the call. With the sun down and the land around me dark, I couldn't see anyone, so it was unlikely I was being observed. The calls from the others seemed to be getting further away rather than closer, as one might assume if they were truly coming toward me as planned. However, the situation had played out pretty much as I'd expected, so I dropped the sack to the ground. Pulling my knapsack off my shoulder, I flipped on my flashlight and dug inside my pack.

After a brief caravan to the nearby state park, our group had set up camp in the late afternoon. I liked these Outdoor Club kids and was glad I had agreed to act as their teacher-sponsor for the rest of this semester. We'd gone on several hikes around the area over the last two months, but hadn't had a chance for any overnight events. Their scheduled camping trip back during spring break was cancelled when their former teacher, Duncan Fowler, was murdered. In the aftermath of the murder and finding the killer, Lester hired me as a substitute for Duncan's biology classes, and Elizabeth and I had decided to turn our short visit into a long-term relocation.

The kids were shocked by his death, but kids were resilient. They seemed to have recovered pretty well, handling the transition to me as their new sponsor without issue. The excitement of planning this camping trip felt like the perfect capstone to the year.

Finished with my preparations out in the forest on my own, I put everything back in my pack, pulled on my windbreaker, and carefully picked up the canvas sack the kids had given me. Swinging my knapsack over my shoulder, I stood and listened. All I heard was the normal nature sounds of the forest at night. I took a deep breath and yelled, "ah-oo-gah" one last time as loud as I could for effect before setting off for camp.

The kids' laughter and yelling echoed into the forest long before I saw the campfire. When I reached the edge of the clearing, I paused to compose myself. With the night getting cool, putting a hand inside my windbreaker seemed natural. Then, holding the canvas sack out in front of me with the other hand, I stepped out of the woods.

"Hey!" I called, not even needing to fake excitement as showtime began.

"Shh! Shh! He's back. It's him," came the kids' voices. Many seemed surprised to see me. Perhaps I should have waited longer or made a lot of noise traipsing around lost in the forest before returning.

Holding the canvas sack in front of me, I marched into the firelight and set it down. "I think I got one," I said excitedly, making sure to take several steps back and show trepidation on my face.

Kim, one of the club leaders and a student in my biology class, looked at the full sack before grinning. "What did you catch?"

I maintained my expression of concern. "I couldn't see things clearly in the dark. Didn't you say snipes were black, furry, and look like a cross between a jackrabbit and a squirrel?" I shivered, keeping my nonverbals somewhere between creeped out and excited. "It was so dark and scary on my own, I didn't want to look until I got back."

As Kim strode toward the fire, Dale Cooper's son, Tyler, looked back and forth between me and the canvas sack containing an obvious lump. "Come on!" His voice sounded doubtful, but he too stepped toward the sack to check it out.

They were two steps away when the sack jumped a few inches into the air.

Kim screamed. Tyler screamed louder and leapt backward, falling on his rear.

Then the sack moved again, causing the drawstring to loosen.

The other kids scrambled back. To Tyler's credit, he grabbed a shovel near the fire and raised it as he stood up. He didn't approach the sack but stood ready to confront whatever came out.

The sack moved again in a new direction.

The group screamed.

The top came undone and something black and furry became visible.

Tyler let loose with a roar and started moving forward.

"Wait! Wait!" I yelled, and leapt forward. I grabbed his arm, stopping him just before he could swing the shovel.

Holding Tyler off, I leaned over the sack.

"Mr. Tyler!" cried one of the other girls in alarm from a safe distance.

Ignoring her, I pulled the bag completely open, revealing the battery-operated, robotic black cat inside. From my jacket, I pulled out and showed everyone the remote control. I grinned while Tyler caught his breath.

Trent Walker started howling with laughter. After a moment, the others joined in.

Tyler blushed, but eased off his attack stance and dropped the shovel before starting to laugh also.

"OMG, you got us so hard," screamed Kim before taking the cat from me. "Look at the cute little fake kitten that Tyler almost killed." She held it up so everyone could see it more clearly.

"How did you guess?" asked one of the kids.

"Guys, this isn't my first campout," I answered.

"But Mr. Trout, Tyler said you told his dad you hadn't been camping. That's how the idea started," said Kim.

"It's not that I've never been camping. He was asking me if I've gone camping here in Arkansas. If I recall correctly, Tyler walked in after his question so he only heard me tell him, 'No, no camping.' Not here in Arkansas at least." I winked at Tyler. "Besides, you know there's this thing called the internet. Don't you think I would have looked it up when you told me we would go on a snipe hunt tonight because it was a full moon?"

Trent clapped me on the shoulder. "That was great. I figured you had something up your sleeve when you agreed to their ridiculous plan so easily."

"Were you messing with us when you kept asking for help and screwing up the tent when we were setting up camp?" asked one of the students.

I grinned again. "I was playing it up to see what you'd try to get me to do." Putting the remote control away, I waved my backpack at them. "I was never a Boy Scout, but I did come prepared."

Trent pointed at the backpack. "What all's in that backpack of yours?"

"Let's just say I'm prepared for a number of other contingencies." I watched as a couple of students exchanged guilty looks. "Just in case."

Trent grinned and then waved his arm at the students. "I mean, come on. Telling him you have to wait until it's dark but you're going to drive snipes toward him and he'll somehow see them coming and catch one in a canvas sack?" He shook his head in disbelief. "Me and my buddies were far more realistic and creative with our pranks when we were your age. Next time loop me in ahead of time."

That roused a chorus of comments and arguments, and the gathering broke down into smaller discussions. Trent and I sat back, enjoying the shared ambiance of the firelight and teenage enthusiasm. After some time, we slipped into a natural conversation about our respective experiences of camping and the outdoors.

It made sense that Trent had spent a lot of time in the woods while growing up in Jenkins. He liked hunting and was skilled at tracking. Over s'mores we discovered a mutual love of hiking and kayaking. Trent even owned his own kayak, which was on my wish list once we had a place to store one.

"Hey, Sniper, pass me the marshmallows," one of the boys said to me.

"Sniper?" I asked.

"Yeah. I think that should be your new Outdoor Club nickname. Sniper, as in one who catches snipes. You know, like smoker is someone who smokes; driver is someone who drives."

Some of the other boys laughed and echoed my new nickname. Apparently, that made it official.

The boy took out a handful of marshmallows and continued, "Mr. Cooper gave us wildlife nicknames when we went camping way back in Cub Scouts. Mine is Tick, because I got a bunch of ticks one year. My mom had to pull them all out one by one. It was so gross." As a chorus of girls cried, "Eww," he pulled his baseball cap off his head. "Wear this every time I go into the woods since then."

From his other side, Kim shyly asked Tyler, "What's your nickname?"

When Tyler didn't answer, Tick yelled out, "Ladybug." Everyone laughed again, although I smiled as I noticed Kim didn't. Their relationship had been slowly building—perhaps so slowly that Tyler hadn't realized it yet.

Tick explained, "He got that name because he used to collect ladybugs when we were supposed to bring back wood for the fire."

Before they started ribbing Tyler too much, I said, "You know there's a famous quote in biology about animals. 'Eyes in the front, animals hunt. Eyes in the side, animals hide.' Next time you try to trick someone about snipes, get your stories straight about whether they are hunters or prey and put their eyes in the right place."

A few grumbles greeted my lesson as I realized they were on summer break and not interested in hearing a teacher's lecture.

Trent leaned over. "Don't worry about the grumbling. Everyone nowadays views me only as a deputy, so they think everything I say is some official sheriff's policy statement or legal announcement. We've got to teach these kids up right. Else, how'll they ever pull off a successful snipe hunt stunt on the next guy?"

Trent and I sat on rocks off to the side of the fire—close enough for some light but far enough away so the kids could forget we were there and enjoy themselves. While the students gorged themselves on chocolate and s'mores, he and I chatted. We both avoided any mention of Elizabeth, but that didn't seem to stall our conversation at all.

One of the boys spoke a little louder than the others, catching my attention. "You know this forest is much spookier at night than during the day. Did anyone else hear odd noises when we were out there?"

Kim narrowed her eyes at him. "Are you trying to trick us with a ghost story?"

"Yeah, who wants to tell ghost stories?" asked Tick eagerly.

The first boy said, "No, seriously, it sounded like something large. Are there any bears around here?"

A few of the kids started looking scared. One girl grabbed her jacket and shifted seats closer to the fire, clearly deciding she was willing to sacrifice one of her friends on the outer ring in the interests of safety.

Trent stood up and stretched before moving a bit closer to comfort them. "Nah, come on, don't worry, y'all. There might be a few black bears way up in the Ouachita Forest, but none down here close to all the crowds and people in Jenkins."

I almost laughed until I realized he wasn't kidding; he actually considered Jenkins crowded.

The noise level rose around the campfire again as the kids started to joke and tease each other about being scared of rogue bears and refocused on their desserts. Trent moved to toast another marshmallow.

Out of nowhere, a gunshot rang out.

Trent dropped to the ground and yelled, "Down! Down! Everybody down!"

Kids screamed and moved in every direction.

Another shot cracked out as something whizzed past me.

A thwack smacked into the tree beside me and something struck my forehead nearly simultaneously.

Half-toppling, half-diving, I fell to the ground.

"Stay down!" yelled Trent. Somehow, he had produced a previously-unseen pistol. Hiding behind a fallen log, he aimed it in the direction of the shot and yelled, "Police! Put down your weapon and come out with your hands up."

Still lying on the ground, I touched my forehead gingerly.

My fingers came away sticky with blood, but not covered with it. And most importantly, my fingers encountered no hole in my forehead.

"Jonas?" called Trent.

I must have been hit by something else. I wouldn't be alive if a bullet had hit me there. Turning my head to the other side hurt a little, but I could see the kids lying on the ground in the dirt and leaves.

Before I could answer, Trent's voice turned strident as he yelled again, "Jonas! You okay?"

"Yes! Just a scratch," I answered.

"Everyone else okay?" asked Trent.

Some conversation broke out, but Trent interrupted. "Check your neighbor and call out if anyone is hurt. Otherwise, be quiet."

The kids quieted down. Fortunately no one else appeared to have gotten hurt.

After a few moments and no further shots, Trent crawled over to his pack and pulled out a police radio. He called in the emergency.

Less than twenty minutes later, we were no longer alone in the wilderness. At least five or six deputies roamed around with flashlights illuminating the surrounding trees and radios squawking non-stop. An ambulance had responded as well, with the paramedics fussing over the minor cut on my forehead.

By this point, the kids were allowed up from their prone positions. They all sat huddled together. No one felt up to standing or even raising themselves up to sit on the logs again. Without tending, even the campfire had died down.

Trent came over to my side. After he looked at my forehead briefly, I followed him as he knelt to study the tree behind me. "Look at this," he said, pointing at a sheared-off part of the bark. "I think this is where a bullet struck. Probably made the bark ricochet into your head."

I raised a hand to touch the bandage on my head.

He looked back at me, but one of the deputies radioed him before Trent could speak. One by one, the deputies reported that they had found no signs of the shooter. I felt relieved that no one was hurt—even my own injury had dropped to just a minor annoyance. I was especially pleased that Lester had not been here tonight and that Trent had stepped in as the substitute.

From the beginning, the kids had seemed happy to swap their principal for a younger man. Any remaining reservations about having a law enforcement officer as their chaperone had completely disappeared. Who would have expected we'd need a gun and police radio for a one-night campout in a nearby state park?

Trent organized the other deputies into teams to escort the kids in groups back to the cars. Everyone was going home to sleep tonight and would come back in the daylight to collect their camping supplies. Before they left, Tyler remembered the fire, and shoveled dirt on it to prevent it from spreading accidentally while we were gone. A forest fire breaking out near Jenkins on the same night that someone had shot at us would have been too much.

As the others were led away, Trent came over to the rock I was sitting on. I hadn't done much since the shot rang out besides help keep the kids calm. Once my role as chaperone was discharged, the reality of tonight's shooting had started to sink in. I was feeling jittery and was fine just watching the deputies secure the area and help the kids.

Trent crouched near me, looking toward the forest. Then he stood and swiveled, looking around the campsite through a professional's eyes.

I watched attentively but saw only the fire, the tents on the other side of the fire, and the logs and rocks off to our left where the kids had been sitting. Trent and I had been by ourselves before he had left to make himself another s'more.

After a few moments scanning the layout, Trent turned back and met my eyes. "Why do you think someone was shooting at you?"

19

Saturday Morning

Jonas

"At you', he said." Elizabeth repeated it more quietly as she stepped through the open frame of our half-built house on the land she had inherited from her grandparents. This morning, we'd felt antsy trapped inside Mary's small house and decided to escape here, figuring this place was as safe as anything. No one knew we were hiding out here, and we'd hear anyone approaching along the dirt road that served as our extended driveway.

"Yes. Trent believes someone was shooting at me." I was almost too tired to engage in conversation. As if she was caught in a post-traumatic loop, Elizabeth had been repeating this phrase ever since I got home last night. I hadn't returned until very late, after making sure that all the kids had reached their homes safely.

Despite the late hour, I had still been pretty amped up when I got back. No one had ever shot at me before, if that was truly what had happened. I'd never given anyone cause to wish me lethal harm and I could not fathom what I might have done now. Elizabeth adding her own energy to the mix when she'd heard what happened hadn't done anything to help me make sense of the situation.

She had many wonderful qualities, but reacting in a calm and reassuring fashion when her newlywed husband was used for target practice was not one of them. Neither of us got much real sleep last night, although we did get into bed eventually. When she did drift off, Elizabeth kept a tight hold of me as I stared up at the ceiling.

Elizabeth was an amazing partner for me—the yin to my yang, or perhaps it was the other way around. It had been a long time since my one college philosophy class, and all I remembered was the two forces were complementary and interacted to form a dynamic system in which the whole is greater than the assembled parts. That characterized us as a couple nicely. Admittedly, Elizabeth would never be confused as the calm one in our relationship.

"One question. Okay, never mind, I never just have one question." Elizabeth shook away any self-imposed limits.

Despite the knot in my stomach, I quirked a lip and flicked a glance at her, but she didn't feel any comic relief from her own inadvertent honesty. She stood staring out the rectangular hole in the front of the house where a window in the home office was scheduled to be installed next week. The construction was moving quickly.

Turning to me, she asked, "Why?"

And there it was. The million-dollar question. I couldn't answer it last night and still had no idea. While Elizabeth had been doing her own reenactment of a stuck record player, repeating the same line over and over again, I had been sorting through all my memories from living in Jenkins, wondering if a killer lurked somewhere in there.

When I didn't respond, she said, "I bet it has something to do with Courtney's murder. It's too much of a coincidence not to be." She tsked. "I mean it's not like some student is going to shoot you. Grades haven't even come out yet."

Although a poor attempt at humor, it was a good sign that she was feeling safer out here. Humor was how Elizabeth dealt with most situations. I ignored her jibe about my students and responded to her first comment. "So who?" Still feeling some residual nervous energy, I walked around the ladder that the construction workers used to climb to the second floor.

Elizabeth wanted a curved staircase for the house. It would be a beautiful focal point, but the subcontractor had run into some problems and the delay meant our main contractor had to build out the second floor without a staircase. With the workers climbing up and down a ladder all day, Elizabeth had convinced the contractor to install a fireman's pole to provide a more fun option for descending. She and I had enjoyed goofing around with it, but since it hadn't been part of the plans filed with the county, it had to be taken out after the last inspection.

"Well . . ." Elizabeth stepped into the bedroom behind the future staircase that we'd planned as a guest room. "Beverly's still a suspect. Or that tough-looking guy. Or the Gradys."

"Didn't your friend say their security camera showed the Gradys had been at home until after Courtney's boat exploded?"

"Maybe there's a secret exit out of their house?"

When I scoffed, she added, "Well, you met with them earlier yesterday and then this happened at night."

"It will be difficult for them to attract an investor if they shoot anyone who expresses interest," I said dryly.

Her laugh made me smile and relax a little. "I didn't say anything unusual—at least I don't think so."

"You didn't have to lie, did you?" she asked, suddenly concerned that I had broken my pledge.

"No. I told him I wanted to understand the numbers before I would make any final decisions about investing. That part's true, even though it seems to make no sense to sink money into a business that barely earns enough to keep up that old, nearly empty property at the end of that road. Sure, it's on the lake, but can you get any further away from Jenkins? Is it even in the same county?" I caught my breath. All this blabbering was a clear sign of my lack of sleep.

"It's just this side of the county line," she explained. "Those dunes just beyond it are across the line."

Trying to picture what she meant, I asked, "The dunes by that little bay?"

"Yeah." She stared at the framing, lost in thought. "Are you sure you didn't ask any questions or say anything that would alert them?"

"No. I didn't have to, since I overheard them yelling at each other when I arrived."

With a hand to her chin, Elizabeth asked, "Do you like the closet here?"

Blinking to keep up with her shift in topics, I moved closer to take another look at the fully-framed closet space. "Yes. It fits nicely, plus there will be a nice big area in the back, going under the stairs, where we can stash things." I held back on mentioning that having the carpenter re-frame the closet would add a delay right as we were pushing to get the house finished faster.

"What things?" she asked, chewing on her lip.

"Well, I'm hoping everything we own won't always fit into your old bedroom plus a few boxes in your mother's garage," I replied, wrapping my arms around her from behind. We'd sold or given away most of our furniture when we flew back to Portland to make the move to Jenkins. Most of that stuff had been from our student days anyway, so it wasn't hard to agree it was time to upgrade.

"Okay, we'll leave the closet here," she said, smiling as she leaned her head back to kiss me. "But I want to move the light switch."

"Deal," I said, noting that the electrician hadn't yet wired this part of the downstairs. Normally I would have been into checking on all these details too, but exhaustion and leftover stress had worn me out.

Elizabeth roamed into the open area that would form a great room combining the kitchen, dining area, and downstairs living space. For our new house, we would take advantage of the same great views, but without the original old-fashioned small rooms and narrow hallways of her grandparents' home. We had agreed to have an unfinished attic like the one she'd loved as a child, but with a more convenient entrance and lights installed rather than a bare bulb dangling from a wire and creating a fire hazard.

"Could Beverly have . . ." Her voice trailed off.

"Do you think she's capable?" I responded. "Does she even own a gun?" Then I yawned. Someone who raced out of a critical PTA meeting because her daughter had been injured at school didn't strike me as a killer who would stalk me at night through a forest and fire two shots at me and a bunch of high schoolers.

Elizabeth held her arms out wide. "Maybe? I don't know. I hadn't seen her in ten years until the other night." She stared at a wall, probably envisioning what art she'd want to hang there while she considered the suspects.

Then she pivoted on her toes. "It could be those mafia guys."

"So you do believe your mother's silliness?"

She waved that off. "I'm serious, Jonas. That enforcer guy could be a sniper."

"Or just a wealthy developer's bodyguard. Why would they want to kill me?" I raised a mocking eyebrow. "I didn't go snooping around in their hotel room."

"No one saw me in there," she retorted, and then stroked her cheek. "Didn't you tell me you had run into them taking pictures and blocking the road?"

"Yes, out along Front Street. The fancy-looking guy was taking pictures of the fairgrounds, or the dunes, or just the water. But so what? Why would they want to kill me for seeing them take some pictures? Plenty of people were driving by."

"Trent told me he was checking into them. We'll just have to trust Deputy Dawg," she said.

"Okay. I'm sure Trent'll do it, then," I said.

She turned a brief, puzzled expression toward me before moving toward the back door. Standing there, she poked around the piles of junk on the floor with her shoe. "Maybe the shot wasn't meant for you at all. Could it have been a hunter?"

I yawned again and shook my head. "Trent didn't think so. It was completely dark, except for our fire—too dark for hunting. And whoever did it didn't answer when we were all yelling. Trent and the other deputies went looking but didn't find any trace of the shooter in the woods. He said a hunter would have rushed out to make sure no one was hurt. And definitely not shot a second time."

"Hmm." She studied me again before turning to look out the large openings for windows that would face our backyard. "I guess it's not even hunting season now anyway."

I nodded, pretending it was normal that I would know the schedule for hunting season. "Trent was going to have some of the deputies help him search for bullet casings this morning, but he thought the shots were taken from a direction that meant they weren't aimed at him or the kids. It might have been an accident, but the gun was aimed in my direction and fired twice. Trent was pretty confident of that."

Out of the blue, Elizabeth commented, "And now you're calling him Trent?" The sarcasm practically dripped from her voice. "What happened to Deputy Walker?" She stared at me and then jerked back in alarm. "Oh, no. You did not go and become friends with Trent Walker, did you?" She smacked my arm, but it was gentle as she was still upset by the shooting.

I was too.

"I told you I didn't want you becoming friends with him." She stepped away and then turned back, eyes narrowing. "What did y'all talk about?"

I gave a noncommittal shrug, knowing there would be no good answer. We passed through the great room and out to where sliding doors would one day connect the living room to the back deck. For now, we had to climb down a short ladder to the ground.

We'd left Daisy safely tethered in the backyard, away from the construction debris, and she'd settled down to gnaw on the bone we'd brought for her. She looked pretty relaxed out there.

Coming up here had been a good idea. I was feeling better, and clearly Elizabeth was as well since she'd started teasing me again. I held her hand as she came down the last two steps and managed to stumble into a hug again.

She wasn't typically clumsy, but the shooting had freaked us out so we both used the excuse to hold each other tight.

I stood facing the house, looking through the spaces where the basement windows would go. The basement would sit only partly underground, so we'd get some nice natural light through those windows. That also made the first floor a bit higher, which only improved our view of the lake and distant hills. Although the basement, like the rest of the house, was still unfinished, I could envision the entertainment area and pool table—or ping pong table, depending on whether Elizabeth or I got our way—that we hoped to furnish it with.

"It's really pretty here, isn't it?" asked Elizabeth, relenting on the questioning and finally relaxing in the peaceful sunshine with nothing but birds and rustling leaves around us.

I released her and turned to face the same direction. It was hard to decide which direction I liked best—the river winding down from the ridge to my right or the lake where the river ended to my left. I checked out both and then turned even further to the left to smile at Elizabeth. No question, this was my favorite direction of all.

I kissed her and then noticed the camping chairs that sat on the dirt near Daisy, in the middle of what would one day be a nice yard. It wasn't quite the cozy two-person swing that Elizabeth wanted built on our porch, but it would do for now.

Gratefully, I sank into one of the folding outdoor chairs, stuck my feet on the footrest, and closed my eyes.

"What are you doing? What if whoever's trying to kill you tries again? You can't sit outside here in the open."

"We'll be fine," I said as my body craved the rest it had been denied last night. "No one knows we're here."

"What if someone comes nosing around? If we're sleeping, we won't hear them coming." Elizabeth perched on the edge of the other chair but didn't lean back.

"Daisy will warn us," I said through a yawn, reaching out my hand to pet her.

Sensing she needed to demonstrate her trustworthiness, Daisy barked.

"Good girl. That's the idea. Now tell us if someone tries to sneak up on us while we nap." I closed my eyes again and rested my hand on Daisy's head.

Through closed eyes, I was aware of Elizabeth getting to her feet. "I've got some more decisions to make in the house while the workers aren't around bugging me. You rest here with Daisy."

Not moving sounded good to me.

20

Saturday Late Morning

Elizabeth

I took another lap around the downstairs of our house, moving slower this time as I envisioned the final product and checked for anything that would annoy me. Mimi and Pawpaw's house had always felt just right while growing up. Building a new house to replace theirs felt like a big responsibility. Although I wanted a more modern design, I felt the pressure to achieve a similar level of comfort and welcome. Basically perfection.

In the guest bedroom, I finalized where the light switch should go and opened my purse to pull out a black Sharpie marker. I'd started keeping one there ever since our house construction had begun. In my purse, my fingers brushed across something hard and rectangular. I grabbed the object and pulled it out. Vanessa's USB drive. With everything else going on over the last couple of days, I'd forgotten to go through it and look at the rest of the emails with Jonas. But now, with Vanessa home from jail, looking through her things without her permission felt like peeping.

I grinned as I realized that I could ask her about them in person. And of course, I should return the USB drive to her. Mind made up, I hurried over to the back door. "Jonas," I called, but he didn't stir. Slumped in the camp chair, he was asleep. Even in that uncomfortable position, he looked too cozy sitting in the sun for me to disturb him. Neither of us had gotten much sleep last night, and although a nap was tempting, I had better things to do right now.

Ever vigilant, Daisy raised her head and thumped her tail in anticipation of whatever adventure might await.

"Stay!" I commanded in a quieter voice with a firm hand gesture. Jonas was right—she'd serve as a great early warning system if anyone nosed around the ranch looking to bother him. I was pleased to see Daisy quickly settle back down. I'd have to remember to tell Jonas he was wrong, that we didn't have to put her through any formal training. I hated to drill the originality and spirit out of her and turn her into some sort of robot dog.

Before I left, I dug around in my purse for a piece of paper to leave Jonas a note but found none. I didn't want to text him in case he'd forgotten to mute his phone before he fell asleep. Finally I grabbed a piece of scrap plywood and wrote a brief note with the marker before propping it near where the back door would be. I wouldn't be gone all that long anyway. Picking my way around the piles of construction trash, I went to my car. A mere ten-minute drive took me to Vanessa's apartment.

"Vanessa!" I folded her into a hug when she answered the door. I'd seen her briefly yesterday, but she'd been exhausted and overwhelmed so I'd only stayed for a minute before leaving her alone with her family. Today, it felt good to see her out in the wide world.

"Come in, come in." Vanessa beamed as she opened the door wider to reveal her mother and Olivia sitting at the kitchen table. She showed off this normal tableau as if she were proudly displaying a sitting for a Norman Rockwell painting. I didn't blame her. I knew how it felt to crave normalcy when you got locked away behind bars.

I beamed back, proud I'd played a small part in this sweet domestic scene. "I won't intrude for long," I promised. "I have something to return and, well, wanted to ask you some questions . . ."

"Let's talk outside," agreed Vanessa, appearing equally reluctant to get into an awkward discussion in front of them.

I greeted her mother and then tilted my head and smiled. "Good morning, Olivia."

"Hi." Olivia returned my smile shyly from where she sat surrounded by an array of drawings and supplies as her grandmother looked on. "Look." She thrust a drawing at me.

It showed a little girl next to a woman in a room with a large fish tank. My eyes teared up as I noticed the woman's hair resembled my own. "It's very nice," I said with a catch to my voice.

"It's fine. You can have it," said Olivia in a singsong voice, dismissing her creation as irrelevant now that she had started on her next project.

"She made me go to the store and buy a new package of colored pencils yesterday evening," said Vanessa as she guided me to the chairs set up in their building's backyard. "I think that's your doing, Aunt Elizabeth."

My eyes glistening, I just nodded and clutched the drawing.

"And what's with the gray trees?" Her teasing tone ended the touching moment.

I laughed, then reached into my purse and handed her the USB stick.

Vanessa drew in a breath and sank into the seat across from me as she palmed it. "Oh, thank goodness. I hoped Olivia had remembered to tell you before the cops found it. Olivia didn't know what happened to it, and I didn't find it in the flower pot yesterday. I was so worried the sheriff had it."

I decided to cover for Olivia. It didn't matter now that she had forgotten to say something, and my Pawpaw's sleight-of-hand training had kept Trent from catching me with it. "The deputies never found it. But . . ." My voice trailed off as I tried to find a way to ask her about what it contained.

Vanessa didn't meet my eyes, instead looking across to the next building, but she understood where I was going with this. "I, uh, hired a private eye back when our marriage was breaking up. I needed to know, you see."

Feeling equally uncomfortable, I mumbled, "Uh-huh."

Still looking away, she went on. "On top of everything going wrong between Adam and me, we were losing clients right and left. It was as if someone was hand-selecting who to lure away. I couldn't believe everything in my life was falling apart at the same time—my marriage and my business."

I nodded, but she might not have noticed.

"The PI confirmed that Adam"—her voice trembled on his name but then steadied—"was seeing Courtney behind my back." She whipped her head back to look at me as her eyes sparked with fury. "She knew we were married too—we had all met a year or so before when we were volunteering for VITA. You know, those are the volunteers with the IRS who do income taxes?"

When I indicated that I'd never heard of it, she explained, "Accountants—and other people—volunteer and help poor people get their taxes done for free." She shrugged. "It doesn't matter, except it explained why Adam had continued volunteering. I'd been too exhausted after the first year. Tax season is the busy time for accountants with our own clients. After a long day, we'd drive over to Ft. Smith to volunteer on some evenings and weekends." She twisted her mouth bitterly. "I should have known something was up. Adam isn't the volunteer type. There had to be something else drawing him to do it again the second year—or someone else."

I swallowed. "I'm so—"

Vanessa didn't wait for my sympathy. "The PI and I showed the results to my lawyer. She said it would help me win an at-fault divorce because of Adam's adultery. I'd get a bigger share of our business, but then that floozy started stealing my clients."

"Couldn't you—"

Again, Vanessa didn't let me finish as she shook her head. "We couldn't prove Adam was involved in it, so the judge wouldn't do anything. So, I . . ."

As she paused, I felt a chill shoot through my veins as a surge of panic struck me. Had I been wrong? Was Vanessa about to confess to killing Courtney?

Vanessa gulped. "I decided to get back at Courtney. If she was going to take my husband and my clients, then I was going to take her clients."

I let loose a breath I hadn't realized I'd been holding.

She noticed and looked at me in surprise. "What? You didn't think I killed her, did you?"

"No, no. Of course not. Never." Maybe my multiple denials only made me sound less convincing since Vanessa's forehead wrinkled while she stared at me.

So I told her the truth. "I was suspicious about whether Adam might have killed her."

"As if." She snorted. "He wanted her." She stifled a sudden sob, adding, "Too much to kill her, at least. They were seeing each other the whole time the divorce dragged on. Besides, with the judge assessing Adam at fault for the divorce, Courtney was the one who would be supporting him. Why would he kill his sugar mama?" Then her eyebrows squished together. "I guess that would be the phrase, right?"

I shrugged, happy I didn't need to know but also sorry to leave her hanging.

Vanessa sighed. "As much as I'd like him to suffer more and go to jail for being a cheating snot, I don't want Olivia to have to deal with that. Although Adam sucked at being a husband, he's a pretty decent father." She sighed again. "He didn't kill Courtney."

"How do you know?" I asked softly. I didn't want Olivia to have a murderer as her father either, but as my mother always said, "Wishes don't make things come true." With the investigation still ongoing, Olivia's mother wasn't off the hook yet either.

She shook her head. "He just . . . Wait, let me show you." She stood suddenly and rushed into her apartment.

Just about when I started to wonder if I should have followed her inside, she burst back outside and thrust a small, pink tablet computer at me. "There. Look."

I looked. It was a short email that read, "Today I walked past New York City. Just kidding! See you soon. Love, Daddy. Sent from my iPhone." Below the words was a photo of Adam Martini clowning around in front of the fake skyline of the New York New York casino hotel in Las Vegas. I checked the timestamp, and Vanessa was right. Adam Martini couldn't have killed Courtney Stanton. The email had been sent at ten-twenty on Wednesday morning. At least, that was assuming he hadn't taken the picture some other time and only sent the email then.

My theory of him flying back to Arkansas, somehow triggering the explosion that killed Courtney in the pre-dawn hours, and flying back to Las Vegas by the early afternoon without anyone knowing seemed busted. For a moment my mind spun with possibilities of how Adam could still have pulled off this scam—he had lined up someone to email a photo from his phone on Wednesday mid-morning while he was in flight; or he'd purchased Wi-Fi from the airplane and sent the photo himself in-flight while hoping no one would call; or he'd . . .

I stopped spiraling.

None of that would hold up to scrutiny from the sheriff. And why would Adam have sent the email to his daughter instead of an adult? What were the odds that the deputies had even thought to ask if Olivia had her own email account and cute pink tablet? No, Vanessa was right—Adam hadn't killed Courtney.

I nodded in agreement and handed the tablet back to Vanessa. "What were all the other files on that USB drive?"

Finally Vanessa grinned. "That was some of my best work ever. Courtney had the Gradys as clients for years. You know, they own the fairgrounds."

I nodded, not feeling like explaining how Jonas and I had recently become quite familiar with them.

"So I approached them about taking over their accounting. I was all prepared to use my standard ploy of undercutting Courtney on price." She shook her head, suddenly deflated, and as an aside, added, "Stupid plan. All that would have done was keep me poor so I'd have to live in a small apartment or move in with my mother forever."

Then a rueful smile broke onto her face. "I guess I won't have to compete on price with Courtney Stanton any longer." She sat quietly for a moment before continuing, "But David didn't even ask me for a quote. He wanted me to analyze his books to see if something was wrong."

"David?" I asked.

"David Grady. I thought you said you knew them?"

I did know the Gradys, especially Grody, but the father had always been Mr. Grady to me. I felt my eyebrows rise as I realized he must have been the DG24 person Vanessa had been emailing. Not wanting to admit that I had read some of her emails, I stayed quiet.

Vanessa was too excited by her accomplishment to care. "I found something. Something big." Her eyes sparkled as she leaned forward. "Courtney had been siphoning off funds from the Gradys for years. Like a lot of money. And"—Vanessa jabbed a finger at me to emphasize her point—"she was stealing from other clients too. I found suspicious gaps and missing money from at least three other clients of hers that I approached after I found the issue with the Gradys."

I blanched. I believed Vanessa when she said she hadn't killed Courtney, but the sheriff would find this all very suspicious, especially that she had hidden this evidence from them. Based on the security camera footage, the sheriff's department had already ruled out the Gradys for the murder—at least if Carlita's info was accurate. If Vanessa wasn't careful, she could get locked up forever just because she was still the most logical suspect.

Vanessa misunderstood my reaction and laughed. "Don't worry. My lawyer knows. We were going to report her to the state board as soon as the divorce was finalized."

"Did you find their money?" I asked, suddenly impressed by this self-confident friend. Thinking of her as my older sister had always made her seem impressive to me, but not like this. She'd discovered her husband cheated on her, went through a rough divorce while still raising an awesome girl, identified a criminal in the act, gotten arrested for a crime she hadn't committed, and even seemed comfortable with the thought of living with her mother indefinitely. Yet, despite all that, she didn't seem any worse for the wear. What couldn't she do?

"No. I couldn't trace where the money had gone." Somewhat cryptically, Vanessa added, "But it's not in a US bank account owned by Courtney Stanton." She merely smiled enigmatically and refused to answer how she knew that.

We sat silently for a moment while I absorbed her story and she looked smug. The smugness was well-deserved, but it annoyed me a little nonetheless. There was no way she could have known Courtney hadn't stashed the stolen money in a bank without doing something illegal. I decided she could remain my honorary big sister and my friend, but I definitely wanted to find a different accountant.

Suddenly my phone rang, breaking the quiet.

"Where are you?" asked Jonas. "Did you go for pie?"

21

Saturday Afternoon

Jonas

"Vanessa figured out Courtney was stealing money and then Courtney got killed! C'mon, that's gotta mean something, right?" asked Elizabeth from the driver's seat of her car.

We were hurrying down the mountain from the ranch to get back to her mother's house to shower and change so we'd make it to her reunion dance. I'd be glad when this weekend was over and I could start my summer vacation in earnest. It had been nice seeing this side of Elizabeth as she visited with all her old friends, and I was looking forward to dancing with her tonight. After that, however, my days would be full of nothing for a while.

"It is a direct correlation," I responded. "But it doesn't have to mean something. It could just be a weird coincidence."

After tonight, I planned to convince Elizabeth to end this investigation and join me in doing a whole lot of nothing. Maybe even go away on vacation for a few days. The timing seemed right. Her friend was home with her daughter. Trent and the other deputies would do a professional investigation, and a jury would scrutinize their results in a trial before anyone would go to prison. The guilty person, I felt confident, would be found—whoever that turned out to be.

I no longer was too concerned about Vanessa—I was more focused on avoiding bullets, either stray or directed at me and Elizabeth. We could leave town for a few days without causing any delays at the house. In fact, without Elizabeth's frequent changes, the contractor might make even more progress. She could focus her extra creativity on the decorations after we moved in.

"Didn't someone say there's no such thing as a coincidence?" Elizabeth asked as she pulled into her mother's driveway.

"Isn't that one of those character's rules from that TV show your mother's always watching?"

"Oh yeah—*NCIS*." Elizabeth sounded disgusted as she blew out a puff of air. "We've got to get out of my mother's house before I start quoting more from Leroy Gibbs."

"I thought you liked that show. Didn't you watch it all the time when you were a kid?" I asked as we mounted the porch.

"Exactly. I was a kid. I've been gone for ten years and the show's still on and she's still watching it. It's ridiculous."

"What's ridiculous?" asked Mary, opening the front door, on her way to somewhere.

I jumped in to answer before Elizabeth could provoke an argument. "Isn't it ridiculous how Courtney could embezzle a ton of money from folks and not get caught?"

"Hmmph." Mary gave me some side eye but accepted my explanation. She was clearly onto my ways. I would have to spend some downtime considering how often I relied on my reputation for not lying and yet still misled people.

"Hi, Mom," said Elizabeth as she breezed past. "We've got to hurry to get ready for the dance."

"I'm off to Lisa Hardy's house tonight. Don't wait up," said Mary from the porch.

Elizabeth stopped and turned. "Wasn't your poker game last night?"

"Yes. Tonight, we're learning to play bridge. Judge Hardy's up for re-election this fall and doesn't want folks talking about her playing poker. Some voters don't care for gambling."

"Are you worried about it too as a county commissioner?" I asked.

"Nah. Probably helps me. Most folks 'round here only want their judges to be saints. They like their elected officials to be normal people." She glared at Elizabeth as she heard her clearing her throat. Keeping her glare in place, she continued, "Besides, never too old to learn new games. You'd be surprised how good old birds like us pick up on things." She turned her glare in my direction, but I maintained my look of innocence.

"Well you have a good time and say hello to all the ladies for us." I held the door open, allowing for Mary's exit while blocking Daisy's escape and gently pushing Elizabeth into the house. I was surrounded by three strong-willed females. No wonder I was so in need of a vacation.

A short while later, Elizabeth walked out of our bathroom wearing only a towel. "Nope, this isn't a blazer kind of event, either. How about your chinos and that cute button-up shirt I like? You know, the one with the vertical stripes." She slapped my hand away when I reached for her towel as she strolled past. "Hold that thought. We've got to get ready."

It wasn't fair for her to keep walking around in nothing but a towel when we needed to go someplace. I sighed and went to change.

"Where do you think it all went?" she asked.

"What?"

"The money. If Courtney stole it, where is it now?"

"Maybe her boyfriend—Vanessa's ex-husband, Adam—took it?"

"Like he used it to go gambling in Vegas?" proposed Elizabeth, getting animated for a moment before deflating. "But then who killed Courtney? No, I already thought about this. He would have needed to be on a plane back to Vegas on Wednesday morning when that selfie was sent to Olivia."

"What?" When had Elizabeth figured out the possible timing for Adam to kill Courtney and get away with it? Getting glimpses of what actually went on inside Elizabeth's head was somewhat amazing at times, but also dizzying, and sometimes downright disturbing.

"Never mind about him," she said with a dismissive wave of her hand as she turned back to the mirror. "Where else could the money have gone?"

"A bank?" I asked, only half caring again as I pulled out her preferred chinos and shirt. It wasn't my money and I didn't have it, yet someone had shot at me. It seemed absolutely unfair.

"Vanessa said Courtney doesn't have the money in any US banks."

Surprised again, I turned around only to see Elizabeth slipping her dress over her head. Somehow I had missed the towel-free moment. I shook away my distracting thoughts. "How would Vanessa know that?"

"I don't know. I'm an artist, not a financial type." She shrugged, then froze. "Beverly is a financial type. We should check into her some more. The others don't seem to fit."

I stood there silently, thinking through the possibilities. "What about Vanessa?"

"Yes, Vanessa figured out that Courtney took the money. Something about the accounting. Vanessa's clever."

"No," I said, feeling a chill down my spine. "Could Vanessa have taken the stolen money back from Courtney? Maybe Vanessa killed Courtney after all?"

"No!" exclaimed Elizabeth firmly. "Not her."

Not as convinced as Elizabeth, I asked, "Did Vanessa look like she was planning to run?"

"It wasn't her, Jonas!"

"Okay, okay." It was just a theory—for now. Someone had taken the money from the PTA, the Gradys, and who knows who else. But until more facts were known, it certainly wasn't worth getting Elizabeth upset tonight.

"Maybe Courtney had it with her on the boat and it blew up with her," she proposed.

I gave it due consideration before I disagreed. "Wouldn't we have seen some of the bits of money all over? And besides, where could she escape to on the boat? It's a lake in the middle of Arkansas."

"Oh, yeah. That was dumb." She snorted. "Courtney should have been disbarred."

"She was an accountant," I corrected.

"Then she should have been *discounted*." We both laughed at this before Elizabeth snapped her fingers. "Do you think the mafia guys found out she had all that money so they killed her and stole it?"

Elizabeth was a good friend to Vanessa. She was really working to solve this. "How would they find out about the money? They're new to town."

"Maybe she stole from them too?" Then she realized how silly that sounded and changed her idea. "They're master criminals. They could have heard it through the grapevine. Everyone else around Jenkins seems to learn everything about everybody's business."

I smiled wistfully—she was right about the power of the Jenkins rumor mill. "So you're thinking there's some sort of worldwide, organized, rumor-spreading service where criminals gather information to scam people?"

Elizabeth grinned. "Yes, it's called Facebook."

We both laughed, and that ended our discussion for the time being. We hadn't solved anything, but we had a dance to get to.

*****

Showered, changed, and having fed Daisy, I was back in the car with the most gorgeous date I'd ever taken to a dance. I pulled into the parking lot outside the school gymnasium where the dance would occur.

"Hold up for a minute," said Elizabeth as I started to open my door.

"What's wrong? Did you forget something?" I asked, looking at my beautiful wife. "You look fantastic, by the way."

She leaned over and kissed me. "Thanks. You too." Then she tapped the clock on the car's dashboard. "We're early again."

"No, it starts right—"

"It's too early to show up," insisted Elizabeth. "We were running late and somehow we got here too early again. It's like a time warp. Let's sit out here for a few minutes so we can at least arrive fashionably on time."

Another car pulled into the spot right next to us. The couple got out, and the man, tall and lean, leaned over and looked at us through the front window.

"Oh, for Pete's sake," exclaimed Elizabeth in a quiet voice. Then she threw on a smile and climbed out of the car. "Hi! Good to see you again."

She exchanged brief hugs with the other couple and introduced me, but I promptly forgot their names.

"Why aren't y'all going inside?" asked the tall man.

"Well." Elizabeth started to hem and haw before blurting out, "I hate getting to events early and being the first one there. I always feel so awkward."

The tall man's wife, dressed in a dark blue dress and heels that matched the blue highlights in her hair, laughed. "Good point. Maybe we'll hang out here with you for a little."

We chatted while several more cars parked nearby. As those people got out of their car, they noticed the four of us standing by our cars.

"What're all y'all doing out here?" asked one of the newcomers as he got out of his car.

The woman in the blue dress yelled back, "We don't want to go in so early."

Another newcomer replied, "Yeah, I hate that." He checked his watch. "I didn't realize the time. Mind if we join you?"

The tall man nodded his agreement as his date greeted the newcomers like long-lost classmates, which I supposed they were.

To be polite, Elizabeth and I followed the first couple to the sidewalk to meet the other arrivals. It felt less strange than standing and talking in the middle of the parking lot like my students did when they were deciding where to hang out after school.

We stood and talked on the sidewalk with the others. The next thing I knew, twenty-five or thirty people were standing around us on the sidewalk outside the entrance to the school gym. Some of the people were familiar to me, but Elizabeth was in her element as she flitted from group to group greeting everyone. I gradually found myself separated from her as I chatted with one of the men I'd met at the underground bar.

After a few more minutes, a glass door to the gym opened and Daniel from Wednesday's check-in table took a tentative step outside. "Hey, why are y'all waiting outside? Is there a problem?"

A woman poked her head and shoulders out the door too. "Something's wrong?" she yelled.

Another glass door banged open. "What's going on?" shouted a guy, and a couple of others followed him outside.

Soon even more people migrated outside, drawn by the movement and crowd standing on the sidewalk. Idly, I wondered whether everyone would have followed their neighbors and jumped off a cliff if one had been nearby.

Sixty or seventy people were now milling around outside, talking to each other and trying to figure out what was going on, when a yellow Corvette Stingray convertible came roaring into the parking lot. It swerved around the lot, barely missing breaking off an extended side mirror of one car, and then fishtailed, skidding past another car, almost sideswiping it. The screeching tires halted all the conversations as everyone turned to watch the entrance.

Seeing the big crowd by the doors, the driver leaned out the window with a big grin and gave a thumbs-up. He was wearing a black tux, one of those low, flat driver's caps with a gray and black pattern, and old-fashioned driving goggles. The driver swerved again and zoomed up to the sidewalk, squealing to a stop by us.

I looked across the crowd and caught Elizabeth's eye. I waved my hand up and down in front of my shirt to indicate the man's tux and bow tie and smiled at her. She'd told me this wasn't a jacket kind of shindig. What would she think of my wearing a tuxedo?

She mouthed the word "tacky" at me and rolled her eyes.

Then from a clump in the crowd, Christy Tomer stepped out to the curb. Tonight, she wore a glittery gold reflective dress that was somehow even shorter and more revealing than the outfit she'd worn to the mixer. She had a pile of some golden, filmy see-through material perched on the side of her head like a bird's nest. I noticed that none of the other men were looking at her hair.

I hadn't seen her arrive. I would definitely have remembered the arrival of that dress.

Christy hollered, "Rick Hoffman! Don't tell me that's the surprise you had for me tonight?" She jutted out a hip and put a hand on it to strike a contemptuous pose. "That lil ole Camaro is too hard for me to get into."

Rick flipped off the ignition and popped out of the car, still wearing his full getup. He staggered toward us. "Hon, hon," he said, both hands patting the air before he pulled the goggles off his face. He stumbled against the side of the car. "This ain't no

Camaro," he slurred, and then turned in my direction, his back now to Christy. His eyes closed and a smile spread across his face as he spread his arms wide in supplication to the vehicle. He swayed from side to side. "This here's a 1969 C3 Corvette with the special LT-1 engine. Three hundred and fifty cubic inches, small block V-8, and only 14.3 seconds to go a quarter mile. This rare bird is the sexiest thing I've ever seen."

Suddenly his eyes popped open as he swallowed and spun back to refocus on Christy. "I mean next to you, of course." But he ruined the effect by stumbling again.

During the sudden silence, Andrew Grady stepped out of the crowd. More people must have congregated on the sidewalk than I'd estimated. "Bruh, that thing's sweet."

Rick bobbed his head a few times in agreement as he stared at Christy and staggered a step toward her. "I rented it from a luxury specialty place over in Little Rock for you." Then he turned to Andrew. "You know my daddy once drove a car like this for a few minutes after he repaired it in our shop. It was Matthew McConaughey's car and he had a breakdown on his way back home to Texas." He paused and then added, "You know, Matthew McConaughey—'All right, all right, all right.'" He stumbled again and waved at the crowd to let us know he was okay.

Christy broke in, "Are you drunk?"

"No, darlin'. Not tonight," Rick answered her in all sincerity. Then he slurred, "I'm high."

Christy put both hands on her hips and struck a pose. "Without me?" Then she shook a finger at him. "You were supposed to wait until after the dance."

"But," whined Rick.

Christy broke in. "No. I don't care about your daddy, your smelly garage, Matthew McConaughey, or some silly car. That thing's too small. I'll break a heel getting in there."

"But," moaned Rick, pulling off his hat and rubbing his head with one hand while the other crumpled the hat in his fist. "I drove all the way to Little Rock to get this for you. That's why I was late and had to meet you here." He swallowed. "Well, and a stop for the pot."

"Hey," said Elizabeth as she stepped toward the car. "That hat!"

22

Saturday Evening

Elizabeth

B efore I could speak again, a black Cadillac SUV pulled up behind the yellow Corvette. Giuseppe jumped out of the passenger seat while his bodyguard exited more slowly.

"Why, hello to all you good people of Jenkins," he said smugly, followed by an oily smile. "I saw the crowd and wanted to join in the night's festivities." He looked from side to side to take in everyone. "It's good to see so much excitement around here. What sort of merriment are we engaging in this lovely evening?"

Someone in the crowd behind me yelled out, "Dance."

Giuseppe smiled and bowed theatrically. "Ahh, how wonderful. I have been known to cut quite the rug."

"It's for our high school reunion," called out another person. "Graduates only."

I heard a familiar voice as Dale Cooper chimed in, "Well, I'm sure we can make an exception just this one time for our honored guests."

I whipped my head around. "What are you doing here?"

"As mayor, it's important I attend all important functions held in Jenkins."

Giuseppe said, "Ah, lovely Liza. Perhaps you will save a place on your dance card for me."

I turned to glare at him, but out of the corner of my eye, I saw Christy's mouth twist into a scowl. Torn between laughing at Christy getting jealous of me for stealing her thunder and yelling at the uninvited guest, I stopped and stared at her.

Her outfit was completely inappropriate for tonight—a gold lamé dress with see-through fabric that barely covered the essential parts along with some sort of ridiculous lace, ribbon, gauze, scrunchy-type thing on her head. The headpiece jogged my memory, and I swung back to point at Rick Hoffman. "I recognize your hat!" I'd seen it in that photo on Vanessa's USB drive.

"What? You?" Rick looked sideways and raised his fingers to his temples as if he was trying to figure out a hard math problem. He shook his head, trying to clear the cobwebs. "What are you even doing here anyway?" He started mumbling to himself.

"Hey!" yelled Jonas, stepping out from the crowd to defend me.

When Rick caught sight of Jonas, his head jerked up and he stumbled back a few steps, as if he'd seen a ghost. His eyes bugged out and his mouth dropped open. He fell back onto his car but bounced up, looking terrified. As sweat beaded on his forehead, Rick moved his mouth a few times before words finally came out. "You, you!" he puffed, suddenly out of breath. "How?"

My voice rose to overcome his. "You worked on Courtney's boat."

Everyone in the crowd seemed to freeze at the mention of her name.

Rick looked like a deer caught in the headlights as he jerked his gaze back and forth from Jonas to me. Breathing hard as he stared at Jonas, he finally stuttered, "He . . . he saw me. At the dock, man. I was stupid, wearing my hat, but I was pretty high that morning." He stifled a nervous laugh. "It gives me courage."

Gripping the car for support, Rick looked at the crowd. "Do you see him too?" He pointed at Jonas. "That ain't no ghost or nothing, is it?"

Stunned, people in the crowd tittered to each other, but no one answered him.

Visibly screwing up his courage, Rick stood upright, turned toward Jonas, and wrung his cap with both hands. "Hey, I'm sorry, bruh. It ain't personal or nothing. You were just staring at me from the water. When I remembered you later, I had to." A great big shiver went through his body. "Please don't haunt me. You can't be real. I saw you fall in the forest, and then the ambulance came and ever'thing."

"Shut up, man," shouted Grody, shoving his way through the crowd to stand in front of Rick.

Rick turned his bleary red eyes to Grody. "Bruh, it's over. He saw me and my hat." Rick waved the crumpled fabric.

"What?" Jonas's forehead crinkled.

I lurched forward and jabbed Rick in the chest with my finger. "You killed her for the money, didn't you? You killed Courtney Stanton. She stole that hundred and fifty thousand for the festival and you killed her to get it for yourself." Not pausing to let him respond, I poked him hard again. "What did you do with the money?"

Rick seemed cowed by the fire in my eyes. He backed up against his car as I kept jabbing him. "She didn't have no money. It was all a lie." He stank from marijuana.

Then my words must have penetrated because he stopped cringing and glared at Grody. "Wait. What's this about a hunnit and fifty big ones? You told me it was twenty-five grand and I'd get ten for my half."

Grody repeated, "Shut up!"

But Rick ignored him as he stared at Christy, tears forming in his eyes. "I'm sorry, babe. There ain't no money. He promised me, but there ain't any. No trip after all." Apparently taking his lead from me, Rick pointed a finger at Grody. "I waited for her on Tuesday night in her home like you told me, but she swore she didn't have no cash on her. I even smacked her a few times, but she only said she had a bit of coin."

Grody flung his hands into the air. "You idiot. She didn't say she had a bit of coin."

"Yes, she did," insisted Rick. "I grabbed her wallet and all that was there was a twenty. She must have buried the money. Maybe out on the beach by Stillwater Cove. Why else did she go there by herself all the time? But no, you wouldn't listen to stupid ole Rick and help me dig out there on the beach for her stash. Thought she was the cat's meow, did she? Well I showed her." He spat on the ground in Grody's direction.

Grody raised a fist and took a step toward him, then stopped as he remembered everyone was watching. "Oh, you freaking idiot! No wonder my father divorced your mother. Your whole family is too dumb for words." Then he barked, "She said bitcoin. BIT-COIN. Not a bit of coin." Grody waved a dismissive hand at Rick. "I don't know why I agreed to give an idiot two grand in advance. What a waste! You've probably blown it all already."

When Rick hung his head, Grody said, "You have, haven't you? Idiot."

I felt rage building in my stomach. I'd had it with both of these idiots. Besides what they'd done to Courtney and put Vanessa and Olivia through, one of them had taken a shot at my Jonas. I growled as I clenched a fist and stepped toward them.

A familiar voice stopped me in my tracks.

"That's quite enough," said Trent, striding forward. "You're both under arrest for the murder of Courtney Stanton and attempted murder of Jonas Trout." I hadn't seen him arrive. There sure were a lot of people here.

Of course, Rick reacted in a most intelligent fashion—he ran. At least he tried to.

Stepping away from Grody, he stumbled down the driveway and lurched past Giuseppe before Trent could get to him.

When Rick reached the black SUV, somehow he was still upright. Drosnic thrust out his leg.

Rick tripped and sprawled to the ground, yelping in a most satisfying fashion.

Drosnic then kneeled on Rick, eliciting a loud grunt as his full weight landed on Rick's back.

Trent grabbed Grody by the wrists. "Don't move," he shouted, even as he dragged him over to where Rick lay on the ground. "Can you hold him down for a few minutes?" he asked, indicating Rick's prone body.

When Drosnic nodded from his position on top of Rick, Trent said, "Thanks, Jimmy."

Trent kept a hand on Andrew and used his other to pull out his cell phone and call 9-1-1. I was glad he hadn't brought his gun and police radio to tonight's dance. He was supposed to be able to relax and enjoy himself like the rest of us.

"Sorry, bruh." Rick groaned as he lay on the ground. "I couldn't lean on that Courtney chick for too long. Deputy Dawg here lived next door to her."

"Dude, shut up already. Wait till we get a lawyer," hissed Grody.

"Sorry," repeated Rick.

In less than a minute, two deputy sheriffs pulled into the parking lot. I'd bet the sheriff had been hoping to catch some drunk drivers after tonight's dance and had them stationed right outside the school parking lot.

I stepped back as the deputies read Rick and Grody their rights and moved them into the squad cars.

Jonas barely beat the "ABC" girls to my side to hug me. He held onto me tightly until we could hear some whispered giggles. As he started to release me, they shouldered him aside and squeezed me into a loud group hug. It felt like old times.

"Oh, you were so brave confronting him like that," said Angela.

"So they're stepbrothers?" asked Carlita.

"Yeah, now I remember," responded Brooke. "From forever ago. That must have been back in elementary school."

I shrugged and shook my head. I went to the other elementary school and hadn't met Brooke, Rick, or Andrew until middle school.

Carlita asked, "What kind of connection does that make them—ex-stepbrothers? Is that even a thing?"

Brooke shrugged. "Who knows? It's like trying to explain second cousin versus first cousin once-removed. No one remembers it anyway."

The three women started to debate the definitions, but Jonas and I moved away. Some concepts are better left alone.

As Trent walked past, Carlita gave him a quick smile and wave, but he didn't seem to notice.

"All right, folks. Show's over," called Stapleton, suddenly making his appearance from the steps near the gym. "Come on inside for the dance and let the deputies finish their work out here." For once, I agreed with the man, even if I still didn't like him.

Still keyed up from all the commotion, I recoiled as someone approached me rapidly from the side, but it was only Kelsey, arriving late as usual.

"What'd I miss?" she asked breathlessly, staring wide-eyed at the flashing lights and crowd.

When I hesitated, Brooke jumped in and grabbed her. "Come on, Kelsey, let's get a drink. Ella Mae needs a moment to herself. Besides, I can tell the story way better."

Then my friends walked off together as Brooke threw me a wink over her shoulder.

They strolled toward the gym along with most of the crowd, leaving me standing outside with Jonas, the deputies, and the criminals.

And those guys.

Giuseppe and Drosnic stood nearby, next to their SUV. Giuseppe looked positively entranced by all the action. Trent returned to where he and Drosnic stood. "So, uh, thanks, sir," he said, reaching out stiffly to shake Drosnic's hand. "That was very civic-minded of you. Thanks so much for your support." And then he suddenly blushed beet red. "Okay, have a good evening."

He abruptly turned away from them. I watched him take in a deep breath and survey the area, his face slowly returning to its normal hue.

As Drosnic and Giuseppe walked to their car, I narrowed my eyes at Trent. What was up with him? That excessive, blushing reaction only used to occur whenever he got caught in a whopper of a lie.

What was he lying about now?

Was he holding something back from me? After I'd solved this case for him, how dare he keep secrets from me.

I glanced around. Everyone else seemed to have gone inside or was headed that way. From the gym, loud dance music started playing. The other officers seemed to be finishing whatever it was they had to do with Rick Hoffman and Andrew Grady. I wondered if Grody's charges—solicitation to commit murder, or attempted murder, or something—would stick. Would Mr. Grady get Andrew off, like he had bailed him out of trouble in the past?

"You know," said Jonas softly, "I don't think Rick has realized that I never saw him on Wednesday. The shadows from the mountains keep the dock darker than the water in the early mornings. When he sobers up, I'll bet he's going to be upset at himself."

I muffled a laugh. Rick never had been the brightest bulb in the box—in fact, he was about as sharp as a marble. With him blurting out a confession in front of everyone, he was definitely going to prison. All over a hat. A hat I had remembered from Vanessa's private eye's surveillance photo of Courtney and Adam.

I wondered if I had known he was the killer when I pointed at his hat. Surely my subconscious was trying to help me out by telling me it had solved the crime. Otherwise, I'd only have been able to prove that he knew his way around Courtney's boat.

I shrugged. It didn't matter now. He was hosed for sure.

The sound of a door slamming made me glance to where Drosnic had just settled himself into the driver's seat. Trent hadn't started blushing until he'd talked to Drosnic. His lying had something to do with them.

I snapped my fingers as I realized what it was. As Drosnic started the car, I turned to Trent. "How did you know Drosnic's first name? You called him Jimmy."

Trent's neck grew redder while he fumbled with his notebook, pretending he didn't hear me.

"Trent?" I demanded.

He merely shrugged but didn't look up.

"I mean it, Trent Walker. You're lying about something. You better spill or . . . or . . ." My mouth gaped open and then closed. After all these years, did I have nothing left to threaten Trent Walker with? Nothing to use as leverage to get my way?

Annoyed at myself, and vowing to come up with something better in the future, I finished, "or I won't let Jonas hang out with you."

I blushed at having to resort to kindergarten-level threats, but my voice must have gotten louder because a few of the remaining alums walking up the steps snorted.

Trent quickly looked up and put his finger to his mouth to shush me.

He did not get to tell me to be quiet. That was not okay. I hollered, "I mean it, Trent Walker. What are you hiding?"

Trent scrambled over to us. "Shh, already." He glanced over his shoulder as Giuseppe and Drosnic's car pulled past. Giuseppe hung his arm out the window, waving and smiling as if he'd saved the day and not his enforcer.

I opened my mouth to give Trent the what-for, but he quickly insisted, "Wait!"

We stood there for a moment. Jonas watched me with a bemused expression while I stared daggers at Trent until Giuseppe's car had left the parking lot, turned onto the main road, and accelerated away.

Trent, who had been standing rigidly, his face tense and expressionless, turned back to me. He released a big gust of air and said, "Okay, fine. It's almost over anyway. But you can't tell anyone."

I raised an eyebrow. For that kind of commitment, it had better be worth it.

"I mean it, Lizzie." Trent's mouth went firm and his blush receded. The tension in his body remained but shifted subtly from a defensive posture to one of power.

I realized he was truly serious, and if I wanted to learn the truth, I better accept this deal. Reluctantly, I nodded, glad that Kelsey and the others had gone inside and wouldn't jump me with questions as soon as Trent left me alone.

He lowered his voice even further so Jonas and I had to lean in. "I screwed up. The bodyguard's name is actually Jimmy Drosnic."

"How do you know—"

Trent interrupted, "He's an undercover FBI agent. They've been building a RICO case against Giuseppe for a couple of years. That's the racketeering charge—"

"I know what it is," I interrupted. He should have remembered I'd watched *The Sopranos* along with him every weekend. Well, at least the TV had been on.

Jonas asked, "Are you sure you should be telling—"

Again Trent interrupted, "It's okay now. Giuseppe's high up in one of the mafia families."

I laughed, blurting out, "Mom was right," as I looked at Jonas.

Trent looked shocked. "How did she know? This was a closely guarded secret."

I snickered. "You know Mom. What she doesn't learn via the gossip mill, she manages to guess. You remember that time—"

"Yes, yes." Trent looked embarrassed again. Then his face twisted into a frown.

"It was just a guess. Don't get her into trouble," I urged him.

"Hmm," he responded noncommittally.

"Trent, please?" I begged, and then he nodded without speaking.

Clearly Trent was eager to share his exciting news with someone because he started talking again. "The FBI gave us a courtesy briefing on Monday that they had an active operation in the area. They've finally got enough on him. Giuseppe, that is. Jimmy is driving him to a meeting tonight. Giuseppe thinks it's a secret meeting with the governor to seal the casino deal. But actually he's going to be arrested and interviewed by a team of FBI agents." Trent looked almost as satisfied as if he'd nailed Giuseppe himself.

"Oh," I said, and rocked back on my heels. I felt really stupid now.

"So the movie thing is all fake?" asked Jonas.

"Yeah. It's just a cover for why they're here," answered Trent. "Sorta hiding in plain sight. Everyone gets so distracted by the possibility of being in a movie that they don't wonder why guys who look like them are in town."

Clever, but I knew a movie didn't make any sense.

"His name's not even Giuseppe," added Trent, now smirking. "It's Joey. Joey Lucchesi from Trenton, New Jersey. When he became a bigshot, I guess he decided it wasn't sophisticated enough—or Italian enough—so he started calling himself Giuseppe as the Italian version of his name, and putting on all those airs." He laughed a little. "I mean, can you believe those shirts?"

Jonas and I both joined his laughter.

"I'm sorry, Trent." I actually meant it too. Calling him out for lying had been a childish thing to do, and it could have gotten Trent into a lot of trouble if Giuseppe had wondered why a Jenkins sheriff's deputy knew his enforcer's first name. Trent was lucky everything hadn't fallen apart when he'd goofed that up. I even promised myself not to hold it over him.

Trent kept his voice low. "Did you see that early morning helicopter flying around?"

Jonas nodded, but I didn't. How would I know anything about early mornings? The one time I got up early this week was to help Olivia. I smiled just thinking of her. Her mother was off the hook now, and her father wasn't a murderer. Still a jerk, but at least Olivia would have him in her life. I'd have to stop by soon and do some more projects with her. Maybe she and Vanessa would come to the ranch and we'd go exploring along the creek. Or I could introduce her to watercolors.

Trent continued, "The FBI was flying reconnaissance flights. They've got one of those LIDAR radars." Seeing my puzzled expression, he explained, "It uses pulsed lasers and can see through vegetation so it finds things that are covered. They thought Lucchesi had a hideout or a stash of drugs or money out here and was coming by to collect it."

I gasped. That was straight out of the movies, not something that happened in Jenkins.

Trent nodded at my reaction. "I know, cool, huh? Well, no drugs, but something else interesting. There was a pickup hidden under a tarp, covered with leaves and branches, just off the beach at Stillwater Cove. We went out there Thursday and dug it out. Courtney had stashed it as a getaway vehicle. The glove compartment had a passport with a fake name, a bunch of cash, and a piece of paper with a bitcoin wallet user ID and password." He shook his head in disbelief. "Blows the whole point of security if you write your password down like that, if you ask me."

"Wait," I said, trying to catch up. "So Rick could have stolen the hundred and fifty thousand dollars and a getaway truck from her if he'd only done a better job of looking around that beach?"

Trent grinned. "Oh, yeah. And there was a lot more than a hundred and fifty grand in her bitcoin account—nearly a million all told. She must have embezzled from other clients and stolen from those poker games she ran for years—all slow and steady so no one noticed. She took the last wad of money that had been collected to pay for the festival all at once. She must have been ready to skip town because that loss would have been discovered pretty quickly. I figure she was planning to run and leave her boat floating loose in the lake to make it look like she had fallen overboard."

Trent paused as the other deputies drove past us on their way to the station and waved at him. "Andrew Grady just happened to get pissed that he lost a bunch of money last Saturday at her poker game. We heard from some of the other attendees that he and Courtney got into a big argument when she wouldn't refund his losses. He must have hired Rick to get his money back. I don't even know if he knew about the other stolen money. Blowing up her boat was a surprise, though. I thought her death might have been a mob hit at first, but then we saw security camera footage of Vanessa walking in that direction and she had explosives experience in her military files. Crazy coincidences, huh?"

Jonas and I both laughed at this but didn't offer any quotes about coincidences.

Then Jonas asked, "Why hire Rick? He didn't seem like the smartest choice for Andrew to bring into the plan."

"They've been tight forever, and Rick's been down on his luck since getting out of the army and his dad's repair shop not doing so well. We were looking at whether his army buddies helped him get some explosives and whether he built some remote control device." Trent jotted something down quickly in his notepad. "I hear he's a decent mechanic. But no clue why he blew up Courtney and her boat. Maybe he got upset he couldn't torture the money out of her?" He shrugged. "Don't need to explain why to send him to prison."

"So I didn't solve the case after all?" I suddenly felt crestfallen—all this work and stress for nothing. "You already knew all this."

Trent's face softened and he reached out to pat my arm. "Nah, you did good, Lizzie. They've been on our suspect list since Thursday afternoon but we didn't have proof. We covered up the truck again and were watching both of them to see if they'd search the beach again or do anything else incriminating."

He laughed. "Never thought Rick's silly hat was the key."

Jonas asked, "Are you going to come in for the dance?"

Trent bit his lip and then shook his head. "No. Sheriff Tucker will want to see my report first thing in the morning. I've got to figure out how to explain everything."

"Thanks, Trent," I said, and then decided to try out this whole acting mature thing. "You know . . . our place up on the ridge is almost finished. We'll have to invite you over for a barbecue soon."

"That sounds very nice," he said without even a hint of snarkiness, and then excused himself.

Jonas put his arm around me. "Ready to go inside?"

"Yeah, in a minute." I took a step away and drew in a deep breath to calm myself as I looked out toward the mountains.

"Still thinking about the gunshot?" he asked. "We're safe now with those two in custody."

"No," I answered, and then turned to look at him. "I'm glad it wasn't Beverly—even if she might be a megalomaniac. That only makes her a politician, not necessarily a killer. She was just acting weird because she was concerned for her kid."

I swallowed and then looked into his eyes. "I'm also thinking about Olivia and Vanessa and Adam."

"What you did was really awesome," he said, but I shushed him.

"It's not that." I swallowed and reached out to hold both of his hands. "Maybe we should start thinking about having a baby." Then I blushed as my words tumbled out. "We'll have all that space in the house and you'd make a great father and maybe I won't be all that terrible."

Jonas cupped my face in his hand. "You'll be a great mom."

"You really think so? No lies, right?" I held my breath.

He smiled. "Yes, I do. You're fun, you're caring, and you're actually really good with kids, even though you don't think so."

I smiled back and snuggled into his chest. "Maybe we should talk about it more, then."

"We'll need more practice," Jonas murmured in my ear.

I pulled away and squinted at him. "Practice being parents or practice becoming parents?"

In Jonas's calm, matter-of-fact voice, he answered, "Practice makes perfect."

*****

Thanks for reading my book. I'd greatly appreciate if you could leave a review for other readers here at Amazon and/or Goodreads. Even a sentence or two helps.

If you haven't read my other series, **turn the page** for a sneak preview of the first book—*Uncle and Ants*—in the *Silicon Valley Mystery* series.

Check out the books in the *Silicon Valley Mystery* series on Amazon:

Uncle and Ants
Chutes and Ladder
Serf and Turf
Hit and Mist

Sign up for Marc's mailing list to receive free content,
learn of new releases, and receive special offers:

http://www.marcjedel.com

Preview: Uncle and Ants—Silicon Valley Mystery #1

Chapter 1. Monday Afternoon

B e careful what you wish for when you're ten years old because it just might come true. I've had a complicated relationship with my younger sister Laney since we were kids, but I never wished for her to wind up hospitalized from a falling drone.

Until the ICU nurse called about Laney, my Monday had rocked. Hard to beat clear blue skies and seventy-five degrees on a beautiful late August day in Silicon Valley, and even though my work kept me stuck inside, at least my latest software build appeared to be bug-free and working well.

I hung up to rush to the hospital, only then realizing I'd forgotten to ask the nurse about Laney's condition. Screwing up phone calls was one of my special skills that only came in handy with telemarketers.

When I reached the hospital, I hurried inside, more concerned than I'd want to admit to Laney. Over the years, our relationship had survived on a steady diet of teasing, and it had only begun to deepen since her husband's death.

She moved to town a few months ago, so she and her two daughters were around more often. I hadn't interacted this much with my sister, or young children, in what seemed like ages. I don't see my own two kids often since they started college across the country, close to where my ex-wife moved. I haven't fully accepted that they're old enough for college anyway. I also haven't fully accepted that I've crossed forty.

An unoccupied information kiosk responded to my query for Laney with a map to room 512. Darting through the crowded lobby, I hopped into an elevator right before the doors closed.

As I got off the elevator and walked to Laney's room, the quiet struck me—no loud beeping monitors or garbled announcements over the loudspeaker. An electronic sign reading "L. Tran" glowed next to room 512. Taking a deep breath to slow my rapid heartbeat, I knocked softly and said, "Hello?"

No answer. I stepped through the door, peeking around a movable privacy partition, and, to my surprise, found an elderly Vietnamese woman sleeping in the only bed.

While I like to tease Laney about her advancing years, she doesn't turn thirty-eight until next month. She's also white. About thirteen years ago, Laney married a nice Vietnamese-American man and took his name. A good guy, he always shared a laugh with Laney over people's reactions when a white woman with long, dark, curly hair and hazel eyes showed up for a dinner reservation under the name Tran.

I did a double-take as it struck me. Why was this old lady in Laney's bed? Had Laney already died and been replaced?

I calmed my overactive imagination, took another deep breath, and stepped back outside the room to double-check the sign. It definitely listed her name. Was it a mistake or software bug? Annoyed, I rubbed the back of my neck and considered my next move. Down the hall past the elevators, a police officer stood talking to a nurse. Perhaps they'd know how to find Laney.

They paused their conversation as I stepped in front of them. The cop was a few inches taller than me, and although I don't usually notice men, I paused at his Hollywood-style good looks. He held himself erect in his uniform, crisp, neat, and fitted to his muscular body like it had come straight from the tailor.

I'd like to think my clothes also fit that well. Other people might comment on some gray in my slowly receding hairline and a tendency toward a dad bod, but I saw none of that when I stepped out of my shower each morning. Self-delusion was another of my skills.

The cop's striking green eyes stood out from his dark brown skin and closely cropped black hair, penetrating me as I started to fidget from one foot to the other.

I didn't think I'd done anything wrong, at least not that the cop should know about. But he looked like he'd set me straight anyway. A badge above the pocket on the left side of his chiseled chest read "Sergeant Mace Jackson."

His name sounded more like an action movie character than a real person. That, combined with his looks, meant that if things ever went south in a conflict, I'd want Mace Jackson on my side. After all, action movie heroes always win.

Under the scrutiny of the sergeant's gaze, I directed my attention to the nurse, whose badge read "Ruth."

"Excuse me. I think there's something wrong with your directory or door signs. I'm looking for my sister's room. Laney Tran? The sign outside room 512 says it's hers, but some old lady is in there."

Nurse Ruth said, "Oh, you must be Marty. I called you earlier." She pointed behind her to room 518. "This is Laney's room."

"Her name is on the sign by the wrong room," I repeated, again highlighting the error needing correction.

The cop scowled and looked hard at me. "Your sister is in the hospital and you're worried about a sign?"

When I'm nervous or worried, or even when everything is fine, I've got a bad habit of obsessing over things that don't work right. Trying to ignore the distraction of the glitch, I said, "Sorry. Is she okay? Can I see her?"

"She's stable and should recover just fine in a few days," Nurse Ruth said. "You can call the doctor for more details or wait for her to come back. I have to check on the other patients. And yes, you can go see her, but she's not awake." The warm smile she was directing toward the cop became forced when she aimed it at me before walking away.

I had more questions and wished she hadn't left me alone with the cop. They've made me nervous ever since a difficult experience during my freshman year of high school. Let's just say that I hadn't yet mastered the U.S. postal system.

Squaring my shoulders, I looked up at Sergeant Mace Jackson, who was standing in the doorway to Laney's room. "Do you know what happened to Laney?"

Instead of answering, he asked, "Can I see your ID please?"

"I'm Marty Golden. I'm a software engineer," I said, as if that explained everything. Well, it did pretty much cover my life. I've got a cool job at a startup. It's not the most successful startup in the world, and I haven't received a big payday yet, but hope can sustain a person for quite a while. Even if that meant work consumed all my time. That's life in Silicon Valley.

"Some ID please," he repeated with an edge to his voice.

I fumbled in my front pocket for my wallet as a light sweat prickled on my forehead. When I pulled out the wallet, my badge fell on the floor. As I bent down to pick it up, Sergeant Jackson reached for my license, almost smacking me in the head. I stood up, holding my license, but dropped it when my wrist bumped into his retracting hand. When I bent over to pick it up again, I heard his exasperated sigh. After standing up a second time, I managed to execute a successful handoff. In one fluid motion, he flipped my license over, reviewed the information, and returned it to me as smoothly as James Bond handles a martini.

Then he pointed at my shirt. "Did you get called back from vacation?"

"What?" I glanced down. I was wearing my normal work attire: Hawaiian shirt and a pair of shorts. Different colors and designs every day, but all Hawaiian-style. Today's was one of my favorite patterns with the leaves on the palm trees in the shapes of different tropical fruit. "No. I came straight from work when the nurse called. How'd Laney's accident happen?"

Noting my defensive tone, the sergeant raised his eyebrow but answered, "She was in a pretty unusual accident. Witnesses reported that she was driving through the intersection of Saratoga and Doyle when she tried to avoid an ice cream truck running the red light. The truck was hit by a falling delivery drone and then your sister's car T-boned the truck. She barely missed getting hit by the drone herself. It would likely have killed her in her little car. It totaled the truck."

I couldn't believe my ears. "A drone?"

"Like I said, it was a pretty unusual accident."

I shook my head in disbelief. Granted, a modern delivery drone was heavy, not one of those lightweight, older-generation drones that were only good for taking videos and annoying your neighbors. But still, this shouldn't have been possible. "That's near her daughters' school. How could a drone hit there? The areas around schools are no-fly zones."

"We're investigating. So, do you—"

My phone buzzed, and I held up a finger to excuse myself. Sergeant Jackson pressed his lips together but said nothing as I stepped away.

"Hello? Marty here."

"Is this Marty Golden?" a woman said in a clipped tone.

"Yes, that's what I said. I'm pretty busy right now. What's this about?"

"Well, now, you don't have to be rude. That's just unnecessary. We teach our children to be polite. It's the right thing to do. Manners start in the home, you know."

I rubbed my nose in confusion. A rogue drone had nearly killed my sister and I hadn't even seen her yet. "I'm sorry. Who is this?"

"I'm Mrs. Quarles, school secretary. Skye and Megan are with me in the office. Their mother hasn't picked them up. We're not a babysitting service here at the Discovery School, you know. You're their emergency contact, so please come get them now."

Trying to take care of Laney and her girls was more than I'd signed up for. Wait, had I signed something? I couldn't be considered a responsible adult. If someone didn't believe me, they just needed to ask my ex-wife. I wanted to tell Mrs. Quarles to call another parent while I stuck around to talk to Laney's doctor and make sure she was okay. "I'll be there soon" was what I mumbled into the phone instead. Probably not the best way to get across my point.

I turned to see Jackson staring at a fixed point on the wall with narrowed eyes and hands on hips.

"I'm sorry. That was my nieces' school. I need to pick them up since Laney is here."

He took another slow, deep breath. "Before we're interrupted again, here's my card." He handed me the first paper business card I've seen in years. "I'd like to talk to her to find out if she saw anything unusual. Tell her to call me when she wakes. But I won't be back until Thursday because I'm on furlough for the next two days."

"Furlough?" I didn't know that word.

"Unpaid, mandatory time off. All thanks to the city of San Jose not having enough money to pay us." He grumbled at this before striding off to the elevators, chest held high like a champion headed off into the sunset.

I looked around but didn't see the cameras or director following our star, then stepped into Laney's room to see her before I left to pick up the girls. She looked to be asleep, with a bunch of tubes and wires running from her to surrounding machines. Bandages covered part of her head, and the rest of her face was bruised. I moved to her side and squeezed her hand, but she didn't respond.

The nylon satchel that she used as a catchall briefcase and purse rested on the chair next to her bed. Her computer, phone, wallet, and some papers were nearly spilling out. Grimacing as I noticed a splotch of blood on the side, I grabbed it all to take home with me for safekeeping. Maybe I would even wash her satchel so the blood wouldn't remind her of the accident. Well, I'd think about washing it.

I used the twenty-minute drive from the hospital to my nieces' school to check in with her doctor and update my own kids, who were away at college. To avoid enticing some elementary school hoodlum to break into the car, I grabbed Laney's bag as I got out.

The desert landscaping that most in the Valley have adopted to deal with the long-term drought prevailed along the path to the office. Assorted cacti, succulents, and rocks decorated the red dirt, creating an eye-catching display, but I still pined for green grass.

My nieces sat talking just inside the glass walls of the school office, their backs to me. Skye, reed-thin and pretty with dark hair and glasses, was a girl with plans. Twelve going on thirty, she liked school and was constantly reading fantasy books. Megan, her younger sister, wore her long hair up with various colored hairpins sticking out every which way. Megan was nine, or eight, or possibly a mature seven. I never could remember. The free spirit of the family, she bounced off the walls with energy.

When I opened the door, Skye noticed me first. Interrupting Megan mid-sentence, she said, "Hi, Uncle Marty. Did you come with Rover?"

From a side room behind the counter, a woman's disembodied voice called out, "No dogs in here! That's simply not allowed."

Before I could speak, Megan chimed in, "You got a dog?" Without pausing to hear the response, she continued, "Hey, where's Mom?"

"Yes," I answered Skye, glancing around and rubbing my chin. What was that voice talking about? There were no dogs in sight.

Megan jumped up and started a little celebration dance at the idea of having an uncle with a dog.

Oops. "No, sorry. I was answering Skye. I didn't get a dog. It's my car, remember?"

Megan's dance ended with a lurch. "Just the dumb car?" She slumped back onto her chair.

"Well, it's not dumb."

A woman walked toward the counter. This had to be Mrs. Quarles, the school secretary. "You gave your car a dog's name?" she asked in a scornful tone.

I'd never met this woman and didn't understand why she felt it was acceptable to judge me, but my parents had taught me to always be polite, so I answered, "I work for a car service called Rover that drives the cars for you. It's like a taxi, but with no driver. We call all the cars Rover. You know, like, 'Hey, Rover, come'—"

"Why not Buddy?" Megan interrupted. "That's a better dog name. Buddy would always be your best friend ..." Her voice trailed off as she hugged herself, thinking of her imaginary best dog friend.

She had me there. "Well, our marketing team decided on the name. Maybe they're not as smart as you and didn't think of Buddy."

Megan looked up at Mrs. Quarles. "Uncle Marty makes the cars go wherever you want."

Skye clarified, "He's an engineer."

I smiled. So the girls had paid attention when I'd told them what I did. Turning to Skye, I said, "I think you'll be interested in a new feature we just added."

Looking excited, she started to ask me about it, but Megan jumped in again. "But wait. If they all have the same name, how do they know which one should come?"

Can't argue with a child's logic. So I did the adult thing and ignored her. "Come on, girls, get your backpacks and let's go." I turned to shepherd them out the door.

Mrs. Quarles called out, "Excuse me. You need to sign the girls out first."

"I'm Marty Golden, the girls' uncle. You called me."

"Yes, Mr. Golden, I am aware of who you are. You still need to sign the form. It's in THE RULES."

I heard the capitalization.

Mrs. Quarles continued, "We all have to follow THE RULES. Please show me your ID so I can verify that you are who you say you are, and then sign this form before the girls can go."

I thought about bolting for the door, but the girls probably wouldn't follow fast enough to make a clean break. Besides, we had to follow THE RULES. I didn't notice any stone tablets with THE RULES etched in them, but the school might have sent them to the mason for cleaning.

After I signed, the girls followed me out the door. I didn't know how to tell them about their mother lying unconscious in the hospital, nor did I understand how this could have happened in the first place. Drones didn't just fall out of the sky nowadays. It's impossible, or at least it should be. Package delivery services worked out all their bugs years ago and were now safer than driverless cars. Fewer random pedestrians or unexpected street construction projects at a thousand feet in the air.

So how did a drone almost hit Laney? I wanted Sergeant Jackson to figure that out now, not waste two days on a silly mandatory furlough.

*****

Read the rest of *Uncle and Ants* today. Get it now on Amazon. Free for Kindle Unlimited readers.

Other Books by Marc Jedel

OZARKS LAKE MYSTERY SERIES

Book 1. Fish Out of Water

SILICON VALLEY MYSTERY SERIES

Book 1. Uncle and Ants
Book 2. Chutes and Ladder
Book 3. Serf and Turf
Book 4. Hit and Mist

Sign up for Marc's mailing list to receive free content, learn of new releases, and receive special offers:

http://www.marcjedel.com

Acknowledgements

Love to my wife and family for their support, but especially my wife since she has to put up with me daily. Sometimes her ability to channel Elizabeth and Mary so effectively is a bit unsettling.

Thanks to my F.I.S.H.Y. (Fabulous, Intelligent, Smart, Human, Yay!) Advance Readers for all their helpful feedback, corrections, and support.

Special thanks to Scott, my amazing "name whisperer." His ability to invent good, on-target names, seemingly at random, for any character I describe made writing more entertaining. I named the "Grody" character in his honor even though Scott in no way resembles him.

I appreciate the good people of Mountain View, Arkansas who've hosted the Annual Bean Fest and Great Ozarks Championship Outhouse Races for over thirty years. I was fascinated and inspired. I want to attend some day, but I'll be sure to stand upwind.

Please support, or even volunteer for, non-profits in your area that run the IRS' VITA (Volunteer Income Tax Assistance) program to offer free tax help to people who qualify. Imagine—the IRS actually helping taxpayers!

Thanks to my developmental editor, Kristen Weber, for her many recommendations. Extra thanks are due to my amazing editor, Cara Quinlan, for the thousands of improvements she made to the manuscript!

About the Author

Marc Jedel writes humorous murder mysteries. He credits his years of marketing leadership positions in Silicon Valley for honing his writing skills and sense of humor. While his high-tech marketing roles involved crafting plenty of fiction, these were just called emails, ads, and marketing collateral.

For most of Marc's life, he's been inventing stories. Encountering more funny and odd people and situations as he's gotten older has made it even easier to write what he knows and make up the rest. It's a skill that has served him well as an author and marketer.

The publication of Marc's first novel, UNCLE AND ANTS, gave him permission to claim "author" as his job. This leads to much more interesting conversations with people than answering, "marketing." Becoming an Amazon best-selling author has only made him more insufferable.

Like his character, Marty from the *Silicon Valley Mystery* series, Marc lives in Silicon Valley, has worked in high-tech, and enjoys bad puns. Like his characters Jonas and Elizabeth from the *Ozarks Lake Mystery* series, he grew up in the South and spent plenty of time in and around Arkansas. Marc too has a dog, although his is neurotic, sweet, and small with little appreciation for Marc's humor.

Visit marcjedel.com, for free content, special offers, and more.

Made in the USA
Monee, IL
13 September 2022

13923487R00152